ST. PETERSBURG WHITE

OTHER TITLES BY GREGORY C. RANDALL

NONFICTION

America's Original GI Town: Park Forest, Illinois

FICTION

THE ALEX POLONIA THRILLERS

Venice Black
Saigon Red
St. Petersburg White

THE SHARON O'MARA CHRONICLES

Land Swap For Death
Containers For Death
Toulouse For Death
12th Man For Death
Diamonds For Death
Limerick For Death

THE TONY ALFANO MYSTERIES

Chicago Swing
Chicago Jazz
Chiciago Fix
Chicago Boogie Woogie
Chicago Back Beat

THE MAX ADLER WORLD WAR II THRILLERS

This Face of Evil
Pawns in an Ancient Game

White Rabbit
The Cherry Pickers
Sector 73

THE DEPUTY JORDAN TYNES MYSTERIES

One Yellow Dog
The Killings in Paradise Valley
Blood in the Yellowstone

ST. PETERSBURG WHITE

AN ALEX POLONIA THRILLER

GREGORY C. RANDALL

WH
WINDSOR HILL PUBLISHING

Cover Design: Gregory C. Randall

This will last out a night in Russia,
When nights are longest there.

—Shakespeare

CHAPTER 1

It was a Fourth of July burned into memories. After the inferno, the mayor of Maise, Iowa, wept uncontrollably. The town—from the train station and ethanol plant on the west side to Elm Street, which ran north and south and split the town—had been incinerated. Its tidy grid of streets and buildings was now a charred abattoir of blackened brick chimneys, gutted and skeletal vehicles, and unidentifiable heaps of what were once the hopes and homes of a community. It would take weeks, the mayor knew, to find all the bodies and even longer to identify them.

The previous morning, Maise had been whole and the clocks hadn't stopped. The day before, life was good. The day before, the ethanol plant hadn't exploded. For more than a century, the town had led a charmed and charming life. Founded by the man from Cirencester, England, Edmund Cornelius Maise, no man-made or natural evil had befallen the town. Never in its history had it been laid low by tornados or arctic blasts. Yes, there were glancing blows to be sure, but nothing as brutal and pitiless as the firestorm. Whereas the day after the fire, the surviving residents knew, deep in their souls, that someone had conspired to murder their village.

The residents were proud of the town's name. Sort of a double entendre, a bon mot, or inside joke—Cornelius/*corn* .

. . Maise/*maize*—corn being Iowa's yellow gold. The region's prospectors—farmers—used steel plows manufactured by John Deere and harvesters designed by Cyrus McCormick to slice open the black earth to gather up its golden wealth.

Maise missed the Interstate lottery by twenty-four miles. America's Interstate 80—three thousand miles long and the lifeline of the nation—passed nearby to the north. The town's beautiful Victorian train station, built by Maise himself, nestled against the transcontinental rail line on the western edge of the village. This edifice, with its bric-a-brac details, sat comfortably in the afternoon shadows of the fourteen 250-foot-tall concrete grain silos that waited, empty and welcoming, for the start of the late-summer corn harvest.

Like other small towns, Maise lost some of its residents to the big cities; those who remained were steadfast supporters and believers in its future. Not only did Maise grow corn for food and ethanol, wheat for bread, and soybeans for export, but also thousands of acres had been overplanted with great turbines that make power from the wind—it was all the stuff of modern life. On the broad flat land and prairie surrounding the village, the colossal wind turbines stood in corn-like rows across the landscape as if giant beanstalks had been pilfered from an old fairy tale. Some in town joked that if Edmund Cornelius Maise were to rise from his plot of land in the local cemetery, he'd change his name to Hightower.

Elizabeth Nelson, the mayor and great-great-granddaughter of old Cornelius, said: "Thank God for the environmentalists. This ethanol thing is a blessing, but it is the wind that frees our souls—and expands our budgets." Everyone on the city council knew the mayor for her great sagacity and Iowan humor. Maise's largest employer, Iowa Power and Light, provided the electrical power for central Iowa. Across northern Iowa, more than a dozen wind farms, with their thousand whirling towers, fed the electric power grid of Iowa and the Midwest. There was a rumor that the energy-thirsty cities in Wisconsin and Illinois would soon be drinking Iowa wind.

The ethanol plant and distillery, located on the western edge of town and directly across the tracks from the train station, was where the carnage began. The ethanol plant's single purpose, both chemically and politically, was to turn Iowa's yellow gold into alcohol—and that alcohol into money and votes. Three distinct American resources are found in America's Heartland: black soil, wind, and the Bakken Formation shale. Boasting two out of the three, Maise stood proud in its effort to support America's future. It was a patriotic point of pride.

Consequently, when the first electrical power outage occurred at 8:08 AM on July 4th, the village was surprised but not overly concerned. During the year, there were often outages due to summer windstorms and winter ice storms. There was concern, not panic. Parts of the four counties that surrounded Maise also went dark. Power at the ethanol distillery failed. Internal pump and transfer stations lost control when their computers shut down; even the backup systems failed. Outside of town, there was no power to distribute electricity from the still-spinning wind turbines to the regional network and grid. Almost every home and business lost power; only those few with solar panels and backup battery systems had electricity. Later, it was learned the skeleton crew at Iowa Power and Light had been frantic; though their initial public face was one of concern and control, they had no idea why the power grid failed.

"We will be back online shortly," the public relations staffer reported dutifully to news reporters. She reported by phone; she was still home with her two children celebrating the holiday. "Sometimes these glitches occur. Nothing serious. It is being handled."

She was right the first time the power went out. Precisely thirty minutes later, at 8:38 AM, the lights throughout the town and the surrounding counties flickered back on. Mayor Nelson left her holiday breakfast and had just arrived in her office halfway through the first outage. She spent the next twenty-five minutes, even after the lights came back on, talking to the county sheriff and the city's police chief, Clyde Dubban. They all remembered the snapped transmission lines after the series of weather fronts and ice storms that clippered through the town the previous January.

"This isn't a storm, Liz," the sheriff said. "It's a beautiful day out there; I've no reports of problems or downed lines. There's supposed to be some strong winds building this afternoon, but nothing out of the normal. Liz, I haven't a clue as to why this shut down."

"Same here," Chief Dubban added. "Nothing. It's got to be in the grid. I have calls into Iowa Power. They say they're looking; I've heard nothing back. Silas and Grundy Counties also reported outages."

Well before the call ended, the lights had come back on and the fan on the mayor's desk began to spin—it was a gift and a replica of one of the wind turbines. The mayor's secretary, dressed for the parade at noon, came into her office and reported that Iowa Power was on it. With it being the holiday, they were short-staffed. They'd report to her in an hour. Mayor Nelson relaxed, no big deal. At 9:08 AM, the power again failed. The fan on her desk stopped. She heard the phones throughout the office ringing; people wanted answers. At 9:18 AM, the mayor left her office and walked out to the city park that surrounded the native Iowan limestone city hall located in the four-block square precisely in the town's center. Floats and other vehicles surrounded the park, waiting for the parade to start; early risers had placed chairs along the curbs in anticipation. Beyond she heard the guttural noise of diesel generators humming. If there was one thing you could count on with Iowans, it was their independence and tenacity. During the year, there were enough weather-related outages that prudent business owners had backup generators to ensure their refrigeration and freezers didn't fail. She was thankful the schools were out for the summer.

The police chief walked toward her across the neatly clipped lawn.

"This time the outage extends outward about twenty miles into the surrounding counties, ten times larger than the one last hour," he said. "I'll tell you, damnedest thing."

They both turned at the sound of squealing tires at the intersection of Main Street and Elm Street in the northeast corner of the square. There was a noticeable bang and crunch as two cars collided. In seconds, yelling voices filled the summer air. People stood and watched. The overhead traffic lights were black.

"Shouldn't they be flashing red?" the mayor asked.

"We took that out of the budget, if you remember, Liz."

"That was dumb."

"It was smart then. With what we saved, we were able to put in that new signal near the train station."

"Which is also out, now."

Dubban nodded. "What about the parade?" he asked.

"We haven't missed a Fourth of July parade since World War II."

"Just asking."

As the chief replied, the traffic signal actuated, and red and green lights flashed. Nelson looked at her watch: 9:38 AM. A strong puff of wind rustled her hair; it was a dry wind from the west.

"Get your boys and girls out to the busiest intersections,"

she said. "I have a gut feeling this is not over. Also, check with the hospital, the two clinics, and the ethanol plant. See if they need anything. I will let you know about the parade."

Nelson took out a cigarette and tried to light it; finally, on the third match and during a calm moment, it took. That was the principal reason she had left her office.

The chief walked away a few paces, raised his radio to his cheek. Then he stopped and looked at the black handset, and then back at the mayor. "The communication system is on the grid. It's out—another budget item. They are waiting for it to reboot."

"My cell phone still works," she said, holding it up.

"What's the backup battery time on those cell towers?"

"Don't know. I'll find out," she said. She started to make a call.

Thirty minutes later, she crushed out her third cigarette and watched as the traffic light and all the storefronts on Main Street went black for the third time that morning. Her phone, even though she knew the time, read 10:08 AM.

"What the hell is going on?"

Her next call was a follow-up to state emergency preparedness; someone finally answered. "We haven't a clue," was the reply. "Just as we locate the spot on the grid where the switches have been shut down, they reactivate, and power comes back into the system. Each time it's different: different switches, different sub-areas. And each time, it gets bigger. The current outage extends outward across fifteen counties."

Mayor Nelson spoke to the county sheriff for the second time.

"We've reports of accidents, nothing serious yet," he said. "There have been a couple robberies at some of the convenience stores near the Interstate. But it's the fire at the plant that's worrying me the most."

6

"Fire? What's that about?"

"A pressure regulator failed, and a valve is stuck open. There's the potential for a serious ammonia leak and release into the air. Jenkins, the plant manager, says he's also concerned about the potential failure of the venting system in the fermenters. He has almost no staff to handle the emergency. There's a fire in a gearbox in one of the grinders. And near one of the dryers, a natural gas line valve is stuck open. The lack of pressure control could cause a problem in one of the boilers."

"What do you mean *could*? There's ammonia and natural gas out there, as well as gasoline and alcohol in some of those tanks." Her phone began to beep, then cut out. "Shit."

She called the fire chief back; he'd been the one trying to reach her. Yes, there was a serious problem at the distillery. He had two of his trucks standing by. She looked at her watch: 10:37 AM. She looked west in the direction of the plant. A plume of black smoke was visible above the treetops; the fast-rising wind was pushing the smoke over the city.

"What's the status of the fire?" she asked. She had to nearly yell over the wind.

"I had to get my guys out. They report a thirty-foot-high gas torch from a broken line is raging near the dryers. We are pulled way back."

As the mayor watched, the lights came back on above the façades of Main Street. Beyond the rooftops, she could see the smoke rip between the tops of the grain silos. It was then that the ethanol plant, with its millions of gallons of distilled alcohol, ammonia, gasoline, and natural gas lines, exploded.

Like a game of dominoes in hell, each fifty-foot-high metal ethanol storage tank exploded and collapsed onto its neighbor. Pushed by the now gusting thirty-miles-an-hour wind, the pressure wave and fire from the cascade of explosions raged, unstopped, eastward into the town. Meanwhile, in the rail yard adjacent to the distillery, on one of the many parallel freight tracks, one hundred double-stacked freight cars were slowly inching their way south. Next to the freight rails sat thirty ethanol-filled tanker cars. Within the freight train were ten double-stacked shipping containers, all filled with highly concentrated ammonium nitrate fertilizer processed in a plant in North Dakota that used natural gas extracted from the Bakken field. These containers were going to Galveston, Texas, where they would be sent on to Uruguay. The burning ethanol from the first exploded storage tank smothered the rail cars; the fertilizer in each shipping container detonated like a ten-thousand-pound bomb.

It wasn't until late that afternoon that the mayor learned from the surviving assistant fire chief that at precisely the moment of the explosion, an Amtrak train was unloading passengers at the train station. The ethanol fireball expanded until the Amtrak train, most of the freight train, and numerous warehouses across the rail lines from the distillery were engulfed. The thirty tanker cars, full of processed ethanol, were knocked off the rails. Some burst open and began to burn. Within minutes, the western half of Maise was on fire. Dumbstruck by the massive conflagration and feeling the heat from the raging wind and advancing fire storm, Mayor Nelson was barely aware of the lights going out again. If she had looked at her watch, she would have seen the time reflected against the wild flames of the fire heading toward her: 11:08 AM.

CHAPTER 2

The next morning, with the smell of burnt wood and chemicals in the air, Mayor Nelson stood at the podium that had been hastily set up in the park in front of the damaged city hall. An odd collection of microphones were mounted to a bracket on the podium with black electrical tape. Each carried a small sign or logo with the brand of the   attending news agency. Behind the mayor, a crowd of public officials in official uniforms—many plastered with large initials front and back—stood solemnly behind her. The mayor's eyes were red from the tears, smoke, and sadness. Fronting the square were dozens of Red Cross vans, emergency trucks, ambulances, and an assortment of state and federal vehicles. The smoldering rubble of Maise, Iowa, was the apocalyptic-like backdrop.

"Thank you for being here," the mayor began. "I do not have to tell you this is a terrible day for our community, for Iowa, and for America. Let me take a few minutes to thank the thousands who came to our town's rescue during the last twenty-four hours. The fires are under control and we expect to have them entirely out by morning. Sadly, we are still looking for dozens of our friends and neighbors who are missing. We are also attending to the injured and working to find shelter for the displaced."

The mayor held up her hand as the reporters began speaking.

"For those in the national media, I will summarize what we know shortly. But first, I will not be issuing any announcements of the number of dead or injured. It is unnecessary and takes away from the horrific nature of this horrible accident, and that is what we are calling it for the moment, an accident. I am concerned, as you should be, for the families of those we lost. If investigations by the state and the federal agencies find other evidence, then this investigation will take on a much different direction. We will schedule twice-daily briefings starting tomorrow. The times are yet to be determined."

Nelson looked out at the faces of her constituents and the various rescue teams. Everyone seemed to be numb, even the hundreds of reporters who had converged on her small town. She knew that over one hundred charred bodies had been recovered from the area around the train station and the ethanol plant. The Amtrak train was still too hot to go through car by car; reports from the scene were of unimaginable carnage. Her police chief, standing directly behind her and in front of the Homeland Security special agent assigned to this scene, had been ordered to discuss the issues of safety and security, potential looters, and traffic only. He was asked by the mayor, as was everyone, not to talk about the dead. There would be time for that later. The Maise fire chief was in a Des Moines hospital where he, along with at least ten other first responders, had been evacuated by helicopters the previous afternoon with significant third-degree burns and other injuries. They were fleeing the plant when it exploded. An empty warehouse was now a temporary shelter along with the high school gymnasium. A temporary morgue had also been set up near the hospital. Homeland had stepped in and supplied refrigerated trailers to hold the dead.

Yesterday had been unimaginable, the mayor thought distractedly. The city's emergency systems were designed for tornadoes and winter storms, not for this type of obscene destruction. Some were calling it Armageddon; she was not going to argue.

"Yesterday morning at approximately 10:40 AM," she began, "due to the recurring power outages and cascading valve failures, the Cornelius Maise ethanol plant caught fire and exploded. During the next five hours, forty-seven blocks of Maise, Iowa, were destroyed."

She looked at the faces. They, too, had seen the destruction; the fear on their faces reflected her own.

"Between the explosions and the fires, almost all homes, outbuildings, and other structures were destroyed or made uninhabitable in the forty-seven-block area west of Elm Street. As I noted, we are searching these ruins for victims. The Amtrak train, taking on and dropping off passengers, was destroyed; the train station is also a complete loss. Dozens of freight cars with their stacked shipping containers were also lost. We are working with the railroad and Homeland Security to determine what is in the remaining containers to ensure ongoing safety. We will also confirm what was in the shipping containers that exploded—it is suspected that it may have been fertilizer."

The mayor took a long drink of water from the plastic bottle someone had placed at the podium; she had not slept for over thirty-six hours. Mayor Elizabeth Nelson had been mayor of Maise for twenty years. She was an excellent mayor and knew almost every one of the town's nearly eight thousand residents. She wasn't sure she would be able to cope with the coming days of funerals and memorials.

"We believe the fire started during one of the strange power outages that began at 8:08 yesterday morning. The current theory is that within the ethanol plant, a pump system failed, pressure built up in the lines, and the system exploded. All other incidental and subsequent damage was caused by a perfect storm of coincidence, timing, high winds, and I have to say it, bad luck. A representative from the county emergency services will discuss this later and provide more details as they become available."

She took another quick drink, feeling her reserves waning.

"I want to introduce Lloyd Desplains. He is the director of the Iowa State Emergency Services Department. Mr. Desplains will bring you up to date on the search for the missing and the process of identification of our loved ones. Please refrain from asking about specific individuals at this time."

* * *

Alex Polonia leaned against the kitchen counter of her new apartment, a cup of coffee in her hand. Stunned by the scenes of destruction shown on the television, her heart went out to the mayor of Maise, Iowa, and everything thrown at the town leader during the last twenty-four hours. The TV showed windshield views, shot by reporters, of the devastating destruction. Empty lots where homes once stood, burnt skeletal trees, smoking husks of cars and other indistinguishable vehicles showed the impact of the explosion and wildfire on the town. Then the TV's image changed to a red and white Boeing 747, with the numbers 944 emblazoned on its tail, dumping orange fire retardant across the rooftops of the Iowa community. The shot of the 747 was obviously from a helicopter and taken the previous afternoon; the camera panned out toward the still-burning storage tanks that surrounded the smoldering ethanol plant. Train cars were scattered alongside the tracks as if some giant's hand had knocked them over. Smoke and steam still drifted upward from some of the buildings. Then the massive airplane rose like a colossal bird from within the smoke, and banked, preparing to make another run. Hundreds of flashing emergency lights punctured the grey scene visible below, all in contrast to the clear and bright blue late-afternoon Iowa sky.

"I want to thank everyone in emergency services," the mayor continued, "and most especially the global supertanker *The Spirit of John Muir*, from Colorado, for helping us slow this inferno last evening so our emergency personnel could get ahead of the firestorm."

Alex remembered an investigation a few years earlier—she was a detective on the Cleveland police force then—of a house fire where five children died. She'd never gotten over the carnage and the smell. To see what had happened to this Iowa town was more than heartbreaking.

The news reports said the Iowa power outages cycled hourly through the region. Alex knew that random outages could occur for a hundred different reasons, but to happen at the same time, eight minutes after the hour, in the same region, every hour on the hour, was unusual—in fact, more than unusual. It had to be man-made. Her mind immediately went to the why. The how was someone else's world, always was. She wanted to know the why and who; that would lead to reasons and the bad guys. She wanted the bad guys, the who, and if she found out why, during the capture, all the better. And seeing the destruction and death, these sons of bitches needed more than to be captured to set the record right; they needed to be put in their own hell.

Beyond the window of her lakefront apartment, the still waters of Lake Erie shimmered in the late morning. The change in her circumstances was both profound and wrenching. To be a successful and respected police detective one day, and an outcast and pariah the next, was a direct result of her asshole husband, Ralph Cierzinski, and his arrest and conviction for running drugs. Hiding behind his Cleveland police detective badge had been an illicit business of narcotics, methamphetamines, and murder. Then, there were more killings during his escape from prison and disappearance. Now, four months later, it was as if he'd fallen off the face of the earth. She hoped to God that he had.

After losing the Cleveland police job, she'd taken a position with Teton Security and Defense, an international security firm. Her new boss, Christopher Campbell, offered her the job and a chance at a new life working as an operative and expert on criminal behavior. Alex willingly grabbed hold, accepting an initial assignment in Saigon, Vietnam. Into the mix had walked the dark and handsome CIA special agent from Waco, Texas: Javier Castillo. Their first chance hookup in Venice had turned more than curious; it evolved into an international terrorist attack and a series of coincidences in Venice she still hadn't fully accepted. Then the Texan broke her fragile heart. To say that the previous four months had been interesting would be to say that swimming in shark-infested waters is interesting—it's interesting, until it isn't.

After returning from Saigon, she'd fully expected Campbell to fire her. *I sure as hell would fire me—even if it was Campbell's damn fault the whole thing almost went upside down.* Both Campbell and Castillo had been dark for the last month—it was as if Alex had been dumped on a desert island and left to deal with the flotsam and jetsam of her life.

She looked back at the muted television and watched a parade of men and women walk to the podium, make a few short remarks, and then move back to the group behind the mayor. One caught her eye—it was her boss, Chris Campbell. He did not go to the podium. *Now why the hell is he there?*

The usual Sunday dinners with her family were otherworldly

calm and weird. Returning from Saigon to her old bedroom in her parents' house, she vowed to be out as soon as she found an apartment. Within a week she found an acceptable solution, a one-bedroom unit that overlooked Lake Erie. Her brothers helped her move in. Her sisters-in-law took her to lunch and shopping and subtly asked her questions about the CIA agent from Waco. They were questions Alex didn't want to answer. It was like reliving her divorce from Ralph Cierzinski, except for the courtrooms, the bad press, and the murders. Yes, it was exactly like that.

She settled into a routine: up early in the morning, spending time in the gym, a light lunch (or a sisterly date), and getting her apartment straight. After the place was organized, she wondered next what to do with her time. After twenty years as a cop, she needed direction and purpose. It came as she started to clean out the coffeepot.

Her phone read, "Chris Campbell." Her head said, "Shit."

She punched in the speaker.

"Hi, Chris."

"Hi, Alex."

There was a mutual pause.

". . . and no," she finally began. "I'm not going to ask about Javier. It will resolve itself when it needs to. Right now, I'm good. Thanks for asking."

"I haven't been able to get a word in edgewise. So, Alexandra, how are you?"

"Just ducky, living the dream here on the shore of Lake Erie. Can't wait for the winter winds to make it perfect. Maybe my ex will drop by and we can share a cocktail and watch the Indians lose."

"Good God, when you get in the dumps, stand back."

"Dumps! I'm just starting. I'm still not over all the crap in Saigon. However, I'm still working for you—I don't think the paychecks are out of pity."

"That's for damn sure. I put you in a bad situation, and you got through it. Bizarre, true—not sure I've seen any stranger couple of months."

"Then why the call? Do you miss me? And I saw you on television, in Maise."

She looked back at the ongoing network newsfeed of the events in Maise; more photos of the burnt town flashed by one after the other. The partially burned city hall stood in horrific contrast behind the mayor as a national broadcast personality was interviewing her.

"It's something to do with the fire in Maise, isn't it?" she said.

"And that's why I need you. I want you in Dallas tomorrow. Catch the morning flight; your ticket is in your email. We have difficult things to talk about. These power outages are just the tip of the iceberg. The press is not reporting the whole story because they don't know the story."

"That will piss them off when they find out."

CHAPTER 3

Ilya Sokolov cupped his hands under the dribble from the sink faucet and splashed the orange-colored water against his face; the pipes, like everything in the apartment building, were old. He vigorously rubbed his cheeks and the stubble of his beard. His headache was diminishing, like a train engine, spitting smoke and fire, slowly leaving the station. He turned back to the kitchen; his two sons sat at the small table. Some sugary, insanely colorful breakfast cereal filled the bowls in front of them. They looked at Ilya, expectant expressions on their ten-year-old faces. They rocked back and forth.

"We've told you not to drink so much, Papa," they said in practiced unison.

"That is my business," Ilya responded, not wishing to reignite this debate. "We have talked about this."

Pavel, the boy on the right, said, "We know it's your day off, and you've said that this is the one day you are entitled. But, Papa, you should not drink."

"You know what happened to Momma," Gavril, his brother, chimed in.

"You know you are not to mention your mother; I've told you this," Ilya said, pointing his finger.

"She is dead. What's the difference now?" Pavel said.

"And you must be more respectful. She had demons," Ilya

said. He drank from the glass of water he'd poured from a plastic bottle.

The boys ate their breakfast in silence, occasionally looking up at their father. The rocking now almost imperceptible.

Since their mother's death, he had been responsible for their care, troubled and difficult care to be sure. But the reality was, he had also cared for them before she died; as her drinking increased, her connections to the real world began to fail. The boys were identical twins. Their mutual diagnosis, at the age of three, of autism, with the potential for Asperger Syndrome, required his constant vigilance. Their brilliance scared anyone who met them, and their occasional odd and repetitive behavior usually forced a quick retreat. Their attachment to him, at times, was dependent, needy, and then suddenly aloof. When they were with him, they were calmer, more malleable. With strangers, they became defensive, though in time they adapted, and grew accepting, especially with outsiders who were older. Ilya hoped is was just an issue of familiarity and comfort. Their lives were one defensive action after another. The two were like halves of the same boy; they watched and cared for each other. They were alike, as only twins could be, in body, mind, and soul. They had no friends, none in the building, and none at school—other children their age might react negatively to the boys, and the boys responded accordingly by ignoring them. Ilya was certain they didn't care. After ten years, he wasn't sure which of the boys was the truly dominant of the two. They were, at times, a tag team of turmoil, madness, and controlled chaos. He had learned that some with this syndrome, now called Autism Spectrum Disorder (ASD), created their own structure in their lives. Yet Gavril and Pavel often adjusted to this structure—first one then the other followed. He also learned that every child with this syndrome was different—there was no definitive blueprint for this form of autism.

18

He loved them with his whole soul, yet Ilya Sokolov was afraid for them and afraid for those who would have to deal with them as they grew older. And yet he knew, in his heart, that they loved him.

"Get dressed. Anya is taking you guys to the zoo today. You need to get out; the sunshine will do you both some good."

The boys looked at each other and grinned. Anya, courageous Anya Belsky, beautiful Anya Belsky, far too young for him Anya Belsky, was a friend and saint to deal with the two of them. Ilya hoped to have a few precious hours to himself, time to decompress, and maybe catch up with some of his work from the institute. He taught advanced computer programming at the Saint Petersburg Computer Institute. It paid enough to keep food on the table and pay the rent, and a little left over to keep the two boys entertained. They attended a private school for the gifted. He wasn't exactly sure why the state offered the tuition and why they were interested in the boys, but he did suspect their unfettered intelligence played a part. However, the staff did provide, at times, some relief and instruction on how to deal with their behavior—behavior Ilya sometimes had trouble coping with.

Currently, the boys were on summer break. During the last three years, Ilya had taken on a lot of the education they didn't get in the school. He brought home books on math, physics, even astronomy. They devoured them. He was sure they both were eidetic; they remembered everything. Soon enough, they would have to care for themselves. Ilya tried his best to prepare them for that day.

Father and sons had evolved into a strange parental relationship. He was anxious for his children; he wasn't sure if they understood what his role was in their lives. Theirs was a war of constant renegotiation. Anya provided a welcome buffer. The boys carefully dressed, moving in unison as if it were a game—there was a definite pattern to their actions—and then sat together on the hall bench waiting for Anya.

The doorbell rang and Ilya showed Anya in. She smiled, said nothing, and looked at the twins. She had them stand at attention, put their backpacks on, and marched them out the door as if it were all a game.

After the trio left, Ilya retrieved his laptop, intending to begin his work. Out of habit he opened the browser and checked the history. His heart dropped. The boys had managed again to get past the new passwords and firewalls. He searched through the list of recent URLs, and he did not understand or recognize any of them. Some had .com addresses, others for Russia and other national origins. The boys had somehow gotten into his computer, again. The institute told him this was impossible with this computer and the security programs the institute's software engineers had installed on this machine; obviously, they were wrong. Nonetheless, the boys had found their way in, and now he was afraid of what they had done.

He continued to scroll through the browsing history. The boys, most probably Pavel, had not dumped the sites from the list: a series of disconnected and seemingly incongruent URLs continued to appear. He was afraid even to try and access some of these sites. As a Russian, it was normal to be concerned about who might be watching or listening. Even the briefest search attempt might lead to serious consequences. He skimmed the list: IP addresses for office equipment and innocuous printers. One he did click on was a place identified as an office building in Moscow. Moscow? He rationalized that the boys were playing, the result of their intense curiosity. They'd done it before, hijacked other computers and caused mischief. This time, however, the thought of Moscow and office machines scared him. Everything in Moscow scared him.

He went to his newsfeed. A peaceful anti-government march

in Moscow had been broken up by a gang of thugs (called patriots); the report showed no sympathy for those beaten. There was concern about natural gas prices and a pipeline from Russia through Turkey; a riot in Ankara in opposition to the route had led to two deaths. And a massive explosion in an ethanol plant had occurred the previous day in a town called Maise in Iowa, in the midwestern United States. Power outages had been linked to the blast. His heart dropped. He scrolled back and looked at the access times on the search history. Even though they connected to places in Moscow, some of the IP addresses came back as government buildings. After mentally adjusting for time zones, the times of the searches coincided with the time of the explosions in Iowa. He did not believe in coincidences when it came to the boys.

He blamed himself for what had happened; if he hadn't gotten drunk and passed out, the boys would not have gotten into his computer. Panicking, he poured himself a drink, and tried a couple of the links. There was a pause, then a message popped up about not being authorized to access. He instantly shut the computer down. He'd failed them again and himself. Now his boys may have caused deaths and destruction—and he was to blame. He made a few notes, refilled his glass, and considered his options. He expected that someone might be watching for Internet contacts to the American FBI or some other government agency. But a library, innocuous and unrelated to most Russian concerns, might prove a conduit. After running scenarios through his head for twenty minutes, he rebooted the computer and then looked up the website of the Maise public library. He wrote a short letter to the director of the library in English, hoping that someone would read it and get it to the proper authorities. He needed help—help he would not get from anyone in St. Petersburg or Moscow.

* * *

Christopher Campbell waited in the American Airlines baggage claim arena at Dallas–Fort Worth Airport. He spotted Alex as she came down the escalator. He waved; she waved back.

"Luggage?" he asked.

"One bag, other than my handbag and backpack," Alex said. "How are you?"

"Good, I guess. Carousel Two."

They walked together and waited until the bags began to drop on the carousel. Alex grabbed her bag.

"What's happening?"

"We'll talk in the SUV," Chris said, inclining his head toward the exit. He led the way outside to where a black Chevy Tahoe waited at the curb. A Latino man with military bearing stood next to the vehicle.

"Hi, Alex," Jimmy Cortez said. "How ya doing?"

"Not sure yet, Jimmy," Alex answered with a smile.

Cortez put her bags in the back of the Tahoe and climbed into the driver's seat. Alex climbed into the rear seat; Chris took the seat next to her. A work table separated the seats. Two coffees sat in the cup holders.

"Black, no sugar," Cortez said.

"Thanks, Jimmy," she answered and turned to Chris. She gave him a questioning look.

"We'll start with this. Please read it. It's a copy sent to me through Homeland and the CIA."

He watched her scan down the paper.

"Holy shit," Alex said. "This is all we've got? There has to be more."

"Right now, that's it."

He'd read the one email so many times, he'd memorized it.

> *To the director of the Maise, Iowa, library. Please*
> *tell the authorities that it was a mistake; it wasn't sup-*
> *posed to happen. It was an accident. I'm so sorry; I need*
> *help. They are after us.*

Alex looked over at Chris. "Any idea who this is from? Who is *us*?"

"None. Some believe it's a disillusioned or remorseful hacker or hackers. Others suggest an opportunist trying to get into the United States—the Internet is full of conspiracies. We don't know if they may or may not be the ones who hacked into the control and distribution systems of the Iowa Power grid—and that's the current theory. The one thing that was discovered is that Iowa Power and Light has more holes in its system than a sieve. One of the NSA guys joked that a child could have found a way into the system. The routing of the email leads us to believe it's from Russia, the St. Petersburg region. CIA and NSA are trying to find who or what the *us* is. The strongest idea is a radical group opposed to Putin."

"Well, shit. And I'm here because?" Alex said.

Campbell was silent for a few moments as they exited the airport parkway and Cortez piloted the SUV onto the eastbound Interstate toward downtown Dallas.

"This explosion was not the result of an unfortunate accident at the plant. We'll go over everything at the meeting; it's at noon," Chris continued. "What I can tell you now is that IPL is shutting down all external access, including their website, emails, and even their bill-paying site. It appears someone found a way into their system through an HP desktop printer in one of their private offices. They used the wireless connection to get to a manager's desktop; from there, they accessed schedules and switch routines. After that, who the hell knows?"

"That easy?" Alex asked.

"They believed they had enough firewalls and protections," Chris said. "They didn't. Whoever it was blew through the safeties like they were simple annoyances. Once NSA found the path, they duplicated it. It wasn't hard, but then again, they knew where to start. Their opinion was that the original hacker just got lucky."

"That kind of luck is scary."

"That's why Linda Monroe, our technologist, thinks it was more than luck. She believes it was an attempt at vandalism and mayhem."

"Looks like more than an attempt," Alex said.

"No kidding," Chris added. "Other things could have been done, like stealing customer data or payment records—none of that appears to have happened. This seems intentionally done to cause havoc. And they succeeded. The repetitive power shutdowns caused backup surges in the pumps; eventually more pumps and valves failed. That failure then led to the cascade; the cascade blew out a natural gas pipeline fitting. The ethanol, adjacent to the gas line, and under extreme pressure, ignited, and from that point on . . ."

. . . *a small hell was unleashed*, thought Alex, when he didn't finish. "There had to be safeguards, system checks, check valves, backflow preventers?" she asked him.

"The power outage caused them to fail," Chris said.

"The best-laid plans of mice and men," Alex said softly.

Chris nodded soberly. "Failure is to be expected. Designs must deal with the possibility, but sometimes budgets force system compromises. Even after the explosion, the locals believed it could be contained. Unfortunately, between the wind and the explosion of a hundred thousand pounds of fertilizer, the cascade of events caused the inferno."

"And people died."

"Sadly, yes."

"How many?" Alex asked, not wanting to hear the answer.

"Right now, they're saying at least one hundred and fifty, and over four hundred in hospitals with severe burns; many may not make it. Thank goodness it was a holiday. This is why there's a massive federal effort. It is being called, unofficially, terrorism."

"Then, why am I here? There are too many cooks in this kitchen already."

"Your detective skills," Chris said. "Also, there's something weird about this, the contriteness of the email, the unburnished admission, the plea for help. Not something you'd expect from a terrorist."

Alex nodded. "There would have been more bravado, more in your face, a celebration of the act as if a trophy."

He gave her a tight smile. "Right. I need someone whose first reaction is to consider the situation, not shoot the first person that moves."

"And the other claims? There has to be a lot of groups wanting to take credit," Alex asked, looking back at the email.

"Yeah, the usual from ISIS, the Palestinians, a couple of religious nut jobs, a militia in the Rockies, and even a fringe environmental group from the UK," Chris said, ticking off his fingers as he spoke. "All are claiming they were responsible. I think they all should be chased down and shot, but that's just me. No, I think this email was the real thing. But I'm very willing to be proven wrong."

"The library site is being monitored?"

"Yes, for many reasons."

Russia? It was a strange place to begin, Alex thought. Of course, there were implications all over the Internet about hackers, extortions, and even messing with elections, all pointing to Russia.

"If it is Russia," Chris said, echoing her thoughts. "But this is murder, plain and simple."

Alex took a sip of the coffee Cortez had provided; it was now lukewarm but still mildly comforting.

"And all assuming this attack has not been sourced somewhere else and bounced around the world before landing in Maise," Chris said, mirroring her act of reaching for the coffee. He took a long drink. "For now, we are going with Russia and Saint Petersburg. And, just so you understand, we are not part of an officially sanctioned action. Linda believes the Russian Federal Security Service, the FSB, and their techies are chasing this hacker down with as much effort as we are. And . . ."

". . . assuming this is the case, they want this person as much as we do," Alex said. "I assume that this person of interest would not be thrilled to be found by the FSB. They're asking for help, our help."

"Linda has co-opted the library site; it is no longer involved. He will believe he is still in contact with the library."

"Why us?" Alex asked. "I know you are tight with the CIA and NSA, and especially the FBI. I saw an agent with FBI in bold letters on his jacket standing in the line behind the mayor of Maise at the press conference yesterday, near you. So, why us?"

"That was Special Agent Robb Case; he will be at the meeting this afternoon. We are on board because if it is Russia, the government wants as much buffer as possible between them and the United States. We can act differently than the Feds—at least I think we can. Again, there is something unusual about this, especially the contact through the library and not using other channels."

"Did we respond to the email?"

"Yes, or at least the FBI did. Our response was: *We can help you. Please respond to the new email address.*"

"Pretty basic," Alex said. "Like a hostage situation."

"If the guy is smart, he won't believe any of this. I think he'll try another route; they are raised to be paranoid in Russia."

"Rightly so. Any idea how?" Alex asked.

"No clue, but we are waiting."

They had reached their destination, a nondescript aluminum-clad two-story building in a Dallas industrial park on the city's west side near the intersections of John W. Carpenter Freeway and North Stemmons Freeway. They both fell silent as Cortez wheeled into the parking lot and backed the SUV into an unmarked spot.

"I'm setting up an action group under the White Team. Jimmy will remain here at the logistic center, and we will head to the club where you will be brought up to speed this afternoon," Chris said to Alex as they exited the SUV. "I'm going to Washington immediately after our meeting." He came around to her side of the car. "I wanted to see you and ask you personally about this assignment. I know what you're thinking."

"There you go, making assumptions," Alex answered. "Damn it, Chris, you do not know what I'm thinking. Right now, you want me on White Team; I go where you send me. You hired me as a law enforcement professional; that is what I am. We can hug and do Freudian analysis together sometime in the future. Right now, we need to stop this son of a bitch and bring him to justice."

CHAPTER 4

Dmitry Ivanovich flipped through the pages of the reports that his assistant director, Tanya Golubev, had placed on his desk. The assistant director was tall, blue-eyed, with hair the color of late-summer straw. She was from Moscow and grew up not ten kilometers from the Kremlin. Director Ivanovich was friends with her parents for over thirty years, connected party officials; they believed in a broad education with a robust political upbringing. After her university graduation, Tanya spent more than a decade in the military as a policewoman and investigator. She joined his department as a junior staff member; that was four years ago. He was impressed, by her determination and the simple fact that she'd stuck longer than any other assistant he'd had since becoming director. Her dark grey suit had a militaristic appearance, while the blue scarf around her neck broke decorum; he liked it. Standing at attention, three paces back from the front of his massive walnut desk, she slowly turned her head and looked out the fifth-floor window of the Center for Information Security at the corner of Lubyanka Square in Moscow. The early morning traffic beyond the square was growing.

"Are you sure this time?" he asked.

"Yes, Director." Her head snapped back. "The electronic trail began in an area of the eastern suburbs of St. Petersburg, was bounced around between servers in Amsterdam, Madrid, and Buenos Aries until it ended at our servers here in Lubyanka. The Internet connection re-established itself every half hour, starting at precisely 4:08 PM Moscow time. We are trying to establish the exact location of the attacking computer. However, it does resemble an earlier attack, though that attack came from a different IP address."

"There are similarities?"

"Yes, Director," she said with a slight smile. "I believe it is the same hacker."

Ivanovich's eyes skimmed the report as she continued.

"This time the hacker accessed our systems files. There was special attention to the encrypted folder for *Zapadnaya Zima* [Western Winter] and *Paslen* [Nightshade]. Somehow they were able to access and then activate the programs."

He looked up at her, startled by the remark. "You must be joking. I have been assured there is no way that anyone other than myself, and maybe two others, can access that program. It has a complex series of passwords."

"Obviously, we were incorrect."

"A lot of fucking good that does. What happened?"

"By accessing our program, the hackers were able to manipulate the electric power grid in Iowa. That's in the United States."

"I know where Iowa is. In fact, the whole world now knows where Iowa is."

"We believe the loss of power led to a pumping failure in an ethanol plant. The result was that hundreds are reported, by American news outlets, to have died. You saw the reports during the briefing this morning."

"What you are saying is that someone found a way to access our top-secret programs and used them to blow up an ethanol plant. Can this be traced back to us?"

"The point is the plant was not the target; it was collateral damage from the shutdown of the electrical grid in that part of America. And no, I do not think it can be traced back to us."

"Who else knows?"

"The world knows about the power grid collapse and the explosion. From what we see, the trail currently points elsewhere."

"Why wasn't the hack more extensive? Our experiments have performed this operation many times: Ukraine, Poland, even Turkey." He knew he wasn't telling her anything she didn't know. But why had the attack been so isolated, and why the United States? "It was not sanctioned from here," he said, a fact they both well knew.

"I understand," she said calmly. "With respect to the American grid, it's the nature of their systems. It's a collection of dissimilar operating systems, most developed during different decades. Many are uncoordinated. Their governmental standards leave most regional systems to their own specifications. Very inefficient."

"Yes, I know. That's one of the reasons it's been difficult to build a model that would take down their entire grid at one time."

"We are still working on that," she answered.

"It was your program that they hacked, Assistant Director Golubev. What are you going to do about it?" Ivanovich stood so they were eye-level. "And are you sure this attack was not sponsored by some other Russian agency or rogue operator within the political wing of the FSB or the party?"

She met his gaze. "I am certain that it was not. Third floor has checked, and there weren't the usual lines of code and signatures that we know. The intention of this attack on our system appears to have been harmless, a probe, an experiment as evidenced by the target and the result. The fire and destruction in the American town looked to be ancillary and accidental. While it did take a considerable amount of computer and math skills as well as the creation of algorithms that facilitated the hack on the printer—which were ingenious, I might add—we believe it was an amateur."

"An amateur? Really? They must be a fucking genius."

Director Ivanovich moved to the window and stared out at the street below. Traffic filled the street; new construction was underway a block away—he had heard it was for a private company owned by one of the president's favorites. Nothing changed in Russia, maybe the names and the people, but nothing really changed.

"Agreed," Tanya said, coming to stand beside him. "It was the consequences of the hack that makes this so terrible. The explosions and the firestorm were not predictable. It was a cascade of misfortune."

"You sound so Russian when you say that, Assistant Director Golubev," the director replied, still gazing out the window. "You see now why I am concerned. It is like a small earthquake on a faraway island that produces a surge in the ocean that builds into a tsunami that wipes out villages hundreds of miles away . . ."

". . . or coastal naval and military bases," she added.

"Exactly. One small, almost innocuous event can become a force of unimaginable terror and lead to the collapse of entire defensive systems and operations. That is why your group and others here in the Counterintelligence Service are developing scenarios exactly like the earthquake. A snowball rolling down a mountain becomes an avalanche."

"A small act leads to chaos and terror."

Ivanovich looked at the assistant director. "You think this actor is in St. Petersburg?" he asked.

"Yes, we are certain the hack originated there," she said

without hesitation. "There is the suspicion that it was from a listed laptop owned by one of the universities. We are chasing that lead now. I have formed a task force to find this hacker— they will not make any attempt to contact this person or persons. I want to know everything before we apprehend them."

"Excellent."

He removed a lighter and slim cigarette case from his jacket pocket, ignoring the flicker of disapproval that crossed her features as he lit a cigarette.

"After they are detained, make sure they understand that they are not under arrest," he said. "I don't want to spook them. They may have left traps and backdoors that would prevent us from using their algorithms and programs. And more to the point, they may have left time bombs . . ."

". . . that may infect or disable our systems. I will do as ordered, Director Ivanovich."

"Proceed, Tanya. I also want you to personally ensure the usual legal paperwork is in order in case we stumble into an action by another agency. I do not want that embarrassment again. Keep me posted. In fact"—Ivanovich took a long drag of his cigarette, and smiled at the assistant director's expression that openly said the stench was nauseating—"when you think you are close to finding this person, let me know. I will join you. I want someone with these skills working for us, and if they don't wish to work for us, I do not want them working for anyone else."

* * *

"The first contact email from our Russian friend was real; he's back," Chris Campbell said. "We still don't have a name or a motive."

He sat at the head of a large wooden table in the primary

conference room of the Dallas home office for Teton Security and Defense, aka the "Country Club." The room had no windows, and the security systems enfolding the room would mask any attempt at eavesdropping. The system TSD had developed was now standard at many American embassies and regional CIA offices.

Chris passed copies of the new email around the table.

"I'm starting before Micah Lynch arrives because SA Case has to get on to Maise," Chris said. "Robb was passing through Dallas, and I asked him to join us. His team is being assembled from across the country. Micah will be here shortly. His connection at Heathrow was delayed. His plane landed ten minutes ago at DFW."

Five people were in the room: Chris Campbell, Jake Dumas, Jimmy Cortez, and Alex Polonia were with Teton Security and Defense. FBI Special Agent Robb Case was based in the Washington, D.C., office and had spent the last two days in Maise. The tardy member was Micah Lynch. Based in Berlin, Lynch was the White Team leader for Northern Europe. Chris had subdivided the TSD world into ten teams, Black, White, Red, Green, Blue, Violet, Orange, Charlie, Baker, and Flashlight. Red was for Southeast Asia, from where Alex had just returned. The White Team covered Eastern Europe northeast of Switzerland and across Russia.

They all read the email.

"And we believe this guy?" Dumas said. He was in Dallas reporting on the changes underway for the Southeast Asia Red team that he led.

"Yes, as far as it goes," Agent Case said. Case was medium height, broad-chested, large muscular hands, bald head, a thick bushy mustache, and he wore black horn-rimmed glasses. "I'm here as a liaison between Homeland, the CIA, and the NSA. Chris wanted only me. Too many roosters in the room, you said, and I agree."

He smiled and nodded to Campbell. He held up a paper. "The email you all just read came in an hour ago."

> *Thank God for your response. We have much to talk about but can say little. My family and I are in great peril. I have no one else. I trust no one. I assume that I'm being watched and monitored. The power failures were an accident. I did not want to cause any harm. Help us.*

"Sounds like the emails I get from that prince in Kenya," Alex said. "Wonky, out of context. Is anyone trying to contact this guy? Have you confirmed that he's even in Russia?"

"No to both," Agent Case said. "We do not have enough information. The CIA is searching to find if he might be on their radar, but they also don't want to put a spotlight on the guy. If they did, the FSB would be on him instantly. And Homeland wants the guy's head; no one gets away with killing Americans—anywhere. They want this disaster to be declared a terrorist attack and kick open the doors, send in the Seals. The president wants the perpetrators found and brought to justice. We get it. I have twenty FBI agents in Maise, and more coming—though I'm not sure what they can do in Iowa. For us, the real question is who did it? When the president points a finger, we want to make sure it's at the right person."

"And you're certain it's not state-sponsored?" Alex asked.

"No, we are not. But we are leaning toward believing this guy. If he has the skills that made this happen, a lot of people want him, us included."

"He's a goddamn murderer," Dumas said. "I've got a few ideas on how to resolve this conflict; a bullet is one of them."

"I understand, assuming he's a man," Case said. "But that's

not how we do things."

"I'd still shoot her," Dumas answered.

"Really?" Cortez said with a wry smile. "There's a few Al-Qaeda and ISIS true believers with their virgins who'd argue that fine point of American retribution."

Case ignored Cortez and turned to Campbell.

"Chris, the reason I'm here talking with you—"

He was interrupted by a tap on the door.

Chris looked at his iPad. The face of a bookish man with wire-rimmed glasses looked back at him. Chris went to the door and ushered the man in.

"Robb and Alex, this is Micah Lynch. Micah, you know the boys. It's good to have you back."

"Thanks," Micah said as he shook hands with everyone. He glanced twice at Alex, then said, "I read the after-action reports on Saigon. Not sure how to respond. Jesus, what a mess. But for your first assignment, well done. Lots to talk about."

"Alex and Robb," Chris began, "Micah was born in Zurich, and then spent his first sixteen years in Moscow and other cities in Russia. His parents were with the U.S. State Department. After West Point, he spent four years in Army Special Operations. I believe he has been to more countries, hot spots, and watering holes than even Jake here. Micah's been with us since 2008. He took over White team two years ago."

"Jesus, I feel like an underachiever," Alex said. "Again, not sure I know why I'm here."

"Patience. All will be revealed," Chris said. "Robb, please continue."

"We are working up various scenarios," the FBI agent said. "Contingencies run from snatch to elimination. Homeland is the most aggressive when it comes to that last option, especially if this is state-sponsored. We are trying to confirm who this guy is, what he knows, and what he wants. Then we can act accordingly. That is why I'm here talking to TSD. If this leads to action inside Russia, we need to be extremely careful. As you are all aware, things are not that wonderful between us. If the Russians even thought we were running an operation inside their motherland, all sorts of political hell would fly. Chris?"

"Robb, as the president's representative, has requested that we be ready to move quickly into Russia to 'rescue' this terrorist," Chris said. "The president believes the CIA and other governmental agencies are too public. The FSB and the Kremlin have excellent systems to identify and track foreign agents in their country. I don't need to tell you that they are using AI—artificial intelligence—closed-circuit TVs with facial recognition, massive databases, even moles in our own agencies. For all we know, they know our guys better than we do. And, of course, there's interagency self-interest. The CIA does not want us to use their in-country assets; it's taken too long to place them where they are. However, they may be able to help if we need them. We've run this scenario before."

"Yemen, Tehran, Mumbai, to just name a few," Dumas offered. "But we had to be so nice to those CIA guys."

Alex looked at Dumas and then Campbell; both men smiled.

"The hope is that we can get in and out without being caught?" Alex asked.

"And if caught, respond with plausible deniability," Jake said. "Where have I heard that before?"

"Yes, there's that. That's why we get the big bucks," Cortez said.

"It's a day for clichés," Micah added. "In for a penny, in for a pound."

An hour later, after Cortez returned from taking Special Agent Case to the airport, the group met again.

"There's something that's bothering me about these emails," Alex said. "In both, he refers to his family. But we don't know how many, ages, genders, anything. We go in expecting maybe two people, and we end up with six or seven. The whole plan can go wonky real fast."

"We're pressing the FBI for more information," Chris said. "It's very fluid. That's why I asked you to be part of this. It's one thing if it's a guy and his laptop; it's something else if there's a wife, a couple of kids, maybe a grandmother in a babushka. We need a different perspective."

"It sounds like babysitting to me," Alex said.

"Not as far as I'm concerned. Our team must be small, two people, no more. Micah has people in Russia who can be moved around if we have enough time. They also can provide documents and papers. But, like the CIA, I don't want to lose them. They have taken years to place and they are friends."

"And we aren't?" Alex said. "Really? I had enough babysitting in Saigon."

Chris opened the double doors of a wall-mounted cabinet that hid a flat-screen TV. He picked up his iPad and began moving his fingers quickly across its surface. The TV screen lit up with a map of the Baltic Sea.

"Our first scenario assumes the target is in St. Petersburg, here." A red light moved to indicate the sprawling metropolis. "We work on ways to get in and then get out with our man. Family scenarios included. No weapons, no force, no debris left behind. This will be a snatch with a willing target. In, then out. That's why I want you in on this, Alex. A man and woman team, less suspicious then two American military types walking the streets all macho-like with military haircuts."

"Hey, unfair," Dumas said.

"I wasn't pointing to you," Chris said. "And besides it would take too much time to grow your hair out."

"I can't speak the language," Alex said. "I know a little street Spanish and can carry on a conversation in Polish, thanks to my grandmother, but that's about it."

"Micah is fluent in Russian and even some of its regional dialects," Chris said. "He's a language hobbyist who's been translating Pushkin in his spare time."

Lynch smiled and held up his hands.

"Now, I'm even more depressed. A babysitting job with a savant," Alex said.

"Micah, will you go through the first scenario we talked about?" Chris said, ignoring Alex's crack.

The bookish-looking man took the iPad from Chris. "Poland is here; then we've got Lithuania, Latvia, and Estonia. As you know, all independent now from the old USSR. However, we believe there are hundreds of old connections to Putin's KGB in its new reality as the FSB. So, passing through any of these countries may be filled with potential problems."

"Why not just fly into the St. Petersburg airport?" Alex asked.

"Several reasons. First, they have CCTV, and we assume facial recognition everywhere. This has more to do with their Chechen and radical Islamic problems than Western interference. Besides, I think my face is in their database, so I must be careful."

"Aren't you located in Russia?" Alex asked.

"No, I'm in Berlin. We have people in Russia, extremely low-profile, and not connected with the United States government—and I need to protect them. Second, if we come for just seventy-two hours, tourist visas are easier to get. Even Russians enjoy the reduction of paperwork."

"I believe there are four ways to get into Russia—plane, boat, drive, and train," Alex said.

"Correct. I'm not a fan of a plane and the airport—too many layers of security. By boat is either by cruise ship or ferry. Smaller private boats take too long, and besides, I get seasick."

"You, seasick?" Dumas said.

Ignoring the remark, Lynch continued. "Driving can be a disaster. Let me remind you the roads inside Russia are dreadful. The borders are watched and sometimes take hours to get through. And it's not so much for getting in; it's the getting out. And once inside St. Petersburg, the traffic can be just plain awful. Some days, it's quicker to walk across the city."

"That leaves the train," Alex said. "I like trains. They are comfortable, run on time, have beverage carts." She pointed at the TV screen. "My geography is a bit challenged; is that Finland there above Russia?"

"Yes, wonderful, civilized, clean, and honest Finland," Lynch replied. "In all my years of dealing with White team, I've never had a problem with Finland."

"So?"

"In one sentence: We fly into Helsinki, take the four-hour train ride into St. Petersburg, find our target, take the train back into Finland, meet our CIA contacts at the Helsinki airport, clear Finnish customs, then fly us all out and safely home."

"How delightful. I can only think of maybe a dozen things that could go wrong," Alex said.

"Me too," Lynch agreed, "but I want this son of a bitch. Someone has to pay for what happened in Iowa."

"Be careful with the vengeance thing, Micah," Alex said. "It will cloud your thinking. Chris, regardless of what Micah said, the Russians aren't going to be thrilled with us sneaking into their country and kidnapping their citizens—even if the victims are willing. From what we heard from SA Case, the Russkies want this guy as much as we do. So, unless you have a secret underground railroad moving people out of Russia, we need to make sure that every step is covered. I assume we have more resources and someone to answer questions?"

"Yes, we do," Chris said. "He will be here later this afternoon. He grew up in St. Petersburg, knows the city as well as anyone. In fact, he's written two books on the history of the region and teaches Russian Soviet history at Texas A&M."

"You always know someone."

"After your meeting, you and Micah have less than twenty-four hours to get everything together. Tomorrow night, at midnight, you leave for Helsinki."

CHAPTER 5

That afternoon, Alex and Micah spent four hours with Professor Ivan Denisovich Kazakov. At the end of the briefing—which turned out to be more of a lecture on political theory and Russian history—Alex wasn't sure which was more screwed up, Russia or America's version of Russia. She learned it was the twenty-first century in Russia's cities, with all the trappings of modern civilization including traffic jams, bad television, and CCTVs. In much of the rest of the country, it was still pre-Lenin nineteenth century. She understood that the internal politics would take years to understand and that an underlying paranoia permeated everything. It was this paranoia that could contribute to the failure of their mission.

"Please remember this," Professor Kazakov said. "The Russian political body believes that everyone is after them, and they will do anything and everything to keep in power. They will protect Mother Russia and their dream of her future. It is a great place to make money, but do not cross the government. Hence the current post-Soviet institution, the powerful and ubiquitous Federal Security Service. The FSB exists to protect the government at all costs. Understand this, and you will begin to understand how to act when confronted by its operatives."

* * *

Twenty-four hours later, Alex and Micah climbed down the steps of the TSD Gulfstream G280 to the wet and glistening tarmac of Helsinki airport. It was almost midnight, and a cold summer rain left a sheen over every hard surface. They had spent the last fifteen hours in transit between Dallas and Helsinki; their one stop was for refueling at the St. John's Newfoundland airport. TSD employees Jack and Linda Monroe were the crew. Jack flew the jet; Linda was the attendant. Alex learned that Linda could take the controls if needed and was TSD's senior technician. She was also an excellent cook. The coffee on board had been fresh, and they were served a delicious dinner of Atlantic salmon and roasted potatoes somewhere over Iceland.

"This time of year, summer, the sun almost never sets in Helsinki. The same goes for St. Petersburg," Micah said as he and Alex jogged through the rain to the small glassed-in lobby of the private air service building, The Helsinki sky had a somber grey overcast that surprised Alex.

"This time of year, there's about three hours of partial darkness, then over twenty hours of daylight. It can really mess with your head," Micah told her.

When they entered the lobby, a woman in uniform met them.

"Welcome to Finland," the woman said in English. "I am with Finnish Customs. Please offer me your passports."

Alex and Micah handed over their passports and customs cards, and after a cursory review, the customs agent marked their passports with a small stamp.

"Your reasons for visiting Finland?" she asked.

"Business," Micah offered. "We are meeting with a manufacturing group in Helsinki, and then on to St. Petersburg for a short vacation."

"You will be returning here to Helsinki?"

"Yes, in about a week," Micah said. "Possibly sooner if we conclude our business."

"Where are you staying in Helsinki?"

"The Radisson near the train station," Micah answered.

"You have been before to Helsinki?" the agent asked.

"Yes, a few years ago. Beautiful city in summer, a little too cold in the winter."

"Yes, I agree, but it is my hometown. Enjoy your stay, Mr. and Mrs. Stapleton."

The customs agent left and climbed into a compact electric car parked at the curb; Alex watched as she drove off into the night. Their two bags were carried into the lobby by the air service's attendant. Alex took a seat in the lobby, slipped off her black leather backpack, and inserted the Stapleton passport into the front pocket next to her phone. She zipped it closed.

"The pilots are not waiting?" Alex asked. She watched through the window as the plane slowly maneuvered on the apron.

"No, Jack and Linda will fly onto Berlin tonight. Chris will meet them there. He's flying commercial in from Washington in two days, or at least that's the plan."

"A very busy man, as I've found out."

"I don't control his schedule; not sure anyone can," Micah said. He took out his phone and tapped the screen. "Our Uber will be here in five minutes."

He looked across the lobby to an alcove and spotted the vending machines. "I'm famished. There's a late-night restaurant a couple blocks from the hotel. We are already checked in at the Radisson; I suggest dinner. My blood sugar is already low. I'll get us reservations."

"At midnight?"

"I know people."

"Of course you do."

The drive into downtown Helsinki was, for Alex, as strange as the day she arrived in Saigon. It was raining then as well, but the chaos and confusion in that South Asian city were lacking here. There were few cars on the road and certainly not the thousands of motorbikes that clogged Vietnam's largest city. After a ten-minute drive, they traveled on city streets that were, compared to Ho Chi Minh City, empty and, to be honest, boring. The late-night yellow and green trolleys still wound their way along the streets; all were almost empty. A few taxis were parked along the curbs.

The restaurant Micah had chosen faced the area of Helsinki's harbor where the cruise ships and ferries berthed. Currently, only one of the vessels was tied up to the long pier; it's lights blazed in the near dark. It was a ferry.

"Some days, there are four and five of those massive beasts," Micah said as the Uber driver let them out in front of the restaurant. "Ten to fifteen thousand tourists suddenly descend on this poor village."

Alex remembered being in Venice and the comments about the cruise ships that dominated the town. She was well aware that she wasn't in Cleveland anymore.

Two hours later, Micah was spot-on about everything, especially the food and the service. However, the Belvedere on the rocks and her share of a bottle of Burgundy had gone straight to her head. She barely remembered the walk, the hotel lobby, and collapsing onto bed in the suite they'd rented. She did not forgive her phone for ringing; the screen read *Micah* and *9:05 AM*.

"Time to get up," Micah said. "Meet me in the coffee shop. Thirty minutes."

"Aye, aye, captain, my captain."

"It's cool and dry. Dress warm."

"You've been up?"

"Three hours, four-mile jog, call with Chris, and two coffees."

"I hate you, Mr. Stapleton."

The plan they had initially developed in Dallas and expanded on the flight over was simple. Then again, all plans were simple until they failed and became complex and took you to the edge of disaster, or worse, thought Alex. The night before, Lois and Robert Stapleton from Dallas, Texas, had arrived in Helsinki. Alex was even pleased with her passport photo. Their cover was a meeting with the Helsinki sales division of a company that "Robert" worked for in Dallas. The company was real, an Internet communications firm that was funded through the CIA. "Lois," if asked, worked for a Fort Worth security company as a manager. She carried business cards in her handbag. The firm also was real; however, the phone went through a switchboard controlled by TSD. Lois was on holiday while her husband attended meetings. As they told the customs agent, after Robert's sessions, they were taking the Allegro high-speed train into St. Petersburg to spend a few days as tourists. The travel agency TSD used had procured the temporary visas they needed. In the old city built by Tsar Peter the Great, they were staying at another Radisson hotel, less than a mile across the Neva River and the St. Petersburg Finlyandsky train station where, according to one of the plans, they were to meet their quarry.

Using an encrypted satellite phone, Micah was in regular contact with their TSD base in Dallas and with Chris. Alex and Micah both carried satellite smartphones. However, in Russia, one of Micah's local TSD operatives would pass on a pair of clean burner smartphones for their use in St. Petersburg. All contact with the hacker would be through his new contacts with the email address the American team had given him, which would then pass on the information to TSD. Then, via the encrypted sat-phone, to Micah. They would, until the initial meeting, avoid any contact directly with the hacker; this would avert the FSB from discerning any connection with the tourist couple named Stapleton traveling in Russia. Alex and Micah were there strictly to meet, question, and then, if required, extract. If at any time the hacker decided to bail, they would do their best to convince him to come with them. They were not to use force, or as said in the meeting, any other means of coercion that might drag the Russian authorities into the conversation. Alex wasn't sure if Micah was given different directions in the event the man walked away. She wanted to ask; however, she did remember the last conversation they had with Jake Dumas in Dallas.

"That means you can't kill the son of a bitch," he'd said.

"You sound disappointed," Alex said.

"Part of me feels there's a right way and a wrong way to go about this mission," Jake said, "my personal feelings aside. We're not like the current regime, who shoots their enemies on a bridge and leaves them there as an object lesson. Just try to make him see the advantages of coming with you."

"Good, since we *are* going in unarmed," Micah said.

After Alex dressed, and before she headed to the coffee shop, she read her email, including a message from Chris. The hacker had sent a new email:

> *Thank you for understanding. I also know there is much I have to atone for. We are not at fault for the accident in Iowa, but I know who is. I think I'm being watched. I am afraid for my family. Please help us.*

The American team responded with four questions:

What shall we call you?
How many in your group?
What do you want?
How do we contact you?

"I assume we didn't ask about a place to meet so that we can control the location?" Alex said to Micah in the coffee shop. "We are still not sure who this hacker is?"

"Exactly. I want all the control I can get. This could be an FSB attempt to probe our reactions to this crisis or a way to ferret out our people here in Russia. This wouldn't be the first time they've tried it, and this type of activity might make them believe we'd lower our guard."

"We will need to contact the hacker sometime," Alex told him.

"Let's see what the response is. We're four hours away from St. Petersburg. If this guy is real, we can meet him shortly after we get off the train. The longer we stay in Russia, the greater the chance of compromise, discovery, or worse."

Alex didn't need to be told what "worse" meant. The Russians had a problem with anyone meddling in their domestic affairs. If she and Micah were caught, there would be significant political blowback—"and our asses in a Russian jail," she said, finishing her thoughts aloud. "I'm not interested in a TSD version of *Mission Impossible*, where our existence is denied. We get in, make contact, and extract. It's simple. I had the same thing happen with a CI in Cleveland. But in that case, the informant was playing both sides against the middle. He was offering us information about a drug gang at the same time he was feeding our information to the gang. We found out all of his dealings after we fished his body out of the Cuyahoga River."

"Don't jump to any conclusions, yet." Micah poured more

coffee. "Our train leaves at sixteen hundred hours. It gets into Finlyandsky station at nineteen twenty-seven."

"So, you decided not to go to your meetings tomorrow?"

"What meetings?" Micah said, momentarily confused. Then it came to him: their cover.

Alex smiled. "You need to work on that; it's an easy trip-up. I assume the Finns are less paranoid about their foreign guests than the Russians?"

"That's a fair assumption. The less time we stay in one spot, the chances of us being discovered are also reduced. You have a few hours this morning to sightsee if you want. Helsinki is nice, though a little stark for my tastes. I lean to the southern European cities. When we get to St. Petersburg, you will notice some resemblance; the Russians controlled Helsinki and Finland for more than a hundred years. Like most of Europe, the First World War changed Finland. It's been an independent country since then, maybe one of Europe's oldest. It's also been a political and institutional battlefield between the West and the Soviets since the end of World War II. The Russians have not given up their political interest in this country."

Alex smiled again. "Politics aside, or maybe not, I saw a Starbucks around the corner. A latte and Wi-Fi connection will do. Then a nap. Where do you want me to meet you?"

"Hotel lobby, fifteen hundred hours."

She nodded. "Do we get to eat?"

"We will be in St. Petersburg for a late dinner. I have just the place."

"I expected no less."

CHAPTER 6

Ilya Sokolov nervously rubbed his thumbs against his fingertips. The laptop sat open in front of him; the email reply to his earlier message was direct and straightforward.

> *What shall we call you?*
> *How many in your group?*
> *What do you want?*
> *How do we contact you?*

The questions were simple, too simple. What could they do to save him? he wondered. Group? They believed him to be part of some group? Would they take the boys? And what the hell did he really want? The very last question was the easiest. The bigger question was who else was reading these messages. He felt his shoulders twitch. Once sent, he had no control over who might read the emails.

The summer heat reached in through the open window above the sink. It filled the apartment. He'd taken this unit on the eighth-floor south-facing side because experience had taught him that the winter sun would produce the most warmth and reduce his heating bill. The hot summer was the price to pay. He glanced at the clock; almost noon. They would be home precisely at 1:00 PM—the boys would insist. He had an hour. He rubbed his fingertips again, then let his fingers float over the keyboard. He typed a reply:

Fyodor, troika, svoboda, email.

His life had been a tragedy, one that would have matched Fyodor Dostoevsky's miserable life—the writer's name was the first that came to him. Ilya Sokolov was thirty-eight years old, the only son of now-dead parents. His father had died in Afghanistan during the war, killed when the Mujahideen overran his base camp. Later, one of the survivors and a friend of his father said the carnage and disrespect to the fallen were unimaginable. Ilya was four years old when his father didn't return. Sonya, his mother, the love of his young life, drank. She drank until one morning she didn't awaken when ten-year-old Ilya brought her tea. After his mother's death, he was placed on a train by a government agent and sent to an aunt living in St. Petersburg. That was thirty-two years ago.

Fyodor, three, freedom . . .

Within a few years of his resettlement to St. Petersburg, Ilya Sokolov watched as the old Soviet state collapsed. The ruble changed value daily, food was scarce, and he and his aunt lived in fear of the gangs wandering the streets. Slowly, order was restored, and when he entered high school, he discovered computers. His teacher said: "Engineering built the Soviet Union. We were great then. Computers and technology will now lead this new Russia into the future." Ilya Sokolov, loving the simple zeros and ones of computers, became a nerd.

His life was simple for a while. His tech aptitude gained him an undergraduate position at the university, and then additional degrees. Eventually, he was offered a job at the university and taught classes on integrated systems and programming. More than once, he was asked to join a group that he knew to be spamming internationally, stealing credit card data, and selling stolen personal information. He refused, even though he needed the money—which was desperately true—it just didn't seem right. An extraordinary principle in a country where morality seemed to have been lost, forgotten, or worse, rationalized. He would be a multimillionaire if he'd gotten into the pornography business. Russia, he often thought, was losing its soul.

In the advanced programming class he taught, a student, Ingrid Smolenskaya, caught his attention. She was older than the other students. She was beautiful, only a few years younger than he was, and she was fun. She grew up in Shlisselburg, an hour east of St. Petersburg, and her past was as complicated as his. She, too, was an orphan; her parents died in an automobile accident when she was eight years old. Her grandmother raised her. After high school, she went to St. Petersburg, where she enrolled in the university after making enough money to pay the tuition. They dated for a year, married, and nine months later she announced she was pregnant. Ilya's position at the university allowed them to move to a larger apartment; life seemed to be looking up. There was talk of abortion, but he convinced her to have the child. Three months into the pregnancy, they learned they were to have twins.

Gavril was the oldest by ten minutes. Both children, late in their first year, were slow to meet benchmarks, and by the time they were eighteen months, it was determined that both boys were potentially autistic. Both boys had exhibited hand-flapping behavior as toddlers.

By the time the boys were three years old, Ingrid was a disaster. She could barely take care of herself and her sons. She blamed Ilya for this, the boys, their condition, the demands on her. She'd known the boys were "damaged"; that's why she wanted the abortion, she claimed. She began to drink excessively. Some nights she went out alone. Sometimes she stayed out all night. Ilya's position at the university was in jeopardy because of the time he had to take off to care for the boys.

One winter morning, when the boys were age seven, police officials knocked on the door of his apartment.

"Are you Ilya Sokolov?" a man in a dark suit and full fur-lined hat asked as he held up a badge. A uniformed policeman stood a few paces away in the hallway.

Stunned, Ilya looked back into the kitchen where the boys were eating their breakfast. "Yes, Officer. I'm Ilya Sokolov."

"I'm Detective Orlov. May I come in?"

"What's this about? I have to get my boys off to school."

Ignoring Sokolov's comment, Orlov walked into the apartment and stood in the doorway leading to the kitchen. The boys ignored the man. The boys were picking their bits of cereal out of the bowl, one piece at a time. Pavel rocked back and forth, and each time he leaned toward the bowl, he took a piece. Gavril rocked side to side and did the same thing. It was as if they were moving to music, music only they heard. Orlov watched, then turned to Ilya.

"What's their problem?" Orlov asked.

"My boys are autistic," Ilya said. "They are eating breakfast to a tune I taught them when they were younger. Some days, it's the only way they will eat."

"Shouldn't they be in an institution or something?"

"They are highly functional; I've been working with them. Besides, there's not much out there from the state anyway. Detective, why are you here?"

Orlov inclined his head toward where the boys sat and then looked pointedly at Ilya. The two men stepped into the sparsely furnished outer room, out of immediate earshot of Ilya's sons. The detective removed a photo from the inside of his jacket. "I'm sorry to ask you this, but do you know this woman?"

Ilya looked at the photograph; it was Ingrid. Her right cheek and right eye were heavily bruised. Her left eye stared blankly at the camera. Ilya looked toward the kitchen, steadied himself with his hand on the back of the one upholstered chair in the room. "My wife," he whispered.

"I'm sorry for your loss," Orlov said. It had the tone of a phrase said far too often. "Do you have any idea why she would be at the—"

From the kitchen, there came a yell. Pavel had pushed away from the table and was jumping up and down. "Won, I won, I won," he yelled. "Won, I won, I won . . ."

"What the hell?" Orlov asked.

"He's all right. It's a game he plays with his brother. The first to finish wins."

"Wins what?"

"Bragging rights. Nothing else matters."

The men watched as Gavril took one of his remaining pieces of cereal and placed it in Pavel's bowl. He tapped his brother on the shoulder and pointed.

"Shit," Ilya said, and quickly walked back into the kitchen.

Pavel saw the single ring-shaped blue Froot Loop in the bowl and instantly began to bang his hands against the wall, screaming. "Won, I won. I won, I won." He repeated it over and over.

"You do not do that, Gavril; I've told you that. Gavril, look at me. Gavril, look . . . at . . . me." Ilya pointed two of his fingers toward his own eyes and then at Gavril. "Do not do that to your brother. You keep your cereal in your bowl."

"I win now. Empty, empty, empty," Gavril said, seemingly oblivious to his father as he picked up his bowl and held it high over his head.

Ilya reached into the box of cereal and took a handful of the colorful cereal and put more in each bowl. "Now both of you are tied. Start over. I'll be right over there with that man."

Pavel stopped his yelling, and both boys turned and looked at the detective; it was as if they were seeing him for the first time.

"Who is he? Is he a stranger?" Gavril asked.

"No, a friend. Both of you, finish your cereal. You have to go to school. When you are through eating, go get your coats."

Ilya walked back to the detective; an immense sadness overwhelmed him. "Ingrid is dead, isn't she?"

"Yes, her identification papers were found in her purse. There was no money."

"She had no money, or at least any that I knew of. Where?"

"In a courtyard behind Dumskaya Street. Some tourists found her."

Ilya was still holding the photograph; he looked at it again. "She would spend the day with the boys while I worked. Then leave soon after I got home. Some nights, I wouldn't see her until morning."

"So, you don't know why she was there?"

"Yes, I know, to get away from them and from me. This was all too much for her—they were too much for her. She said she needed a life; it was my fault the boys are"—he gestured toward the kitchen, where the boys had resumed their eating race. "Detective, she stayed longer than I thought she would. Nonetheless, she did not deserve this." He looked again at the photo.

Now, three years later, Ilya looked back at the screen of the laptop, wishing that an email reply would come before Anya and the boys returned. There were already questions asked about the boys, questions that came from the school they attended. There were other autistic children in the program, some even gifted. However, twice the boys had been caught using the computers in the school's library. The director of the school called it playing, but Ilya knew better. For Pavel and Gavril, the keyboard was like a doorway, a dark and dangerous doorway they used to access the digital world.

CHAPTER 7

The woods were thick and evergreen. Alex watched the Finnish villages zip by as the train seemed to almost silently slide on the rails to St. Petersburg, its modern design effortlessly adjusting to the sharp curves of the route. The small electronic sign above the connecting door read *210 kph*. Their first stop was Lahti; it was brief. For the next hour and a half, they stopped three more times, the last time in Vyborg, a village just across the border in Russia. Alex's Starbucks stop, just before they'd boarded the train, provided an opportunity to check out the passengers on her way to and from the tiny restroom in their car. Almost all were tourists, American and European. Only one of the passengers in the car she and Micah occupied looked like a businessman. He'd laid out pages of notes and diagrams on the small table mounted in front of his business-class seat. He wore earbuds and whispered on his phone.

"Any spies?" Micah asked as she took her seat.

"That couple over there, I swear they are working for MI6," Alex answered. "The perfect cover. He's portly, drinking a beer; she's in a colorful dress reading a Michelin tourist guide for St. Petersburg. It's all extremely suspicious."

"Exactly what you'd think of MI6." Micah looked up at the electronic sign. "Twenty minutes, Mrs. Stapleton. When we leave the train, I'll check the emails. The Radisson is just across the river, a short taxi ride. We will walk a few blocks—I don't trust any taxi at the station. Keep any comments innocuous and touristy. I'll respond accordingly. Be excited or act tired; it all works for me."

"Me, tired? We've come halfway around the world and are now clicking along at high speed, on a train I didn't know existed three days ago, to a city that all I know about I saw on World War II documentaries, and even then, it was called Leningrad. I'm tired, hungry, and still want to know why you dragged me here."

Micah leaned in. "That may be laying it on a little too thick."

"Which part, sweetie?" She kissed him on the cheek. The businessman looked up from his papers and smirked.

Alex believed that to enter Russia there might be a strip search somewhere in the process. The customs agent, a tall, officious woman, walked through the car looking at passports. The uniform, vaguely military, did not hide any of the curves and assets of the agent. When she reached them, she briefly looked at both passports, smiled, and in remarkably good English said, "I hope you have a wonderful time in St. Petersburg. I've heard so much about Texas. I have a brother in Austin at the university."

"Lovely town," Micah said. "And thank you. I'm sure we'll have a delightful time." He reached up for their passports; the agent smiled and handed them to Alex. She then went to the next row of seats.

Alex whispered in Micah's ear. "FSB?"

"Most probably."

"And you think I'm paranoid."

Arriving in St. Petersburg, they walked through Finlyandsky station. Micah pulled out his phone and tapped on the screen. Wondering what he was doing, Alex followed him out to the street. They walked to the corner of Komsomola and Botkinskaya; she only knew this because that's what the signs read. Half were English, the others Cyrillic. Across the street, a park-like plaza extended away from the station. A massive statue of a man, right arm thrust out, stood in the center of the plaza.

"That, Alex, is a statue of Vladimir Ilyich Ulyanov," Micah said, gesturing toward the blackened figure on its dais. "Better known to us as Lenin. He is the man who launched a thousand revolutions and probably, directly and indirectly, the deaths of a hundred million people. This same train station is where, in 1917, he entered Russia from Helsinki. While the revolution had been fermenting for years, it was his coming back to Petrograd, as it was called then, that really started it all." He shrugged. "The Soviets love their monuments."

The evening temperature was warm, the traffic busy. A tour bus passed through the intersection and stopped at the curb that fronted the Lenin plaza. From where Alex and Micah stood, a block away, they could hear the Chinese narration. A dozen people stood in the open upper deck of the bus taking pictures.

"The new revolutionaries meet the old," Alex said as she watched. The bus moved on.

Two minutes later, a Mercedes sedan pulled up to the curb; the driver rolled down the window.

"Mr. Stapleton, I presume?" the driver asked.

"Otto?"

"That's me, boss. Radisson?"

As they wound through the streets, Alex asked, "I thought we were taking a taxi?"

"I assume that everything we say is heard, everything we do is watched. That's why the change. Besides, this is Yuri; we've worked together."

"You called him Otto."

"I go by many names, Mrs. Stapleton. Otto, Yuri, Sergei,

whatever."

Alex turned and stared at Micah; he gave her a big smile.

"And besides, Uber Black is a good cover; this ride is unregistered," Micah told her. "Anyone watching will see the window sign and begin to try and track the Uber license plate. The license is real for the car, but for the next twenty minutes, we should be untraceable. Call him."

Alex clicked on her sat-phone, tapped a number, and waited.

"Chris, we're in St. Petersburg," she said and clicked on the speaker. "Anything new?"

"Our guy sent a response," Chris answered. "*Fyodor, troika, svoboda, email.*"

"Three and freedom," Micah said. "Fyodor, is that his name?"

"We are guessing that it's an alias. We are also waiting for another response. How's the weather there?"

"Warm and pleasant," Alex answered.

"It was thirty below the last time I was in St. Petersburg," Chris said. "Enjoy it. I will email you the next piece of information. I don't have to tell you, when the time is right, to be ready to jump."

"We'll be ready," Micah said.

"Is Yuri there?"

"Hi, boss. I'm here."

"Keep them safe. In and out, no complications. Got it?"

"Got it, boss."

* * *

At the tap on the door, Director Ivanovich looked up from the thick file open and spread across his desktop. Tanya stood there, smiling.

"News?"

"Possibly. Between the cameras worn by our customs agents, the cameras in the cars, and the CCTVs mounted in the Finlyandsky station, we have an anomaly. We have a face that does not match a name."

"Or a name that does not match a face?"

"Both." Tanya placed three photos on the desk, turning them so they were right-side up from Ivanovich's perspective. "This one"—she tapped the top photo with a slim finger—"was taken earlier on the Allegro train from Helsinki. The couple, identified through their passports, are Robert and Lois Stapleton, American. Tourists, according to the customs agent. These others were taken at the Finlyandsky train station. The first is when they walked through the station, and the second is on the sidewalk in front of the station. They caught an Uber, a Mercedes."

"Damn American businesses," Ivanovich swore. "They will destroy us."

"The face of this Stapleton man matches a suspected agent connected to the United States government; one we know well. He is traveling as an independent contractor of some type. The face matches others we have on record from public buildings in Moscow and Volgograd and St. Petersburg. It matches at least three other passports."

"Busy man. And the woman?"

"No idea, nothing on file, and the name Stapleton does not match any we cross-reference to."

"Thoughts?"

"The timing is what we would expect. The incident in Iowa was five days ago. There has been time for a team to be assembled and sent to St. Petersburg. I assume there has been some contact between the hacker and the Americans. That is possibly why 'Mr. and Mrs. Stapleton' have come to St. Petersburg."

"On any given day, Tanya, ten thousand tourists arrive in St.

Petersburg. They come by cruise ship, ferry, train, and airplane. Why do you think we should be watching this pair?"

"Because we know this man; I know this man. We have thought he was CIA or NSA, but we were never able to confirm that suspicion."

Ivanovich glanced up at her. "You know this man? Who and how?"

"His name is Micah Lynch," Tanya said. "Twenty-three years ago, we both attended the Anglo-American School here in Moscow. My parents believed it was in my best interests to get a quality education. We are the same age. He left the school when his parents were transferred out of Russia. I later learned they were stationed in Berlin. It was no secret that his parents were with the American State Department—I will verify that. We were never close, but he was a good-looking American, so I took an interest."

"Fascinating, and you are sure it's the same person?"

Tanya gave him an odd look. "It was a long time ago, and I was a teenager. In this case, nonetheless, we are researching his identification. His gait and physique at the age of thirty-seven says military training. That's what I would expect; again, we are still investigating."

"You are giving away your age, Tanya."

"Don't be rude. You know exactly how old I am, Director," Golubev said. "There may be other reasons for Micah Lynch to be in St. Petersburg. However, right now, I'd wager that it is to find this hacker. It is the way the Americans act. They need to find the perpetrators, and then they will seek vengeance. And, based on our reports, this is also being done"—she paused—"'under the sheets,' I believe they say. He is not on any official CIA, FBI, or NSA list that we have. He knows Russia and has visited three times, that we know of, during the last five years."

"I want to know what that man is doing here and the woman with him, as well. When can you be in St. Petersburg?"

"I've made reservations on the night train out of Leningradsky station. I will be in St. Petersburg tomorrow morning. I will have our people meet me there."

"Take the jet; it will be faster."

"You know I hate to fly. Besides, I can sleep—something I've not done since this operation began. And you can then reach me anytime."

"You know this man? Fascinating," Ivanovich said for the second time. "When you find him, what are you going to do?"

"Simple—stop him from discovering what we are doing, Director Ivanovich. He must not learn about Nightshade."

"And if you can't?"

"Make sure that he, and anyone with him, can't find out. And if he does, make sure that they tell no one."

CHAPTER 8

Fyodor, troika, svoboda. One out of three, Alex thought. Who wouldn't want a big dollop of *svoboda*? Why would this hacker, this mass murderer, use the term? He was obviously smart, maybe worldly, and had what was assumed to be a family, hence the *troika*. He apologized, wanted forgiveness, and freedom. She was sure of one thing: Forgiveness and freedom were not things that she could give.

The Mercedes passed over a bridge; water flanked both sides.

"The Liteyny Bridge," Yuri said. "This is the famous Neva River. When Peter the Great built this city, he imagined a Russian version of Venice and its canals. There are over three hundred kilometers of canals throughout the city, and these bridges interconnect the major islands that make up the city proper—there are hundreds of them. This particular one connects the Liteyny and Vyborgsky districts."

"Our travel guide," Micah said. "You don't have to tip him."

"Thanks, boss, you don't have to tell her that," Yuri said.

Alex was looking out the car window, her thoughts of the hacker overlaying the view of the five- and six-story buildings that lined the canal. The colorful structures were lit by the late-afternoon sun. Hundreds of boats maneuvered along the canal; many were tour boats. The waterway and the buildings reminded her of the five days she'd spent in Venice. "What?" she asked belatedly.

"Yuri, travel guide . . ." Micah saw the look on her face. "What's up?"

Alex took a deep breath as they reached the far side of the river. "This whole thing stinks. Here we are, ready to snatch some guy off a Russian street and take him back for American justice. He wants freedom. He's not an idiot; he probably believes he's safer here than where we'd be taking him. So, why? And he has two associates or family or, hell, maybe two cats. We don't know. And this Fyodor is just a name pulled out of the air. We need his real name; we need more. You tell me how we will get him out. Passports? Visas? Our visas are good for a month, but if we are not out of here in two days, we might never leave. Or, due to the FSB, never be let out, either."

"Agreed," Micah said. "Our cover will last two days, maybe three at most. We will assume less. When we meet with the hacker, we will need to get him a passport; we will also need to get him a passport for each of his . . . cats. Yuri has that taken care of; all we need are pictures."

"At your service, boss," came from the front seat.

Alex's sat-phone beeped. She turned on the speaker. "Chris?"

"Tonight is one of the last nights of the White Nights Festival," Chris began. "Micah will explain it. Fyodor sent another email. He has asked to meet you at Peter the Great's cabin; it's a tourist spot across the river from your hotel. The time is twenty-three hundred and thirty hours. He will be wearing a blue jacket and yellow ascot; strange, but as he said, he wants to look different. The bridges will be lifted and remain open across many of the canals and the river. Make sure you are on the Petrogradsky side, the side where the cabin is, before the bridges open at about 1:00 AM. It's a fifteen-minute walk from the Radisson. Give him one of the phones that Micah has; they are clean. Our friend already knows that he has to take pictures of the two people who will be traveling with him. He will email these to us; we will see that Yuri gets them."

"Do we know yet who these others are?" Micah asked.

"No—all he would say is they are his family, all that he has. We will know who they are when we get the photos; Yuri knows what to do after we send the photos to him. What I want from you is to take the measure of this man. Alex, I want to know what you think about this guy. Is he real, or is this a big ruse to make us trip up? Give it your best gut feel. Micah, the same."

"Yes, boss. I assume the extraction is still a go?" Micah asked.

"Yes. Tomorrow you will be on the afternoon train back to Helsinki. I've set up reservations for five. Simple—in and out. Pick up this man and his family, get them on the train. It is imperative. We assume that the FSB is also hunting this guy."

"And they have people in Finland . . ." Alex said.

"More than likely. Enjoy the festival. It's quite something— lots of fireworks, massive crowds. Use the chaos and noise to your advantage."

There was a pause. When Chris came back on, he said to someone, "*Danke, es war sehr lecker.*" Then another pause. "Alex, I will meet the two of you, our new friend, and his family at the Helsinki train station. I'm in Berlin right now; I will fly into Helsinki tomorrow afternoon. When all is squared away, we will fly back to the States."

"Then what?" Alex asked.

"Fyodor and his family will become the problem of the United States government and our work is done."

Yuri stopped the car in front of a stately corner building; the signage over the door read *Radisson*. For some reason she couldn't remember, Alex believed that Russian hotels would be something out of one of the scenes from *Dr. Zhivago*: old, musty, threadbare carpets, women in rough clothing washing the floor. The Radisson Royal did not come close to fitting that image. The lobby's intricate marble floor, the modern furniture, and the well-stocked bar off the lobby reminded her of the Principe di Savoia in Milan. That was the hotel she'd been delivered to by that strange retired MI6 character Dugan Mc-Corly. Then had come the three days there with Javier Castillo. This was the first time she'd thought of Javier since landing in Finland. Now, what to make of that? For a time, a few months earlier, she believed she could love the man. Maybe it was the rebound from her marriage, or her age, or hell . . . she had no idea. When your whole world is upside down, you grab for what you believe will keep you upright.

"Your key card, madam. There are two inside the envelope," a voice said, punching through Alex's reverie. She looked at the woman behind the counter and took the small cardboard packet that held the key cards.

"Thank you, Elena," Alex answered, noting the nameplate. "This way, Robert." She slung her backpack and handbag over her shoulder, picked up her small suitcase, and they headed to the elevator. A young man walked up and offered to take their suitcases; she politely declined. As the door to the elevator closed, she scanned the lobby and saw a couple sitting in the warm-grey leather chairs. The woman quickly looked away when she noticed Alex's attention.

"Spies in the lobby," Alex said softly.

"Would expect nothing less," Micah responded, then put his index finger to his lips.

They rode in silence to the fourth floor and continued in silence until they reached their room door. Alex slipped a key card in and out. They entered.

"Not bad, for a Russian hostel," Micah said and walked into

the bathroom. There he turned on the shower and motioned Alex to follow.

"Mr. Stapleton, I will take my shower alone, thank you," she said.

Micah whispered, "Assume this place is bugged. No calls out or in. I'll text Chris."

Alex nodded, having assumed as much.

"Take your shower and take your time," Micah continued. "I'm going to get a few winks; it will be a long night. I'll take the couch. We are out of here at twenty-two hundred. No chauffeur; Yuri prefers not to be stuck on the wrong side of the river when they open the bridges. Besides, after he gets the photos, he has a lot to do."

He headed for the sofa. "What do you want to eat?" he added as Alex shut the bathroom door.

"Not a chance," she said, poking her head out the doorway. "You promised me something nice for dinner. After your nap, we are going out."

The restaurant was the Syrovarnya, a mixture of Italian and European influences.

"You actually do know your restaurants," Alex said a bit wide-eyed over the ambiance and the food.

"I try to please," Micah said. "I ate here about a year ago. The food has actually improved. I'm glad you like it."

As they walked the six blocks back to the hotel on Nevsky Avenue, Micah spoke again about World War II and the impact on the city.

"The siege of Leningrad lasted almost nine hundred days, from September 1941 to January 1944," Micah began. "The city Peter the Great built was utterly destroyed; almost everything you see around us was built from the ruins. More than a million and a half Russians, civilian and military, died. Another million fled the city; many of those also died. The German army swept up through Lithuania, then Latvia and Estonia. The Finns, who were also at war with the Russians, pushed down from the north. For the Germans it was a racial war; they considered the Russians worthless human beings—and being communist, only worth the labor they could be forced to do until they died. The siege was one of the most brutal of the war; Hitler ordered that the German commanders were not to accept surrender. The city was to be exterminated. And they came close."

"Unbelievable. I had no idea. I've found Americans to be somewhat uneducated when it comes to the Second World War."

"What happened here would have repercussions we are still living with today."

Alex nodded soberly. "It doesn't get completely dark here during the summer, does it?" she said after a moment, her gaze taking in the broad boulevard. Hundreds of people walked about. The street was clogged with trolleys, cars, and buses.

"No. There's always a touch of light in the summer sky, unlike winter, when the nights never seem to end."

"The White Nights."

"Yes. A mix of Russian romanticism, geography, marketing, and folklore. I prefer the romance and folklore parts. It's really just a state of mind for the locals. Proms, weddings, even graduations all happen about now. Some stay up all night. Even the cruise ships take advantage of the opportunity and allow their passengers to enjoy at least one evening walking the canals, taking in the sites, watching the fireworks. All for us and our faux romantic evening."

"And the bridges that Chris mentioned?"

"Starting about one o'clock, they keep them open until about five. It allows the bigger ships to move up and down the river. And the subway is also down at midnight, too."

St. Petersburg White

A block from the hotel they stopped at a Starbucks. Over espressos, Micah opened a map and laid it on the counter. "We'll take this route and cross over here; it's a leisurely walk. After our meeting, I have a surprise for you."

CHAPTER 9

Ilya watched his sons eat their dinner; he'd brought home a large pizza from the shop on Chkalovskiy Prospekt. It was the boys' favorite food; Ilya was certain they would eat cheese pizza every night if he allowed it. Down the street was a KFC, their second favorite. After tomorrow, he wasn't sure what they would eat. Using his phone, he took photos of the boys and a couple of himself. They were in the face-on look the Americans requested. He emailed them to the address they had included in their response. He then deleted the photos and the email and address from his phone.

The response from the Americans to his four words was curious, no questions about the reason for the name he'd given or his statement of three people. Not even a question about his request for freedom, which in his mind was more about asylum and protection for his boys than real freedom. In Russia, real freedom came when you were dead.

Gavril took another piece of pizza and folded it over onto itself. Pavel watched and did the same. Then they both tried to put the whole slice in their mouths.

"Boys," Ilya said, "do not do that. You will choke. Take that out, smaller bites."

The boys looked up at their father and then slowly spit out the pizza onto the plates in front of them. They each took another slice and began taking small bites from the edges. Pavel rocked back and forth as he ate. Soon Gavril joined him. As they continued to eat, they swayed to a tune only they heard.

"How was the zoo today, Pavel?" Ilya asked.

"Elephants were very big; the giraffes were very tall; the seals were very noisy."

Gavril began to bark. He sounded remarkably like a real seal. "See, Papa, I can bark like a seal."

"Gavi's a seal, a seal, a seal," Pavel began.

"That's enough, Pavel. And you, too, Gavril. Did you study your books this afternoon?"

The boys looked at each other as if passing between them some sign or secret message. Then to his father, Gavril said, "Yes, we read the books. They were wrong a few times. They got to the right answer, but their . . . log . . ."

"Logic."

"Yes, Papa, logic was wrong, and the numbers were not pretty. Pavel wrote a much better answer. His are so much more pretty."

"The word is elegant."

"El-e-gant," Pavel said. "Elegant, elephant, elegant, elephant."

"Anya is coming over later to watch TV with you this evening. I'm going out for a while. I want you to stay away from my computer. I've said this before and you must pay attention. You can only use the computer when I am at home and sitting with you. Do you understand? Gavril, look at me."

Gavril turned his head and imitated his father's gesture of pointing two fingers. "I am looking."

"Good, do you understand? Pavel?"

"Yes, Papa, no computer. You must be here."

"Gavril? Gavril?"

"Yes, Papa, I understand."

"Go wash your hands. And, Gavril, please put what's left of the pizza in the refrigerator."

Pavel continued to rock slowly back and forth; he began a rhyme, his voice slowly rising.

> *Tra-ta-ta, tra-ta-ta,*
> *The she-cat married the tomcat,*
> *With Catovitch tomcat,*
> *With Piotr Piotrovitch.*
> *The tomcat is strolling on the bench,*
> *He holds the she-cat by the paw*
> *Tap-tap on the bench.*
> *Scratch-scratch from the paws.*

It was a nursery rhyme Ingrid taught them as babies. When they were stressed, they rocked back and forth, often repeating the verse in a singsong manner. Even to Ilya, it was mesmerizing. While learning the rhyme from their mother, the boys had mimicked a cat scratching. It was one of the few endearing things Ilya could remember about their mother.

"Where to, Papa?" Gavril said. "Where to, tonight, Papa? Where to?" Gavril began to singsong and repeat himself.

Pavel continued to sing even louder. Ilya closed his eyes and took a deep breath, then slammed both his hands flat on the table. It broke the singsong momentum. The boys, wide-eyed, looked at their father.

"That is enough," Ilya said. "I am going to take a walk; I will be back before the bridges open. Do you remember what happens when they open the bridges?"

"Fireworks."

"Yes, fireworks."

"Too loud, too loud," Gavril said. "But pretty."

"El-e-gant," Pavel said.

"I will be home before the fireworks; Anya can take you to the roof, and you can watch the fireworks with us."

"Too high," Pavel said.

"You sit on the roof, like I showed you, and watch from there. Then both of you to bed."

It was a mile from the apartment to the cabin that Peter the Great used as his base of operations while the old city was under construction. It was small and now faced with red brick; the cabin was claimed to be the oldest structure in the city. A small park fronted the cabin and overlooked the Neva River. The crowd in this part of St. Petersburg was mostly locals and tourists. They stood shoulder to shoulder and lined the river to watch the boats and the fireworks. As Ilya walked to the cabin along the canal that encircled Peter and Paul Fortress and the Cathedral with its magnificent golden spire and angel top piece, he believed that he would never, after tomorrow, see these places again. He passed the monument to the nine-teenth-century revolutionary movement the Decembrists; it was here the tsar hanged the leaders of the failed movement. The rest were sent to exile in Siberia. Why did it feel like going to America was like he was sending his family to Siberia?

He adjusted his coat and the ascot; he felt the fool for wear-ing it, but looking at the thousands walking the embankments, he knew he'd chosen correctly. When he reached the small park next to the cabin, he wasn't sure what to do next. He was fifteen minutes early; the fireworks in this part of the city would start at eleven. On his second tour of the park—it was well past the appointed time he'd told the Americans—a man wearing glasses, a baseball cap, and a lightweight jacket stopped and stood in his path. Next to him was a striking blonde wom-an; she looked Russian. Ilya's heart began to beat furiously; the adrenaline pumped; his breathing came in short bursts.

"*Fyodor, eto ty moy staryy drug? Gde ty byl, my skuchali po tebe,*" the man said. The woman smiled.

The man's Russian was excellent, almost perfect, with a

touch of a Muscovite accent. Friend? Old friend? "*Staryy drug?*" Ilya echoed. "*Ya mog by zadat' vam tot zhe vopros, gde vy byli?*" (I could ask you the same question; where have you been?) "*Vy vse yeshche govorite po-angliyski?*" he added.

"Yes, we speak English. We were caught up with the crowds on the other side of the river, my friend. I am Robert Stapleton, and this is my wife, Lois."

The man reached out to shake Ilya's hand. Ilya held back.

"You will need to trust us, Fyodor. Your emails did make it through," the man said. "You said you have three to travel with you to freedom. These are family members?"

Hearing the faux name, Ilya relaxed. "Yes, my two boys. They are ten years old."

"Boys?" the woman asked. "Are they twins?"

"Yes. Unfortunately, their mother died three years ago. They are all I have."

The woman looked at the man, said something about it being manageable.

"Did you take the photographs and send them on as directed?" the man, Robert, asked.

"Yes, they were sent." Ilya took a deep breath. "What's next? Considering what has happened in Iowa and your government's reaction, and the potential interest by my government, I need to get my family out of Russia, now. I hope you have a plan. I have no money. I can't even buy a train ticket. The thought of a passport, visas, even food for the boys is more than I can afford. I can assure you, though, that your people will be interested in what I have, very interested. I'm fortunate that I've not been arrested."

"How would the Russian government know what happened?" the woman asked.

"How would they find you?" the man said.

"There might be some connection to a government computer that I am allowed to use as a part of my teaching."

"You used a government computer?" Robert Stapleton asked. "This all happened with a Russian computer?"

"It is a Chinese-made Lenovo. Very powerful."

"Jesus Christ."

"What do you teach?" Lois Stapleton asked, deflecting the conversation, as they continued to casually stroll around the park, which insulated them somewhat from the crowds filling the walkways along the river.

"Integrated systems and programming at the ITMO Institute. I have been there for almost eleven years. I started there a year before the boys were born. It's a good job; the pay is the shits."

"Then, why the attack?"

"It was just a game I built. I'd written this program that dealt with operating systems. I was fooling around, and it accidentally worked its way into the Iowa power grid. You know what happened then."

"Over one hundred and fifty Americans are dead because of your playing around," the woman said. "We should leave you here for the FSB."

At the mention of the police, Ilya's heart again began to beat faster. "There are other things that need to be understood by your government, important things, dangerous and evil things."

"And they are?" Robert asked.

"Things that need to be talked about with persons at your CIA and NSA, not you two. These things need to be known at the highest level."

"This is not a negotiation. You came to us, remember?"

"Well, right now it is a negotiation. There will be a trade: my information for *svoboda*—simple. Get my boys and me out of Russia. Give us freedom, and I will tell you what I know."

For a moment, Ilya wasn't sure what these Americans would do. They could turn around and walk away, leaving him to his fate. Or they could string him along and when they got him to the United States, dump him in prison. Or, they could just shoot him. For Ilya Sokolov, alias Fyodor, the options were bad and worse than bad. Any dreams of leaving this behind him rested on these two strangers and faith.

The sound of sirens broke the relative quiet of the park; they came from both the left and right and were getting louder.

"What the hell?" Robert Stapleton said. "Is this your doing, Fyodor? Are these your people?"

"I don't know what's happening. I didn't call anyone."

The seesaw wailing continued to get louder. Ilya could see that the two Americans were nervous. The woman turned to him.

"You better be sure those photos were sent. Without them, you go nowhere," she said. "We will meet you in front of the Lenin statue at Finlyandsky station at two o'clock tomorrow afternoon. Bring everything you need, nothing more. And be on time."

Flashing lights could be seen; the whine of the sirens bounced off the surrounding buildings. Ilya looked every-where, expecting to see police officers running toward them.

He looked at the woman. "We will be there. Two o'clock. Finlyandsky station. I must go."

Without saying anything more, Ilya turned away and quickly left the park. Within moments, he melded into the throng of people along the riverbank.

* * *

Alex watched "Fyodor" leave.

"Strange man," she said. "Nervous and a little paranoid."

"Live here long enough, and you will become paranoid as

well," Micah responded, speaking just loudly enough to be heard over the sounds of the approaching sirens. "That's the result of a hundred years of someone looking over your shoulder, arresting your neighbors, or just shooting everyone in your village. The Russians have perfected the not-so-subtle art of institutional paranoia."

The sirens were almost upon them; from each direction an ambulance appeared. They stopped directly across from the park, where a small crowd had gathered along the river wall and railing. A woman stood holding a flag on a long stick—she was standing next to someone lying motionless on the sidewalk. There were two dozen others grouped around the body; the EMTs quickly went to work.

"Tour group. Damn, that's not how I want to end up," Micah said. "On a sidewalk in St. Petersburg with a tour guide waving her sign over me. Shit, no way." He put his hand lightly on Alex's elbow. "This way. We need to get over the bridge before it opens—we have maybe twenty minutes."

They pushed their way through the crowds. The vehicle traffic had slowed to almost nothing; the drivers knew when the bridges opened and which side of the river they needed to be on. The crowd had swelled at the bridgehead, anticipating the opening. A gate had already lowered, barring pedestrians and vehicles from the bridge. Alex and Micah looked at each other; they were on the wrong side. Across the surface of the river, on both sides of the bridge, hundreds of boats gathered and jockeyed for position, waiting for the opening.

"Shit," Alex said as they watched the center of the span break and then slowly rise. "Too late."

Surrounding them were hundreds of people, mostly tourists. Many held their smartphones up to catch the slow rise of the bridge. A thin crease of orange light held on the horizon; purple-blue tones blanketed the sky. Nearing one o'clock in the morning, it was like nine o'clock on a late-summer evening in Cleveland. Alex turned and saw that Micah was finishing a phone call; he was smiling. He answered her questioning look with another history lesson.

"So much history of Russia surrounds us," Micah said, using his arm as a pointer. "And most especially the last one hundred years. We've left the cabin of Peter the Great, which was his construction trailer for the start of this city. Over there, with its golden spear-like tower, is Peter and Paul Cathedral, where most of the tsars are buried. There, across the river is the Hermitage, once the home for more than two hundred years of Russia's emperors and empresses. It's now a museum. This bridge, a new French design, carried tens of thousands of protestors from here in the Petrograd District to there"—he pointed across the river—"to the parks and plazas of the palace, all to overthrow the government and Tsar Nicholas II. And there"—he gestured again, this time pointing west across the narrow canal—"is the massive Peter and Paul fortress that was never needed. I'm still amazed by the resiliency of the citizens of St. Petersburg."

Alex followed Micah's arm gestures as he did a complete circle, pointing and talking as he went. Across the river, every building from the far end of the Troitsky Bridge to the bridge downriver that Micah called the Palace Bridge was illuminated with thousands of lights. Blue and yellow façades lined the shoreline from bridge to bridge.

"And my guess," Alex said, "is whoever controls the electrical power of this city may control Russia."

Micah looked at her and smiled. "Yes, that's a good guess, but in today's world the power isn't for the lights; now, like back in the time of the tsars, one man controls the electricity that is Russia." He looked out toward the river. "Our ride comes."

"What?"

Alex followed Micah to a stairway leading downward a hundred yards from the bridge. A three-masted frigate floated another hundred yards farther. The steps of the landing disappeared into the river. A motor launch slowly approached; a big man stood at the controls.

"Good evening, Yuri. Thanks for the ride," Micah said as he and Alex climbed over the gunnel.

"You were right. You did think you might get stuck on the wrong side." The Russian maneuvered the boat out into the flow of water traffic. When he saw an opening, he cut diagonally across the river.

"You knew we would be stuck?" Alex said.

"There was a chance, and besides this city must be seen from its canals, and at night—it's quite a place. And if there is a chance we were followed, they can't follow us now. Yuri, down the river to the Admiralty Canal, then I'll leave the rest of the tour to you. Alex, sit back and enjoy."

"Boss, there's champagne and caviar in the cooler. Help yourself," Yuri said as they slowly motored past the multi-columned blue façade of the Hermitage.

Again, Alex looked questioningly at Micah.

"In about twelve hours, all hell will possibly break out," he said. "So, we have a few hours to enjoy this city, be tourists for a while. Have a glass of bubbly and Russia's finest fish eggs, for tomorrow, who the hell knows?"

For the next hour, after crossing the Neva River, Yuri followed dozens of other launches, yachts, and tour boats up and down the canals that transected the Kazansky and Kolomensky islands. Alex was as lost as she had been six months earlier in Venice, and like then, she didn't care. They pulled to the side of the canal to get out of the flotilla and called Chris. After bringing him up to date, they continued to the Anichkov Bridge and the nearby landing. They left Yuri at the stone landing along the wall of the canal.

As they walked up Nevsky Prospect to their hotel, Alex was both exhausted and exhilarated. It was three o'clock in the morning when they entered the hotel and the mostly empty lobby; one man sat in the lounge area off the lobby, and he looked asleep.

"I'm beat. Long day yesterday, and I expect an even longer one today," Micah said. He nodded over to the sleeping man in the chair. "My guess, FSB. Our little secret may be out."

They walked through the lobby to the elevators.

"Breakfast is at 9:00 AM," Micah said as they entered their room.

"We get to sleep in, goody."

Ten minutes later, Alex was out like a light.

CHAPTER 10

Tanya Golubev exited the Moskovsky railway station in St. Petersburg. Even though it was six thirty in the morning, the sun was well above the eastern horizon. The air was damp; she felt and tasted the presence of the sea. To a Muscovite, the taste and aromas of St. Petersburg were as foreign as ice and snow to an Arab. At least the temperature was mild, anticipating a warm, humid day. The three hours of sleep on the high-speed train had helped. She hiked her leather bag higher on her shoulder and scanned the plaza. A dark blue BMW X5 sat at the curb. A broad-shouldered man leaned against the car. He was smoking a cigarette. His thick black hair was combed back, and he wore sunglasses, the mirror type. The man had the look of a Cossack about him. Good, no bullshit.

"Your name?" she said, approaching the vehicle.

"Stepan Kushnir, Assistant Director."

"Excellent. Where is your home?"

"The Crimea. It is good to be back with Mother Russia."

Hearing the password phrase "back with Mother Russia," Tanya walked to the passenger-side door. Stepan opened it and waited while she picked up the envelope lying on the seat and got in. Moments later, they were traveling down Nevsky Prospect.

"To operations, Assistant Director?" Kushnir asked.

"Yes, but first breakfast. The food on the train was terrible. Coffee, and at least a roll or an egg."

"I know a place on the way." He glanced over at the envelope she held. "That is the latest information we have on Micah Lynch. There are photos and a short dossier."

"The woman?"

"Still looking. Nothing so far."

"Do you know where they are staying?"

"Yes, Director. We just passed it, the Radisson Royal. I have a man inside watching. They returned to the hotel at 3:05 this morning. If either leaves, we will follow them."

"When did you discover their hotel?"

"The middle of the night, when the data was forwarded from tourism. They are using the name Stapleton. As per instructions, when this was known, we activated our people. Our observer watched them return to their hotel."

"So, for at least ten hours after they arrived, we do not know what they were doing or with whom?"

"That's correct, though as soon as we learned where they were, we placed an observer at the hotel. It is being coordinated with the usual tourist agency people who monitor the hotels. We have the inside and outside covered. As I said, they have not left the hotel."

"Shit. Ten hours."

"Director?"

"Nothing. Call operations; I want a full extraction team waiting at my hotel in fifteen minutes."

Kushnir tapped the earpiece in his right ear and began talking to someone. Tanya didn't care who, just as long as the team was there when they arrived.

Tanya and Director Ivanovich had talked at length about the situation. The director had decided the hacking incident was too big and too dangerous to be swept under the political rug. There was too much at stake. That someone had accessed FSB files considered impenetrable proved his point. He told his superiors this when the initial operation was proposed. Higher-ups screamed about costs—look at the potential political mess now, they said. Tanya's job was to clean it up or make it go away.

"Anything that relies on the Internet can be discovered, even accidentally stumbled on," Ivanovich told her. "The best digital security can be defeated, and at some point, it will happen. Then what? Are you prepared for the international reactions, the blowback, the internal politics, the finger-pointing, and the eventual headhunting?"

The only way to make this go away was to find this hacker, seize every piece of software and hardware used, and make sure the break-in could not happen again. The ten missing hours meant the Americans probably had made contact with the hacker. They knew who he was. There was no time to play this out, no spycraft, no elaborate schemes, no dancing and winding ribbons around the Maypole. The Americans knew who the hacker was; the answer was that simple. She would demand they tell her whether they liked the idea or not.

* * *

Fortunately, the shades in the bedroom of the suite could be closed tightly against the all-pervading Russian morning daylight. When her phone alarm buzzed, Alex was quickly on her feet and within ten minutes was dressed, groomed, and in desperate need of coffee. Entering the central part of the suite, she found Micah sitting at the desk and engaged with his iPad.

"Wi-Fi?" she asked as she crossed the room.

"Yes, but I expected your first word would be 'coffee.'"

"Coffee first, Wi-Fi second."

"The Wi-Fi from the hotel is surprisingly slow." He held up a prewritten note: *Staying off the sat-phone until I need it.* He then added, "As regards coffee, there's a breakfast place across the street, the coffee is excellent, and they usually have a good selection of breads and sweet rolls. Preference?"

"I can go."

He motioned her to him and spoke directly into her ear. "I need to stretch, and besides you don't speak the lingo. No reason to alert any spectators in the lobby that you don't speak Russian. Give me a few minutes to bring Chris up to date through the Hong Kong email server. Jake is monitoring it; he will pass on messages to Chris. If our friends track the IP address, it will have them shaking their heads."

Alex nodded silently and went to stand by the fourth-floor window; it was a comfortable and surprisingly spacious corner suite. The sunshine directly pierced the window, and she had to squint to see out. The sign on the building opposite and facing the hotel read in English: *Restaurant Palkin.* The restaurant owners didn't miss a marketing trick; the sign on the opposing corner was in Russian. Looking down to the busy street, she saw more signs in both Russian and English that advertised breakfast. Her stomach growled.

"I heard that," Micah said.

"I wonder who else might have heard it?"

Micah smiled, then closed the cover of his iPad. "I'll get a selection of rolls and a large coffee for you. Then we have the morning. I can show you the land side of St. Petersburg. It is quite a city considering its history, and a remarkable feat of survival and even heroism as well."

"Like Saigon and Vietnam," Alex added. "That war had a profound effect on all the generations that followed." Her stomach rumbled again. "If they have anything with cinnamon and raisins, I'd be forever in your debt. Lunch is on me."

"There's an enchanting restaurant near the Hermitage. I'll make up for this meager repast then."

"Come to Russia, and now we speak with fancy words. Don't forget your key, and your passport," Alex said. She turned back to the window; she heard the door click shut.

She welcomed some time alone. She was still processing how her life had changed since Christmas—one foolish fuck-up after another was one way to describe it. And a bizarre march around the world: first Venice, then Cleveland, then Washington and Teton Security and Defense, Dallas, then Milan, Dubai, Saigon—and now Finland and Russia. Every stop a revelation, a challenge, even a miracle. Now she was negotiating with a man responsible for the deaths of more than a hundred and fifty Americans in a small town no one had heard of a week ago. And the man had twin boys to deal with—meaning she had to deal with another babysitting job. Well, at least ten-year-olds could carry their weight. She thought of her brother Rick and his son, who would turn nine this summer, a great kid. She had other nephews and nieces. John, her other brother, had one in high school already. All solid, good kids—good kids came from good parents. "I guess that's why I don't have any," Alex said out loud.

She looked back down at the street. Passengers were boarding the electric city bus that now sat in front of Restaurant Palkin. The traffic in the wide intersection was backed up at the stoplight. A white panel van sat against the curb, lettering on its side along with images of hand tools, hammers, saws, and a vise. She saw Micah standing at the corner opposite the restaurant, waiting for the crosswalk sign to change. He stood among a dozen others waiting to cross the street. Something about the whole scene reminded her of Euclid Avenue in Cleveland—the crowds of people crossing the busy downtown avenue to get to an Indians game. It made her smile. Then a man aggressively bumped into Micah's back. She watched the man lean in and say something to him. Micah didn't turn his head. When the crosswalk light changed, they both started walking. Reaching the opposite corner, they turned left and walked to the panel van. She lost sight of Micah behind the van. A moment later, it pulled away from the curb and accelerated down the street, leaving no sign of Micah, no man, nothing. She lost sight of the van as it sped past the electric bus.

CHAPTER 11

"Shit."

Alex quickly surveyed the suite, her brain firing off a hundred thoughts. In the bedroom, she stuffed the clothes she had laid on the bed back into her nylon bag. On top of those, she put the small toiletries case. Then with a towel she wiped down every surface they had touched, shower handles, the toilet seat and handle. After sanitizing the bedroom, she returned to the shower, turned on the water, and tapped a number into one of the burner phones.

"Yuri, they grabbed Micah. I'm clearing out. When can you be here? . . . Ten minutes? Where? . . . Got it. Two blocks, Vladimir Church, gold onion domes. I'll wait for your call . . . Don't be late."

She looked at the map Micah had used the previous evening; once oriented, she stuck it in her handbag. Moving to the main room of the suite, she stuffed Micah's clothes and sundries into his bag. Then every surface was wiped, counters, TV remote, door, and drawer handles. How much time she had before they would knock on her door, she didn't know. She jammed Micah's sat-phone in her bag; he had his passport, visa, and cell phone, not that they would do him any good now. She shrugged into her backpack, hung her handbag on her shoulder, and gathered up the luggage, then took one more look around the suite and opened the door. A quick look-see up and down the corridor revealed no one. She and Micah had used the elevator to enter the hotel that morning; she would not retrace that path. Exit signs were posted at each end of the hallway. With her and Micah's bags slung over her shoulder, she turned right and quick-walked to the door at the end of the long corridor.

As she neared the exit door, a room door opened. A tall, thin man stood in the doorway, a cigarette in his hand. Alex hid her surprise at his sudden appearance by pointing to the sign below the exit sign. "No smoking, comrade," she said in English. The man, visibly chagrinned, backed up and shut the door. A second later, Alex was through the exit door and taking the stairs down to the ground floor.

At the ground floor, she stopped and took a deep breath. The last thing she wanted was to spend the rest of her life in some Gulag somewhere. Through the double-glass exit doors, she saw another man. He, too, was smoking. Forcing herself to appear calm, she reset the bags on her shoulder, opened the door, quickly exited, and passed by the man. She went left. She didn't stop, yet with every step she waited to hear someone yell, or worse, hear the pop of a pistol. Each place ahead of her was a goal: the end of the block, crossing the street, onto the next intersection, then the church.

The golden domes of Vladimir Church appeared to flare in the morning sun. Rising just above the rooftops, the sun's angle was low and dramatic, and the white trim and butter yellow of the church exterior glowed in the light. A small enclosed courtyard fronted the building. The church was gorgeous, though its beauty was merely another fact Alex observed as she glanced around to see if anyone followed her. She crossed the street and entered the small garden. Hedges wrapped the courtyard. Flowers filled the beds; a group of benches was nestled in one corner; she took one. No one could see her from the street. For the first time in fifteen minutes, she partially relaxed. She redialed Yuri.

"How long? . . . Five minutes? . . . In the courtyard. Single tower?" She looked up. "Got it. I'll watch for you."

Sitting perfectly still just inside the garden's entry, she watched the traffic. Taxis, buses, and trucks made the turn. It was a long five minutes before a black Mercedes slowed and stopped against the curb in front of the church. Uber stickers were pasted to the front and rear windows. Yuri stepped out and scanned the road and the sidewalk. Alex casually walked to the car, said "Otto?" loudly enough for a couple of pedestrians nearby to hear. Yuri nodded and said "*Da.*" Alex climbed into the back seat. Yuri took his place behind the wheel and slowly pulled out into traffic.

"What the hell just happened?" Alex said.

"Obviously, they have been watching the hotel," Yuri said. "Why they didn't go for both of you at the same time is puzzling. Then again, not everyone is as competent as me. At least you got out; in ten minutes, the place will be surrounded. I'll take lucky over skill any day."

Alex's sat-phone, buried deep in her backpack, began to buzz. "Chris? . . . Speaker?"

"Yes, I want Yuri in on this," Chris said. "All I can say is whoever this Fyodor hacker is, he must have scared the shit out of the FSB. With what you told me after last night's meeting, there's a lot more to this, especially if he's negotiating. This brazen snatch of an American tourist off the street says more about the hacker than what he told you last night. They don't know who *you* are, other than through your Stapleton passport. Do you still have your own passport?"

"Yes, boss," Alex said.

"For now, use that. Yuri, she'll need a tourist visa under that name."

"Got it, boss."

"You have all the other paperwork and passports for Fyo-dor and his boys?"

"Yes, boss," Yuri said. "All neat and tied in a bow. They are on the seat next to you." Yuri looked in the mirror. "I don't know your name."

"Alex Polonia."

"Good Russian name, excellent, *otlichno*. I like you even more."

"Yuri, focus," Chris said.

"Yes, boss. Aleksandrina, *moya sladkaya*, the envelope has appropriately aged passports for the father and the two boys, proper visas for traveling to Finland, and some other papers to add validity to who they are, even a driver's license."

"Not sure this guy knows how to drive," Alex said. "I like the 'Aleksandrina,' but what does *moya sladkaya* mean?"

"Yuri's getting fresh. He's incorrigible," Chris said.

"What are we going to do about Micah? I can't leave him here," Alex said.

"Micah is a big boy and can take care of himself. My guess—by now they've put together a dossier on him; he's certainly not unknown in Russia. I'll do what I can from this end. The State Department owes me some favors. Right now, your only concern is to get that man and his family out of Russia. If what he's hinting about are even half-truths, he could be valuable."

"And the boys?"

"Tell him that we will protect them. They will be safe; just get that man out of Russia. I will be waiting for you in Helsinki. This is your operation now, Alex. You once said you had to fly on your own sometime—this is it. Good luck."

The phone went dead.

"There he goes with the luck thing," Alex said. "Personally,

I'd rather believe in fate."

"You are beginning to sound Russian, *moya sladkaya*. You look Russian. Your last name is Polonia. Very nice. Maybe there's some Russian in you?"

"Polish, Yuri."

"No one's perfect."

* * *

They crossed three canals. Alex was as confused as to where they were as if she were on the far side of the moon. Yuri made two phone calls, mentioning her name twice. He pulled to the side of the street, asked for her passport, took a photo, then emailed.

"The visa will be ready shortly," he said. "We will pick it up."

"I need something to eat. Something tells me this will be a very long day."

"That it will be, Aleksandrina. I know a place."

"I assumed you would."

As they drove through the neighborhoods, all the architecture had the same style and look. Only the churches provided relief. Yuri stopped at a small food shop on a side street; Alex waited nervously in the car. Her faith in this man extended from Chris. Her concerns trumped her fear, and she was very concerned. Yuri came back to the car, placed two plastic grocery bags on the front seat, and then drove on.

"Just a few minutes," he said. "I bought some local delicacies, a bottle of Georgian wine. The day is nice, though the weather reports say that a front is coming in from Sweden and Finland. Rain by midafternoon, or sooner. Other than last night, you have had no time to enjoy St. Petersburg. For the next few hours, I'll do what I can to make your stay memorable."

"Memorable? Yuri, already it's more memorable than I want. Right now, I want to be out of here as fast as possible. And how can you be so calm? They took Micah, your friend."

"If Chris says he will take care of it, he will. We will have some lunch. Then I will take you to the train station. You will meet with this man, whoever he is."

"Do you know why we're here?"

"No, this is on a need-to-know. I'm to keep you safe and get you on the train. I do what Chris asks. I am what you would call in deep cover. I have other responsibilities, and my schedule varies. You are the first assignment I've had in months. Chris or Jake come through, I drive, I provide security."

They drove another five minutes, neither saying anything. Then Yuri stopped at an intersection and a young girl walked up to the car. Yuri rolled down the window, said something in Russian; then the girl casually dropped an envelope inside. Yuri then said something loud and obviously rude. The girl, dressed alluringly in a tight dress, flipped him off.

"And I have your travel visa for Alexandra Polonia," Yuri said, holding up a small envelope. "It's a good job. I take my work seriously, *moya sladkaya*."

"What does that mean, *moya sladkaya*?"

Yuri turned his head, a big smile on his face. "It means, 'my sweet.'"

"Great, just great, now I'm being hit on by a Russian Uber driver."

"I'm a Georgian, big difference. My parents came here from Georgia when I was a child; I was raised here. But my heart is with Georgia. I keep it secret; the Russians get suspicious of the Georgians. That was my parents' shop where I bought lunch."

Alex sat back in her seat and watched the city flow by. It all reminded her of a Russian doll a childhood friend had shown her. As you took each layer apart, another, almost identical but smaller, doll appeared inside, layer on layer until you were holding the smallest, yet the most beautiful, of all the dolls—layer on layer on layer.

Yuri was true to his word; he parked in front of another magnificent church, golden dome and all. He carried the grocery bags to a bench and gestured for Alex to sit down. Placing the bags between them, he retrieved, one by one, a collection of delicacies in small plastic containers, and placed them on the bench. The bottle of wine had a twist-off top. He poured the wine into two paper cups.

"We have two and a half hours," Yuri said. "The train station is a few kilometers from here—twenty minutes at the most. My mother made this feast. There are *pampushkis*, dumplings, cabbage rolls, pickled herring, and slices of rye bread with thick butter. There's another bag in the car for your trip this afternoon."

"Thanks, I'm famished," Alex said. "That church?"

"That is St. Isaac's Cathedral. Even today, no one knows whether to call it a cathedral or a museum. The continual battle between a religious non-secular nation and a secular government. It is a church to me, a great church. You can rent it for marriages, or so I've been told."

Alex took a sip of wine and set her desperate need for coffee to one side. "This is very good. From Georgia? Where is that?"

"South, more than two thousand kilometers from here, near Turkey and beyond the Caucasus Mountains. Its most infamous claim is the birthplace of Stalin."

"How did you meet Chris?"

"That, *moya sladkaya*, is above your pay grade, as they say. Just realize that we have known each other a very long time."

Alex bit into the dumpling. It was delicious, and she told

Yuri so. The wine was a light-colored red; she couldn't read the label.

"A rosé," Yuri said. "From the Saperavi grape, an old variety found in the region. My cousin owns the vineyard."

"Delicious." She took another sip of the wine. "Are you sure there's nothing we can do for Micah?"

"He's a big boy, but you, *moya sladkaya*, have a real big problem. You told me that Micah has his passport. They now know he's traveling under the name Stapleton; they must also know you have been using the same name. They will have alerted every Russian checkpoint. They will stop the train before it reaches Finland if they think you are on board."

"As Chris said, I'll use my Alex Polonia passport with my new visa. Did you get one for Micah if we need it?"

"Yes, with yours, if need be. Everything else is in the envelope with your target's new passports and visas. The name they are traveling under is Fyodor Popoff. A common enough name. The boys' names are Boris and Vadim. All common enough. But they will be looking for you, the American tourist Lois Stapleton. Micah may be able to bluff them for a while, giving you some time, but you can't outrun a phone call or a database. They will have the name Stapleton on every checkpoint and customs computer; they will also try and use facial recognition."

"I will be traveling under my name."

"Well and good, hopefully, long enough to confuse them. But what we need, you and this family, is a diversion. So, this is my idea."

They finished lunch, then spent time driving around St. Petersburg with Yuri trying to raise her spirits with stories of the tsar and the revolution. He drove past the train station a few times to see if they could spot any obvious observers. There were other Mercedes, some with Uber stickers in the window, also waiting.

"Aleksandrina, *moya sladkaya*, I will leave you here," he said, pulling to the curb on the far side of the train station. "You have an hour before Fyodor will arrive. It will take me thirty minutes to get there, and at least twenty minutes after that before all hell breaks loose. Take care, move quickly, but do not call attention to yourself or the family. I don't have to tell you that. Let's hope this works."

CHAPTER 12

Yuri slowed the Mercedes and maneuvered between the buses and dozens of other cars picking up and dropping off passengers. The sign on the building he parked in front of read: CUSTOMS. The Customs building backed up to the waterfront; six immense cruise ships were docked in the U-shaped harbor. Hundreds of people were entering and leaving the one- and two-story buildings that segregated the vessels from the port and the city of St. Petersburg.

He walked through the glass doors to the counter and rang the hand bell. Five people looked up.

"Can anybody here help me? Come on, comrades. I've got a problem." He rang the bell again.

"That's enough, buddy, just stop," a man in uniform said. The customs agent stepped to the counter. "What's your problem?"

"Hell, it's not my problem. It's one of the fucking passengers on one of those damn ships; it's their problem. Me, I don't give a shit, but one of them left their passport in my car. I'm just trying to get it back to the rightful owner." He removed a passport from his pocket and placed it on the counter.

"And how did you get this?" the agent asked, looking at the American passport.

"I fucking stole it, comrade customs agent," Yuri said, then stopped and reconsidered his remark. "No, not really. I'm an Uber driver. This morning I picked up a couple from one of these ships; it was right out there at the curb. They wanted a tour of the city, then to be driven right back here. I gave them a price; they said good. So, I did—even stopped for lunch. Must have put two hundred kilometers on my car. It's the Mercedes over there." Yuri pointed out the window.

"And what do you want us to do about it?"

"Get the fucking thing back to whoever owns it. I've traveled some. They will have a hell of a time getting back into the United States if she doesn't have it."

"She?"

Yuri pulled the passport back and opened it. "You speak any English?"

"Some," the agent said. "Why?"

"Then you read it; I can't." Yuri held it up to the face of the agent.

"Lois P. Stapleton. So?"

"Look, comrade. They were nice, gave me a big tip. It's the least I can do so as not to wreck their vacation. Here are twenty euros; buy a drink for the gang after work. Just try and find out who this belongs to, okay? It's not a big deal; do something nice for a fucking change." Yuri reached into his jacket pocket and pulled out his phone. "I've got a pickup," he said, as if reading a text. "Come on, help them out, international relations, be a fucking hero. Maybe they will give you a gold star or something."

"What's your name?"

"Why?"

"For the form."

"For fuck's sake, a form? Just call the pursers on the ships, look on your computer; maybe somebody already posted something. Do your job." Yuri looked at his phone again.

"Name?"

"Shit, Otto Pavelski. Okay, comrade? We done?" At that, Yuri turned and walked out of the Customs building. By the time he reached the car, he was whistling.

* * *

Alex looked at her phone; the text message was from Yuri. The time read 1:50 PM.

The seed is planted, now let us watch it grow. Good luck with your garden. I hope you have many flowers.

She wondered if she would ever meet Yuri, Otto, whomever, again. Another text message appeared on her phone.

In Helsinki, waiting. Good luck. Travel safe. Trying to find your partner. CC

The now somewhat familiar statue of Vladimir Lenin dominated the small railway park. In the misty rain, it glistened like it had been given a coat of wax. The Finlyandsky train station, broad, low, and brooding, was behind her. She sat under a cheap umbrella she'd purchased in a gift shop in the station. Her thin raincoat, the kind that came in a small bag, at least kept her dry. Her hair was a mess; then again, she was a mess. Everything was going in a thousand different directions, and it all was a mess. She had carefully picked a place to sit and watch. If anyone was looking for her, she wanted ample time to spot them before they arrested her, or maybe even have a chance to escape. Then again, where? She was surprisingly calm; it reminded her of stakeouts just before the tacticals—in their black gear, vests, and helmets—were brought in to take down the suspects. She took a deep breath.

It didn't take long. A man in a dark trench coat and a broad-brimmed hat took a seat on a bench on the opposite side of the park. Every fifteen seconds, he would look up from his newspaper—it was getting progressively wetter—and scan the people in the park. Alex wasn't sure how long he'd been in the area; then again, it had only been ten minutes since Yuri's gardening tip. She watched as the man placed his hand against the side of his head, tilted it, concentrated, abruptly stood, and walked back toward the train station. Then a woman exited the station and walked up to Mr. Trench Coat. She said something to him, turned and raised her arm. A dark grey automobile pulled away from the curb and slid to a stop next to them; both climbed into the back. The sedan drove away into the mist.

Gardening can be so much fun, Alex thought.

A blue and white city bus stopped at the far end of the park, and four people climbed down the steps, a man, a woman, and two boys. The man carried a large nylon bag over his shoulder. The woman also carried a bag—hers was black. Alex expected the man, Fyodor, and the two boys, but the woman was a surprise. Was she with them? They walked into the park, passed by where the man in the trench coat had been sitting, his wet newspaper still on the bench. Fyodor looked around, clearly inspecting the faces of the people heading to and from the station. The flowerbeds were in full summer bloom; the fountains, even in the rain, added a soothing sound to the backdrop of the city noise and bustle. Lenin, coat open, hand to his lapel, right arm outstretched, wasn't helping Fyodor recognize Alex, who remained seated, studying the boys. The woman, in the middle, held a hand of each of the boys. Alex folded the umbrella, stood, and walked over to Fyodor.

"I'm glad you could make it," she said. "After last night, I wasn't sure if you would go through with this."

Taken aback, Fyodor stopped, and then furtively looked around again. "Where is the man?"

"Funny thing about that—he was arrested this morning. Why would they do that? Do you know?"

"*Arestoval yego?*" Fyodor said to the woman, "*My ukhodim, eto slishkom opasno.*"

"What did you just say?" Alex asked.

"We are leaving. This is too dangerous," he said.

"Who is this woman?" Alex said.

"Her name is Anya . . . Anya Belsky. She helps to care for the boys. She is coming with us."

"Not a chance, no way," Alex said, looking at the woman. "Tough enough with three."

"I can take care of myself," Anya said in English. "I have since I was thirteen. The boys need my help. Ilya can't take care of them every hour of the day. But between us, we manage."

"Ilya? Is your name Ilya? Ilya what?"

"Ilya Sokolov. This is Gavril and Pavel."

The boys were in constant motion, even more so than other kids if that were possible. They looked in every direction, not focusing on any particular thing.

"Your sons are autistic?" Alex said thoughtfully. Ilya hadn't said anything about that, doubtless aware it would complicate traveling undetected.

"Would you have helped if you knew?" Ilya said. "I obviously can't leave them here in Russia, and I need Anya's help. No one knows about her. After we leave, there is nothing for her here. So, she comes with us. I don't know why your partner was arrested," he added.

"Your action in America has caught the attention of people in your government. They were expecting us. They figured out that we were coming"—Alex paused, and then looked in Ilya's eyes—"unless you told them."

"Me? No, not me. I need to protect my boys. I don't care what happens to me, but they must be protected. This is the only way it will work."

"You gave as little information as possible. You tricked us."

"And yet, here you are. Aren't you afraid that the police will catch us?" Anya said, interrupting the conversation.

"Very afraid; that is why we must go now. The train leaves in twenty minutes. I have tickets for five people."

"How did you know there would be five?"

"One of the tickets was meant for my partner, Robert Stapleton. I have your new passports and visas; I will give them to you in the station." Alex looked at the woman; she guessed her to be about twenty. "And you?"

"I have my travel documents. I traveled when I was in school. I have been to Helsinki."

They left Lenin, crossed the park, and entered the train station. Off to the side, in a quiet corner, Alex gave the documents to Ilya. The covers of the passports were a rich dark red. To Alex, they looked real.

"Your name is Fyodor Popoff; the boys are Boris and Vadim," she said. She looked at the boys. "Can they read?"

"They read and write Russian exceptionally well," Ilya said. "I will keep their new names to myself. It will confuse them if you try to call them by those names. I'm also surprised that they are so quiet. By now, they would be acting up. They are curious, distracted, I guess. I have asked them to be patient and quiet. For once, they listened."

Anya said something in Russian to Ilya.

"The boys need to use the bathroom," he said to Alex. "I will be right back. You two should get to know each other. It will be a long day."

The women watched Ilya and his sons turn the corner where the international sign for restrooms hung out from the wall.

"How much trouble are they in?" Anya asked. "It must be something awful for Americans to come all this way to take them out of Russia. It will be difficult for them if they are caught."

"You as well."

"Yes, but . . . this will work out," Anya replied, as if reassuring herself. "I told Ilya that he needs me to help with the boys. I know them, their moods, their issues. They are very smart, too smart for me. Some days, it's a game of wits. And they look so alike; most people cannot tell them apart, so, they ignore most people. Gavril and Pavel are fine with that; they don't care for people that much either. Besides, I needed a change." She half smiled at Alex. "So, Mrs. Stapleton, why are you here?"

"How do you know my name?"

"An assumption. You said your partner's name was Robert Stapleton. I assume you and he are traveling as husband and wife, a simple deduction."

. . . *and a smart-ass one as well.* This was going south too fast. Alex wasn't sure how much to tell the woman. "It came to our attention that Ilya has skills and abilities that would be helpful. He asked for help, and I am here."

"I'm sure there are hundreds, probably thousands, in America who know computers and systems. I know what he does; it's boring—too much to be made of nothing. I do not like computers. But I love the boys; they are special. So, that is why I'm here."

"He is fortunate to have such a loyal friend."

Anya looked knowingly at Alex. "You think we are lovers, no? We are not. Besides, he is too old for me. Men bore me, especially Russian men. All the macho this and tough-guy that." She smiled again. "I'm a poet in my heart."

The boys came back around the corner and ran to Anya; Ilya followed in their wake.

Anya looked at the large clock on the wall. "This way; the trains to Finland are over there." She pointed, and the group headed to the left.

As they retraced her steps from the day before, Alex stayed a pace or two behind, like a shepherd with her flock. She did not want to chase after two boys if they decided to bolt. Anya led them to the train standing next to the platform. They walked its length until they found the appropriate car that matched their tickets. Ilya placed the bags he brought in the overhead rack, keeping one bag next to him. The two boys sat together, facing Ilya and Alex. Anya took a single seat across the aisle. To all intents, the foursome sitting together looked like a happy family group. The boys were quiet, self-contained. Alex wasn't sure what that meant; at the moment, she wasn't sure what any of this meant.

She took out her phone and typed in a short message.

On the train. Leaving in five minutes. See you soon. AP

When she looked up, both boys were looking at her. The one on the right, possibly Gavril, said, "*Telefon.*"

"That's right," Alex answered in English.

"*Telefon, telefon, telefon,*" the boy repeated. Then his brother joined in. They were both swaying backward and forward. "*Telefon, telefon, telefon.*"

"Ignore them," Ilya said. "They love phones and computers. I think they are trying to get into your head. It will pass."

CHAPTER 13

The train gave a slight lurch and began to slowly back out of the station. The boys started to say, "*Poyezd, poyezd, poyezd . . .*"

"Train," Ilya said. "They love trains, too." He looked at the boys; they stared back at him. He put his finger to his lips; they stopped talking.

"Your sons are well behaved," Alex said.

"For now, there's a lot to see. It's when they get bored that the difficulties begin."

"What difficulties?"

"I'm never sure."

Alex sat back in her seat and regarded Ilya's sons. Anya was right; Alex wouldn't hazard a guess as to which was Pavel or Gavril. Boyishly handsome, blond hair, broad foreheads, bright blue wide-set eyes, and soft, clear, almost transparent skin. Neither had the slightly pinched eyes that had given those challenged with this unfortunate condition its worst and mean description, Mongolian idiot. Alex's police experience in Cleveland had resulted in her having profound empathy for these children and their parents. It began one afternoon when she and two others served multiple arrest warrants for the managers of a group home on the south side of Cleveland. Not knowing what she was getting into when they knocked on the door was the best of it. Inside they found seven children, all autistic, used as an income source for the managers and the owner of the derelict house. The children had been thrown away by their parents. The city believed that in three instances, the children had been sold to these monsters. It wasn't until a naïve social worker, not clued in to the situation, inspected the house and alerted, first, child services and then, when that was glossed over by someone saying, "We are fully aware of it; it is not your problem," the social worker secretively met with the DA and warrants were issued. That was twelve years ago. Alex knew that three of the children rescued from that house were well and living on their own. Two others, the most severely challenged, had to be institutionalized. And the others had, like so many, disappeared off the grid. The group defrauded the city, state, and federal governments out of more than two million dollars. She wished she had been in the prison yard when the woman who masterminded the operation had been beaten and crippled by other inmates, who had different opinions of what should be done with autistic children.

The boys' father pulled from his bag two small blue players; they looked like Nintendos. Each boy eagerly began to thumb the units; Alex heard squeaks of delight.

"They love the things," Ilya said. "Don't know what I'll do when they finally break. Maybe they have them in America?"

"It's possible," Alex said. "They seem somewhat independent."

"Yes, they are to a degree. Their condition tends away from classic autism. It is a form called Asperger's. I have had to find all this out on my own; there's little support and services for autistic children in Russia. From what I've read, maybe I can find help in America. Their language skills are quite good, due to Anya's help. They learn quickly, and thoroughly. But I cannot let them out on their own. They get lost, confused. Once, not a month ago, they both had what we call a meltdown at the same time in a department store. The noise, the lights, the crowds, it all just exploded. Then they fed on each other's panic. I had to carry them out of the store. Those are the bad days."

"You are a smart man. You know why we, I mean me, are here. You asked for protection; many want vengeance for what you did."

Ilya looked out the window at the blur of the cityscape; the rain had begun in earnest. "There's much to atone for, but my boys are my greatest concern," he said. "Once I know they are safe and protected, I will help as much as I can. It was an accident; it was not intentional. Until then, I ask only for your patience and understanding."

Alex saw that Anya had been listening. "Do you understand what's going on?" Alex asked her.

"Only that Ilya says this is a way to help the boys. I believe him when he says this. I have little else; maybe something is waiting for me in America, too."

The compartment door slid open, and a woman in a uniform walked into their car. Alex was glad it was not the same customs agent she'd dealt with the day before. The agent went from seat to seat, looking at papers and passports. She was officious, talked little, did her job. She seemed sullen; the weather probably didn't help.

When she reached Alex, she took her passport and glossed over it. A good thing, too, because there was no stamp of Alex entering Russia on its remarkably empty pages. But one stamp did catch the agent's eye. "Dubai? You have been to Dubai?"

"Yes, just a few months ago, business."

"I've wanted to go there. The buildings are so big. Here in Russia they are flat, and it's cold, and it's so boring. Someday, I want to go to Dubai." She handed the passport back with a smile and then took Anya's, perused it for a moment. "You are going to Helsinki? What's your business there?"

"I am the governess for these two boys; they are autistic. We are going to a summer school there. We will return to St. Petersburg in October." She reached up for her passport.

"*Da, U moyego brata yest' odin is nikh. Ochen' slozhno, oni kazhutsya normal'nymi,*" the agent said.

The two continued to talk. Alex, concerned, leaned toward Ilya. "Problem?" her expression said.

He shook his head. "Her brother has an autistic child," he said softly.

The agent turned to Ilya. "*Pasports. Tvoi I deti.*" He did as she asked and handed her their passports and visas.

Alex held her breath.

After looking at the pages, she said, "*YA zhelayu vam vsego nailuchshego, blagosloveniye Boga na vas, udachi.*"

"*Spasibo I za vashi molitvy,*" Ilya said.

Anya was smiling. The customs agent walked on to the next seats, another group of American tourists, spent a few minutes, then left the car. There seemed to be an audible sigh from throughout the car.

"What did she say?" Alex whispered to Ilya.

"She wished us luck, and that she would pray to God for us."

Alex saw Anya nod her head in agreement.

"A prayer to God from our avowed godless country. Things have certainly changed," Anya said.

They stopped briefly at Vyborg; Alex saw their customs agent walking on the platform, headed away from the train. No one else got on or off. Thirty minutes later, they passed, without incident, through the Russian and Finnish border. The Finnish agent was friendly and quickly went about his business.

When the agent left the car, Alex told Ilya she was going to use the lavatory and find something to eat. The traveling had made her incredibly hungry; she wanted something more substantial than Yuri's cabbage rolls. Ilya nodded. The boys, still engrossed in their games, paid no attention to her. Anya was leaning against the window; her eyes were closed. As Alex walked through the train to the dining car, she noticed that the speed was 218 kph. She guessed that would be about 130 mph in her head. Outside, thick evergreen forests and brief glimpses of farmland flashed by.

Fifteen minutes later, she returned with drinks and bags of chips and sandwiches. She saw that Ilya was asleep, Anya was missing, and the boys held a laptop between them, immersed in whatever they were doing.

"Damn it, Ilya," she said sharply, startling the boys, a few people near them, and most especially Ilya, who woke out of his sleep. The boys began to shake and wave their hands.

Alex leaned toward Ilya and said under her breath, "Turn that computer off, right now. Why didn't you tell me you had a computer? We told you to bring nothing other than clothes. This is bad."

Ilya waved his fingers at the boys in a come-this-way manner.

"*Vy znayete, ya skazal, chto vam nuzhno razresheniye, chtoby poigrat's etim. Day eto mne.*"

Gavril handed the computer to his father. Ilya held down the off button until the screen went black.

"Now pull out the battery," Alex said, "and give it to me."

"We don't have to do that."

"Ilya, please. Now."

Ilya did as ordered. Alex slipped the battery into her backpack.

"Why all the fuss? The boys were just playing," Ilya said. "I told them not to go on the Internet."

"I don't care, they may have compromised us. You said the Russian government owns that computer. That's why we wanted it left in Russia, so we wouldn't be accused of stealing state secrets. But right now, it could be something worse."

Anya arrived, holding a cup of coffee. "What's worse?" she asked.

"The boys were on the computer, Ilya's computer. When they turned it on, its GPS and IP address doubtless went live. If anyone was monitoring that particular computer, waiting for this to happen, they now know exactly where we are and have a good idea where we are going."

Ilya, the closed computer upside down on his lap, looked at Alex. The weariness showed in his eyes. "I'm sorry," he said.

CHAPTER 14

Christopher Campbell stood in the vaulted concourse of the Helsinki Central Train Station. The Allegro train from St. Petersburg would be arriving in fifteen minutes. The station monitors read that the train, as always, was precisely on time. Linda Monroe stood next to Chris.

"We will head to the platform when it's announced," Chris said. "I'll be glad when this is over; there's much to do to fix this. I hope this hacker understands what he's faced with."

"The deaths of one hundred and fifty people, that's what he's facing," Linda said.

"All due to a series of regrettable events."

"He proclaims his innocence," she said, "but if the grid hadn't been shut down, none of it would have happened. In this case, the government isn't going to want a manslaughter conviction. The people want a murder conviction, but that's not my place to decide. You said SA Case would be joining us?"

"The FBI wants in on this; that's why they brought us in originally," Chris said, voicing what both of them knew. "Micah needs to be gotten out of Russia. Obviously, their security systems have become better, and they have always been good. Once we have this guy, they should turn Micah loose. If not, we might need the help of the FBI and the State Department."

Special Agent Robb Case would be flying into Helsinki that night, Chris told Linda. The FBI agent had been in contact with the Finnish Security Intelligence Service—"they will assist us once we have the hacker in our possession," Chris said. "If it gets dicey with the Russians, they want to keep it low-key. It is a long-term relationship between Finland and Russia. Finland has the facilities to detain the man and his family until all the legal issues are resolved. Our Justice Department wants this as clean as possible; once we have him, the world will be watching."

The train from St. Petersburg was announced. Chris and Linda took the escalator down to the arrival platforms and waited. Hundreds of people were leaving or filling other local trains. It was cool for the early evening; the glass roof over the train platform provided some protection from the rain that had moved in that afternoon.

Linda leaned in toward Chris and tilted her head toward the end of the last rail siding. The Allegro sign overhead was flashing. About two hundred meters up the tracks, the nose of the Allegro train came into view.

"Thanks, I see it," Chris said.

"No, not the train. Those three standing against the building. We have company."

"You know them?"

"No, but they are waiting for someone. Two military types and an obvious Russian blonde. Step in front of me."

Chris did, then turned to face Linda, who was taking pictures with her phone. He started to say something, but she held up a finger to stop him. "One minute." She typed expertly into the phone.

"Got them," she said. "I sent their pics to Dallas. Let's see if any of them pop on the facial recognition database. I suggested the FSB and Russian bases first."

"Good thinking," Chris said.

The train slid into the station, its sleek flanks glistening with rain. As soon as the train stopped, the doors opened, and dozens of people disembarked. They all had to pass Chris and Linda to reach the concourse. It was a mix of tourists and businesspeople. Children in strollers and a few older tourists with canes worked their way among the crush of passengers. After five minutes, the flow dwindled to none.

Linda looked at her screen and smiled.

"Our friend over there is FSB Assistant Direct Tanya Golubev; she is one of FSB Director Dmitry Ivanovich's most trusted associates. Dallas believes she controls significant portions of the internal and external data and digital universe of the FSB. Your hunch that the FSB is interested in what's going on has just been proven. In those heels, damn she looks good."

"Professional admiration?" Chris asked.

"Something like that. I'm guessing she's here waiting for our guy, so our adventure has become more complex. Those two guys with her don't look like they're from the Finnish welcoming committee."

Ten minutes later, Linda said, "They didn't get off." She looked at Golubev; the FSB agent was impatiently pacing at the far end of the platform. She was also on her phone. "I'd like to hear that phone conversation."

Chris walked down the length of the train to its midpoint. A conductor was standing on the platform outside one of the open doors.

"Good evening, do you speak English?" Chris asked.

"Yes, of course, may I help you?" the man answered.

"We are here to meet a family that was coming in from St. Petersburg. There were four people, a man and a woman, and two children."

The conductor thought for a moment. "We had a lot of

families on the train today. In car eight, there was a man and a woman, and two boys, maybe ten years old. Autistic, I think? There may have been five in their party."

The word "autistic" took Chris aback. "Yes, two boys," he said. "Five people?"

"I think there was a woman with them, an American. The man and the younger woman were Russian, the kids too."

"Are they still on the train?" Chris asked.

The conductor shook his head. "They were ticketed to go through to Helsinki. The two boys became disruptive, starting yelling. I was called in, but by the time I arrived in the car, they had calmed down. It was difficult for some of the other passengers; they started to ask questions. But the five of them elected to get off the train in Lahti. I told them this was the last train for the day. The woman, a pretty blonde, said not to worry, they were fine."

Chris had already spun around and was walking toward Linda. Golubev and her companions were gone.

"Where did they go?" Chris asked.

"I don't know, but while you were talking to the conductor, she was on the phone. She had a killer look on her face, said something to her boys, and they went out and up the escalator. What did you find out?"

Chris told her. All Linda could say was, "Alex must have had a damn good reason."

* * *

The three adults and two boys stood under the open canopy of the taxi and passenger loading zone of the Lahti train station. Ilya glared at Alex; she glared back.

"We had to do this; they knew we were coming. They will be waiting in Helsinki. We had to get off," Alex said.

"Sure, great, I get it, but now what?" Anya said. "We have almost nothing. It's raining, and the boys are cold." She wrapped her arms across her chest. "So am I."

Above the trees across the street that paralleled the railroad tracks, the top of a six-story white building displayed a sign: *Scandic.*

"This way," Alex said as she repositioned the bags over her shoulder. "Anya, please hold the umbrella over the boys; Ilya, the bags. That's a hotel; we will go there." She pointed.

She was able to get adjoining rooms, the boys and Ilya in one, while she and Anya would share the other. At least her American Express card still worked; it was a TSD card with her name on it. She ordered two pizzas with it. As her companions wolfed down the pizza, she went into her room and sent a text to Chris.

> *We were compromised. Had to leave the train. Now in Lahti. We are fine, no worries. Weather is miserable. We will hunker down here. Exhausted, going to bed. Come and get us in the morning.*

"Ilya, I'm going to take a nap," Alex said. "I suggest that after the boys finish the pizza, they get some sleep. I don't know what tomorrow will be like. Lock the room doors but leave this connecting one between the rooms unlocked."

"We could just live here," Ilya said, looking around. "This hotel room is much nicer than either of our St. Petersburg apartments. Just tell the Americans we will become Finns."

"Good idea—not going to happen, Ilya. And you know that. Please try to get some sleep. I'll check on you in a few hours."

Even though it was almost eleven o'clock in the evening, outside, it was as bright as a midsummer day in Ohio. Alex checked her phone. Chris had responded.

St. Petersburg White

You must have had a good reason. Do not come to Helsinki, FSB everywhere. We will talk in the morning. Waiting out the weather. Get some sleep. See you tomorrow.

Alex stripped down in the bathroom and took a warm shower. At least she had fresh underwear in her bag. She so wanted to change her jeans and sweater, but she knew she could get at least one more day out of them, and then what? She would soon find out. When she came out of the shower, wrapped in one of the guest robes left hanging on the back of the bathroom door, Anya was already asleep on one of the twin beds. Alex wondered about the woman; she showed a lot of dedication for someone who wasn't a family member. The boys seemed to be good guys. They had their issues, but what ten-year-olds didn't? She set her phone alarm for three hours and immediately fell asleep.

The phone's buzzing pulled her from some happy place she was visiting in her dreams; she couldn't remember where or what, just the sense of calm. It was 3:15 AM. Daylight seeped around the edges of the blinds. Anya was still asleep on the other bed. Alex got dressed.

Sticking her head around the corner into Ilya's room, she still smelled the hangover aroma of the pizza. Ilya was asleep on one bed; the other was empty. Panicked, Alex checked the bathroom and even the bathroom in her room. The boys were gone.

Shaking Ilya awake, she asked, "Where are the boys?"

Groggy, he looked around, then said, "Don't know."

"Have they done this before?"

"What?"

"They left without telling you where they were going?"

"It's happened a few times during the last year; they don't go far. Sometimes just a walk."

"Get dressed; we have to find them. Now."

Anya stuck her head around the door. "*Chto proiskhodit?*"

Alex looked at Ilya.

"She wants to know what's happening," he said.

"The boys are gone. We need to find them."

"They aren't far. They are okay," Anya said. "They do this; it happens."

"It's three fifteen in the morning; they could be anywhere. In danger. Injured or worse."

"This is not America," Ilya said. "I'm sure they are okay. But we can look. Anya, please stay here in case they return. We will be back as soon as possible."

They stopped at the front desk. The tired-looking clerk said she hadn't seen the two boys leave. She asked if she should call the police. Alex said no, not right now. She would let her know.

Ilya and Alex circled the hotel. Adjacent to one side of the multistory Scandic was a small commercial complex. A hamburger joint, a gas station, and a small convenience store that reminded Alex of an American 7-Eleven. Across the bottom of one of the windows was posted in English, Russian, and German: *Internet Here.*

"I know where they are," Ilya said.

The store was open twenty-four hours. In the back was a small compact area with a long counter against one wall. The counter held three computers; the twins, still in their pajamas, sat on stools at one of the terminals, tapping keys and chattering to each other. They did not see their father enter the store. Alex wasn't sure if they even cared that he entered. She and Ilya walked up behind the boys.

Above the counter, a television screen displayed the news, a logo for CNN International visible in the lower corner of the screen next to the time display that rolled through time zones around the world: 9:35 PM in New York, 3:35 AM in Finland. On-screen the destruction of the village of Maise was being rebroadcast. The transcription below the aerial images read in English: *Breaking News: Grid collapses again in Iowa. Government is baffled.*

The computer screen in front of the boys displayed an intricate layout of colored lines of text. The boys kept typing; the lines kept scrolling upward.

Ilya reached around behind the terminal and yanked out the power cords to the monitor and computer. The two boys looked up at their father.

"*Ty ne dolzhen byl delat' etogo ottsa,*" one of the boys said.

"What did he say, Ilya?"

"Gavril told me I should not have done that."

"Ask them why," Alex said.

"I already know."

"What do you mean, you already know?"

Ilya ignored her question. "*Idem, rebyata, my vozvrashchayemsya v komnaru.*"

"What did you say to them?"

"I told them we are going back to the room. They need to get some sleep."

Alex looked at the television and then at the two boys. Surprisingly, both children were looking directly at her. She then glared at Ilya. "What's going on?"

Ilya also looked at the television, then back to his boys. "You will find out sooner than later. Up until right now, you Americans believed I was the one who got into the electrical grid system of the United States and caused all the panic and the deaths. That's why you are here to take me to the United States for justice. You are wrong; it wasn't me." He looked at his boys. They were now looking up at him; both were smiling.

"Are you saying it was these two?" Alex said.

"Yes, it was my boys. I still don't know how they did it, but it was their actions that caused the collapse. They know things about computers that I can't even fathom. However, it was not their fault."

"Really, how is that?"

"They did not do it directly. They hacked into the Russian government's security force's computers in Moscow. They used to be called the secret police, the KGB; they are the FSB now. Different name, same people—same brutal people. The boys somehow got through numerous firewalls, and then they turned on systems that activated programs. To them, it is a game."

Ilya sighed and ran a hand through his hair, looking suddenly very tired. "The collapse of the Iowa power grid began immediately. The boys built a program that turned the FSB system on and off every hour. I believe the FSB program was developed by the Russian government as a weapon. So technically, it was my government, accessed by a program my boys created, that shut down the grid in Iowa that indirectly led to the deaths of those people. It was the Russian government that attacked Iowa." He looked up at the television and pointed. "And it is happening again."

CHAPTER 15

Chris tried another text; Alex still did not respond.

"We need to get to Lahti," Chris said. "If that Russian woman is here, she must have a way of knowing where they are."

The weather was clearing, and they quickly decided to make the one-hour trip by car, rather than the slower train ride. "Besides, Jack says the Lahti airport is marginal for the Gulfstream, so he will stay here," Linda said.

Chris nodded. "We drive."

"Alex was smart getting them off the train," Linda said. "Golubev would have had her people all over them as soon as they disembarked here in Helsinki. We avoided an incident on Finnish soil. We have everything set with the Finns to detain them; this could have blown it apart. We'll pick them up in Lahti, then contact the Finns. Bring them here to Helsinki."

"We could just fly them home," Chris said, blowing on his hot coffee. "Just sneak them out."

"Come on, Chris, you know that's not going to happen. The president wants this done by the book. We take the hacker into custody, have the Finns help with the extradition since they are on Finnish soil. Once the paperwork is done, we take them to Washington, two days max. Case and the FBI can handle the extradition."

"A lot can happen in two days," Chris said.

"Don't I know it," Linda said.

Chris's phone rang. "Yes . . . Good . . . We'll be there in thirty minutes. We need a car." He clicked off.

"Was that Jack?"

"Yes, the front is clearing. We'll take a cab back to the airport. He's getting us a rental. Damn, let me check something."

Chris opened his phone, punched in a few bits of text, waited, then put in a few more. "I should have considered this earlier. If Alex used the company American Express card, the charge would have popped up on the company account." He held up the phone. "Scandic Hotel, Lahti, Finland, two rooms."

* * *

As they walked back into the room, the boys led the way, followed by Ilya and Alex. The short hallway leading to the bathroom, just off the room entryway, provided just enough cover. Ilya didn't see Anya. Neither did Alex. Anya stepped out of the tiny hallway and clubbed Alex on the back of the head with a small table lamp. Alex fell to the floor, unconscious.

Ilya was stunned.

"We need to get out of here, right now," Anya said.

"Why did you hit her?" Pavel asked. "She is nice."

"Pavel, she isn't nice. She wants to hurt us, all of us. Ilya, we must leave now. Tie her up; use the lamp cords from the other room. Make them tight. Do it before she wakes. Gavril, help your brother put your clothes and things back in the bags."

Ilya, still shocked, did as Anya told him. He tied Alex's ankles and her hands behind her. He tried not to make the bindings too tight.

"And blindfold her. Use this to make a blindfold from a towel." Anya handed Ilya a small folding pen knife. "Where's her backpack?"

St. Petersburg White

After Ilya and Anya dragged Alex into the adjoining room, Anya searched through the backpack and handbag. She took out the battery for the computer, then checked the pockets of Alex's slacks and found a passport and a small wallet.

Anya opened the passport, then, holding it up and open, showed it to Ilya. "Her name is Alexandra Polonia; she lives in Cleveland, Ohio. I can't find anything about who she works for. She is not this Stapleton woman you said she was. There's about—"

"What the hell are we doing, Anya?" Ilya demanded. "She's done nothing to hurt us; we are here because of her."

"That's exactly right. We are out of that shithole of a country because of her. I'll tell her thanks someday. Right now, we probably have both the CIA and the FSB after us. Actually, they are after you and the boys. Your days of freedom are over, Ilya. Do you think the Americans are just going to accept your excuse that it was all an accident? I know all about what the boys were doing, and I can guess they were doing it again tonight. The Americans have a long memory—ask bin Laden. Wait, you can't, he's dead—how are the boys doing?"

"They are fine, almost done. I don't like this at all."

"You will thank me later. We need to leave, but first, we need train tickets."

Ilya looked around. "For what?"

"Get the computer running. We need train and ferry tickets."

"Tickets? With what?"

Anya held up Alex's American Express card. "With this. It will be good for a few hours before her people shut it down; we need to get as far away as we can. So, please, Ilya, the computer." She looked at the boys. "And keep them here with you." She went back to the room where Alex lay tied up.

Anya checked Alex's bonds. The American was still unconscious. She dragged the woman onto the bed and tied her arms to the headboard; that would keep her in place until the maid or someone found her. She also took another strip of a towel and tied a gag over Alex's mouth. Then she returned to Ilya. He'd found the train schedule for Lahti.

"Get tickets for Turku; we will catch the ferry to Stockholm there," Anya said. "Also get reservations for the Scandic hotel in Stockholm."

He bought tickets for both the train and the ferry and made the reservation. "We have twenty minutes until the train arrives," Ilya said. "We need to leave. They will know where we are now that I've turned the computer back on."

"Transfer the tickets to my phone. You know the number."

Ilya clicked the keys, then looked at Anya. "Done."

"Ilya, they already know where we are—we have to get out of here before they find us. Turn it off and remove the battery. The train ride is almost three hours. We will get food on the train; the boys can sleep."

"Money?"

"The woman has a few hundred euros. It will help. We need to go; get the boys dressed."

"The least you can do is leave her passport and wallet," Ilya said.

Anya hesitated, then stuck the items and the credit card back in the woman's bag.

Ilya dejectedly looked out the window. "The rain's stopped."

* * *

Alex twisted about and attempted to move her arms; they were tied to something. Her hands were twisted back awkwardly, so she couldn't move them either. Her legs and feet were bound. Her head hurt, her eyes were covered with something, and someone had shoved a rag in her mouth. She moved her head back and forth on the bedsheet, working the blindfold. Eventually, the makeshift blindfold slid up and over her forehead. The room was dark; the only light came from thin bright strips of sunlight along the edges of the blackout shade over the window. The clock on the lampstand was out; she guessed its cord was now wrapped around her feet. She had no idea what time it was.

But she guessed what happened. It wasn't Ilya; he was in front of her when they came into the room, so, it was one of two options. The FSB had found them, knocked her out, and had taken the four Russians. The FSB would have come prepared—tape and maybe a needle in the neck. Or it was Anya. Electrical cords and towels? Yes, it had to be the so-called nanny.

What the hell? Why would she clobber me? Wasn't she the family friend, the boys' caregiver? Was she working for the Russians? Oh God, my head hurts just thinking about it.

She lay there for another few hours. For the first hour she vigorously tried to loosen the wires—no luck, and the pain told her to stop. She eventually fell asleep, exhausted from the pain and three days of chaotic travel. She came to when she was jostled by a hand on her shoulder. Chris Campbell was standing over her.

"Goddamn, it took you long enough to get here," she said.

He cut the cords that were secured to the bed, then removed the cords from her legs. He gently untied her hands. "Whoever did this knew what they were doing," he said. "Nice knots."

"When I find her, I'll kill her," Alex said.

"Who?"

"Anya something, the boys' nanny." Alex sat up, touched the back of her head gingerly. "Goddamn her. What time is it?"

"Nine ten in the morning. We need to get you checked out."

"I'm fine. My head's harder than a brick, and right now as thick. Damn it, they've been on the road for almost five hours. It was just after four when we came back to the room."

"Came back at four?"

She explained about the boys and their adventures with the computers, going into as much detail as she knew when she got to the part about the FSB and the Russian program Ilya claimed had hijacked control of the electrical grid.

"Damn, and there was another attack, last night," Chris said. "Then, it abruptly stopped. I'm sorry it took so long to find you. The weather was crap, and the airport here is too small for the jet. We drove up from Helsinki."

"We?"

"Linda is with me. There was an accident on the highway; it was blocked for more than an hour. We knew which hotel; I'd checked it against your credit card charges on the account. Linda is downstairs talking to the manager. The guy at the desk speaks about three words of English, but I got a door card. That cost a pretty penny; these Finns know the value of desperation." He swore under his breath. "And there are more charges on your American Express account: train tickets to Turku and ferry tickets to Stockholm—a hotel."

"Stockholm? What?"

"Looks like they took the train from here to the ferry port of Turku; that's west of here."

"When is the boat going to leave Turku?"

"It left about an hour ago, but it's an eleven-hour trip to Stockholm."

Alex swung her legs to the floor and staggered to the bathroom. She slammed the door behind her.

"You sure you're okay?"

"No, goddamn it, I'm not," she yelled through the door. "At least I'm still alive. Give me ten minutes to get myself together—and shut that other room's fucking door behind you after you leave."

When Alex came out of the bathroom, she hastily sorted through her backpack. At least they'd left her phone and the sat-phones; they would have needed the passwords to use them. The computer and its battery were gone, and all her cash was missing. She was surprised to find her passport and credit cards.

"At least we know their passport numbers and the names on them," Alex said. "Popoff or something like that."

"Names? Numbers? I don't, do you?" Chris asked. "I'll have to get them from Yuri."

"I want to know who this Anya is and why she suddenly has become the savior of this little band of criminals," Alex said. "We need to get to Stockholm and welcome them to Sweden. But right now, the technology makes it easier for the damn Russians to find them."

* * *

Alex settled into the seat of the Gulfstream opposite Chris. She had a cold towel set tightly against the back of her neck. Linda was wrapping ice in another towel to replace it. A glass of vodka on the rocks sat in the holder next to Alex. The remains of a microwaved breakfast sat on the low table. Chris was asleep. He'd been out for about ten minutes. The TV mounted on the panel above him was tuned to CNN.

The speaker was the mayor of Maise, Elizabeth Nelson; she had become the face of the Iowa town. She thanked everyone for their help and prayers, then turned and gestured toward others who were with the city's police and fire departments, praising their efforts to help save the town. She then introduced the secretary for Homeland Security. He took the podium. He was a blustery yet intense man. Alex recognized him as a disgruntled former governor of a western state; she couldn't remember which one. Everyone needed a job—political hack came to mind.

"Ladies and gentlemen, I know you have questions about last night's collapse, again, of southern Iowa's and now northern Missouri's electrical grid. We are trying to find the reasons for this outage; thankfully, this only lasted about forty minutes before the lights came back on. I can assure you that when we find who is doing this—and we know that it was not the fault of our equipment or personnel—we will see that they are lawfully prosecuted. I view this incident in the same way I view the Oklahoma City bombing of 1995, and the other attempts of terrorism against Americans. We will prosecute whoever is responsible to the fullest extent of the law, and like the Oklahoma bomber, Timothy McVeigh, we will see that they are given the ultimate punishment."

Someone from the press corps asked, "Does that mean the death penalty? Will you seek the death penalty?"

"As I said, Bob, I will, through the Justice Department, make sure this killer or killers are held accountable for their actions."

"The death penalty?"

"If it was your family caught in this awful event, what would you want?"

CHAPTER 16

Anya stood on the open bow of the auto-passenger ferry as it slowly turned and backed up to the dock at the port of Marie-hamn on the island of Åland. The wooded hill that rose up above the tidy port and village was the highest piece of visible land, and even that was no more than a hump among the thousands of islands that filled this throat between the Baltic Sea and the Gulf of Bothnia between Finland and Sweden. About two dozen cars waited in the wide holding area to board the ferry. Gavril and Pavel stood next to Anya, excitedly holding to the railing and watching boats move about the harbor. Ilya stood behind them.

"Are you sure we must get off?" Ilya asked.

"Yes, the Russian and Americans must believe we are going to Stockholm," Anya answered. "We will get off here and catch the ferry this evening to Tallinn. Once we reach Estonia, we will catch a train and go anywhere."

"Why would we go anywhere? The Americans said they would help the boys and me."

"Do you trust them? You don't know them. It is a trick to get you to go with them to America. You saw that broadcast on the television—the government of the United States wants to arrest you; you heard what that man said." She looked at the boys. "There they will throw you in jail and take the boys away." She fell silent as the ship moved deliberately and silently toward the long concrete dock.

"Who will take us away, Papa?" Gavril asked.

"Why are we here? Why did Anya hit the nice lady?" Pavel asked for the tenth time. "I like her; she looked like Mama."

Ilya looked at Anya. "Can you answer him that? I understand why we had to leave Lahti; the FSB was coming. I get that. But now, to go to Estonia—why? Tell me, or we stop here."

Anya watched as the hawser lines were thrown to men on the dock; they quickly wrapped the lines around the massive iron bollards.

"Ilya, you are a wanted man. That's why I came along to help you and the boys. You have been good to me; I want to pay you back. When we get to Tallinn, we, and I mean all of us, will board a train and go anywhere we like. That's what I meant. Do you understand?"

"I understand, but I don't understand why. But I trust you; I have to trust someone."

"Did you download everything on the computer to the thumb drive I bought in the shop? And did you wipe the computer clean?"

"Yes, I did it while the boys slept."

"Good. We will leave the laptop here on the ship. It will tell the FSB that we are still on board and heading to Stockholm. We need every hour to get away."

"And that's why we are going to Estonia?"

"Yes, to gain us time. You contacted the Americans after the incident in America; you left the email on the computer. And I know what the boys did. I've watched them these two years. They are incredibly bright, brilliant, even geniuses, but right now, you are all in trouble. The Americans provided the passports and visas you needed to escape Russia. Do you know why? Can you imagine why? They want to be able to find you, take you to America, and put you on trial. Once we are in Estonia, you won't need them. The European Union will allow us to go anywhere, no questions. That's why I did what I did, to protect you and the boys."

"To protect us? Why are you exposing yourself? None of this concerns you."

"I like you and the boys. I can't let that happen to you or them." She looked down at the dock. The ramps were being put in place. "We need to get back to the cabin, get ready to leave. I can buy ferry tickets at the office. The ferry leaves late this evening."

"How do you know all these things?"

"Two years ago, I went to Stockholm and Oslo with some girlfriends. It was a lark, a fun time. We took the trains and the ferry. We came home on that same ferry through Tallinn."

"We could just get off the ferry in Stockholm and escape from there."

"The Americans and the Russians will be waiting. I know it."

"They could be waiting right now, on the dock right here. You don't know."

"Remember you put a hotel reservation on that woman's credit card?—for a hotel in Stockholm. Like the hotel in Lahti, a Scandic. They will believe that is where we are going. When you were with the boys, I also bought train tickets from Turku back to Helsinki. They will be confused."

There was a loud clang as the metal ramps locked onto the ship. The enclosed catwalks moved into place against the hull of the ferry.

Ilya looked down at the dock; he needed to make a decision. "Boys, we will go back to the cabin and get your bags," he said. "Then we will go for a walk. Would you like that?"

The twins looked at their father and Anya. There was confusion on their faces.

"Yes, Papa. When are we going home?" Pavel asked.

"Soon, just a while," he lied. "But soon."

"When, Papa?"

Ilya could see that a problem was building. "Would you like ice cream? There's a shop right on the dock."

A half hour later, they stood on the dock and watched the ferry head back out into the cluster of islands that led to the Baltic. The boys licked their ice cream cones. Somewhere buried in the back of their cabin's closet, under life preservers, was a Lenovo computer connected to the ship's Wi-Fi.

* * *

Tanya Golubev listened on her phone while Ivanovich told her the latest on the possible location of the government computer.

"Somewhere between Finland and Sweden? How is that possible?" Golubev said, not hiding her frustration. "Of course, a ferry. We missed them in Lahti by three hours . . . Yes, the Americans were there just before us . . . I believed they had found them, but the concierge was helpful . . . How much? Petty cash . . . I'm heading to Stockholm. I will intercept them there . . . Yes, then we will return to Moscow . . ."

Tanya had become extremely tired of this game. The Americans had to be orchestrating this. First, there was the now-apparent feint at the cruise ship terminal while the Americans instead took the train from St. Petersburg. Then the laptop IP address went live, but the group had exited from the train in Lahti, rather than going all the way to Helsinki. Lahti had to be a rendezvous point; with the fugitives in tow, this Mrs. Stapleton must have met up with the CIA or some other American agency. At least they had the hacker's new name: Fyodor

Popoff, and the boys, Vadim and Boris. Tanya had been surprised when the technician on the third floor told her the hacker was traveling with two children. The Russian customs agent on the train remembered them; according to her, both children were autistic or at least challenged. And there was the woman—it must be this Stapleton woman, the American agent. Just the four of them, the customs agent had said. The rest in the car were tourists, Finnish citizens, and a few Russians on holiday.

This American woman was smart. Somehow, she'd guessed there would be a Russian reception party in Helsinki; that had to be why she took them off the train in Lahti. Tanya still felt the fool for standing on the platform waiting for the hacker to leave the train. It had taken hours to check the video feeds from the other train stations and spot the man who matched the descriptions from the customs agent and the cameras in the St. Petersburg train station. Lost hours—even with facial recognition, it all took time. Then came the GPS verification of the location of the computer used in Lahti early that morning.

It took even more hours to get to the hotel in Lahti and talk with the manager. It took the third floor more hours of reviewing hacked surveillance videos from the Lahti train station to see that the group, a man and a woman, and the two children, had boarded the Helsinki-bound train early that morning. The manager did let it slip that she was tired of foreign officials coming into her hotel and demanding information about their guests. She said something about this being Finland and not a playground for stupid international intrigues. Tanya asked if these others were Americans; the manager said yes, then told her to leave and then said something obviously rude in Finnish. Four hours later, the computer came on again for about twenty minutes, then turned off. Third floor determined the

GPS location was west of the Finnish port of Turku in the middle of the Baltic Sea.

"They are heading west," Golubev reported to Ivanovich. "They are on a ferry heading to Stockholm. See if you can find them in the train station or ferry terminal in Turku. Let me know."

"Do not let this man go," Ivanovich said. "He cannot let the Americans know what he found."

"Maybe he has already told them; he has been with them for almost a full day now."

"Then why are the Americans still with him? Think this through, Assistant Director Golubev; he must be keeping the information secret, to use it in his bargaining. The Americans certainly want to punish him for what happened in America. He knows this and is using it to protect himself and his children."

"Have you determined who he is?"

"Yes, we have a tentative identification of Ilya Fedorovich Sokolov, St. Petersburg," Ivanovich said. "I am sending two of our people to his apartment right now. We will find out everything we can about this traitor; no one hacks into our systems, no one."

Golubev did not fly into Stockholm's Arlanda International Airport; Bromma Stockholm Airport was closer, smaller, and more convenient. The flight from the Helsinki airport took less than an hour. They parked the department's Dassault Falcon 2000 next to a new Gulfstream G280. As they climbed down the steps, her pilot mentioned something about the jet having American registration. Golubev looked and was impressed; other than the registration number on the port engine, no other identification was visible on the aircraft. She did notice the registration number began with an "N," which meant American. Then again, there were no labels on the French-built plane they'd just landed in, only the jet's registration that began with "RA," for Russia. By the time she and her two associates had rented a car and driven the sixteen kilometers to the Stockholm ferry terminal, they were an hour early. Golubev was not a calm and patient person.

CHAPTER 17

Alex nervously walked about the concourse of the Stockholm Ferry terminal; she was still pissed about being conked on the head by Anya—who the hell was this woman? Anya arrives at the St. Petersburg train station with Ilya and the boys; is vouched for by Ilya. Micah, if he knew, said nothing to her about Anya; she travels with her own passport, and sits on the sidelines watching. The boys know her and like her. Ilya's explanation that she was a friend who took care of the kids only carried so much water. There was something else she couldn't put her finger on. She had many questions for this Anya Belsky; when they had time, she would have Dallas chase the name down. There was something fishy about her; Alex's detective radar said so. Hinky. This girl was hinky.

The flight in from Helsinki to Stockholm's Bromma Airport took an hour, hardly time to settle in or even have a decent drink, and Alex badly wanted a drink. The broadcast of the latest press conference in Iowa troubled her. She hadn't seen such hatred and demand for revenge since the weeks after the attack on the Twin Towers, and that was now almost twenty years ago. But it was there, sharp, loud, and pointed. The Americans wanted their pound of flesh over this attack; she saw it, she heard it. She looked at Chris and Linda sitting in the concourse coffee shop; they both knew that the Russians, or at least their program, ultimately were responsible for the attack on the grid. Alex wasn't sure how much of this information would make it into the public's view. Then again, it was all unsubstantiated, a comment by an acknowledged hacker who claimed his autistic kids had broken into the most secure servers in the world, clicked on a few digital switches, and brought Armageddon to a small Midwestern town. No, she was sure no one in Iowa would believe it. However, Washington might believe it. Washington would make changes to prevent the same thing from happening to their servers. Washington would try and hide it all—to be used later. She chided herself for being so cynical; then again, her experiences in Saigon had proved to her that Washington would do anything to protect themselves. Now, her head hurt to high holy heaven.

The ferry, red hull and white topsides, with VIKING LINE painted in huge letters on its sides, slowly and expertly docked. They would know in fifteen minutes what these four fugitives from St. Petersburg had been up to since Alex's last encounter with them in Lahti. She would like the chance to bonk that woman on the head herself—tit for tat.

They took positions in the concourse where every person leaving the ferry would have to pass. Linda and Chris had photos on their phones of Ilya and the boys, courtesy of Yuri. Their earlier reconnoiter and questions with a female uniformed security agent confirmed that the passengers from the ship from Turku and Mariehamn would exit the doors at the end of the corridor. The three of them waited.

Then, in a mad rush of multicolored T-shirts, shorts, strollers, and suitcases on wheels, hundreds of passengers pushed their way through the doors, down the escalators and stairs, and out onto the plaza in front of the terminal. Some went left, some right. The rush continued for more than twenty minutes; the security officer had said the ship carried more than 2,400 passengers, and it was usually full. Alex and her companions watched, studied, and waited.

Linda and Chris walked across the narrow hallway to Alex.

"Nothing comes close to a couple with two identical ten-year-old twin boys," Linda said.

"They could have gotten past us, but I doubt it," Chris added. "It's a funnel here; we will see them."

Linda looked through the windows of the terminal out to the drop-off area in the front. "Goddamn it, how did she know to be here?"

Alex followed Linda's gaze to just outside, where next to the drop-off curb a lanky woman in a leather coat—with blonde hair that almost matched Alex's own hair color—stood next to a blue van. Two other military types, with short haircuts and leather jackets, stood nearby. They all held a paper and looked at it, then at the exiting passengers.

"You know her?" Alex asked.

"Yeah, Tanya Golubev," Linda said. "She is Russian FSB. According to Dallas, she works for Dmitry Ivanovich, an FSB director in Moscow. She was at the Helsinki train station when we were waiting for you and the Sokolovs. There is no doubt now that she is here for the same reason we are. These people have to be worth a lot for the Russians to have one of their top agents tracking down this hacker."

"The traffic flow is thinning," Chris said. "Should we go over to the hotel they booked, see if they show up there?"

Alex looked at the crowd, then back out at the FSB agents. "I think we've been taken for a ride. This Anya Belsky comes across as smart. If that Russian agent is here, it's because of the computer's GPS and facial recognition in Turku. I'd taken Ilya's computer battery, but they took it from my bag when they left. She may have been turning it on and off to leave a trail. Shit, for all I can guess, Ilya's computer is on that boat somewhere. And the FSB agents followed it here. We know that Ilya and Anya also bought train tickets back to Helsinki from Turku; they may have doubled back. But I doubt it."

The ferry crowd had now dwindled to just a few; most were older with canes and walkers. Alex looked up at the sign above the stairway. It read: *To Mariehamn and Turku.*

"One stop," Alex said. "The ferry made one stop; they could have gotten off."

"Shit," Chris said. "We need to find out what they could do—or where they could go—from Mariehamn. I'll ask Information."

As Chris walked toward an illuminated square green sign with a bold small-case "**i**," Alex turned to Linda. "What did you say her name was?"

"Tanya Golubev; her last name means 'pigeon' in Russian."

"Really? Tanya? Golubev? Pigeon? Well, okay . . ." Alex immediately walked out the sliding glass doors and directly toward the FSB agent. Linda could try and stop her; she didn't. There were spycraft protocol issues involved here. Alex assumed the first was: "If you are a spy, don't let the opposition know it."

"Tanya, damn, it's good to see you again," Alex said in English. "What's it been, three years? Budapest, I think. Yes, Budapest, during Oktoberfest. Great weather. You were with that tall, good-looking Italian, Favio something. Damn you—so lucky. Me, I struck out. That Romanian, he turned out to be a poof." Alex extended her hand to Tanya.

Tanya appeared momentarily stunned and instantly on the defensive. She answered in English with a thick accent. "Who the fuck are you? I don't know you." She did not take Alex's hand.

"Nice way to talk. We had a great time. Me? I'm doing a little traveling again. That guy I married, you remember, the big Polish guy. We split. So, I've got plenty of time and money on my hands. Nice alimony checks."

"Who the hell are you?" Tanya repeated. Her two associates moved in toward them.

"Sandy, Sandy Dumbrowski, Cleveland, Ohio. Well, actually the whole wide world now. Made a few bucks on the Ohio lottery, and now I travel. I'm shocked you don't remember me, Tanya. If I remember correctly, things got a little intimate that night but, hey, I get it, different strokes for different folks. These guys of yours look seriously macho, so I understand." Alex began to back away, her hands up in a gesture of mock surrender. "It was cool to see you, Tanya. Brings back memories."

"Get lost."

"Got it, getting lost. By the way, say high to Dmitry."

Alex went back into the terminal and walked up to Linda.

"What the hell did you tell her? As soon as you turned around, they climbed into the van like the devil was after them. See, they are leaving."

"I left Sandy Dumbrowski's calling card. Kind of a shot across the bow."

"You didn't. You . . . fucking . . . didn't."

CHAPTER 18

Anya paced about nervously at the curb in front of Tallinn, Estonia's Ferry Terminal D. Ilya and the boys sat on a bench and glared at her. She had gotten them this far by using fear as the motivator. Fear of the FSB, the Americans, and fear of the boys being taken away. She hoped, after all these diversions, that she had left their pursuers confused. She needed at least twenty-four hours—one more day, and it would all be over.

"I've booked us rooms in a small hotel near the city square," she said. "I stayed there two years ago. It was comfortable."

"I want to go home," Gavril said. "Now!"

"I want to go home," Pavel echoed.

"We can't, not right now, boys," Anya answered. "Just a few days more. This is a vacation—aren't you having fun?"

"I want to go home, now."

"I want to go home, now," was repeated.

"Ilya?"

"I'm not sure what you've accomplished. The American woman is likely very upset over what you did. She will not give up until they catch us. Then I don't know what I'll do."

"If we are caught, they will put you in prison," Anya said and looked at the boys. "You will never see the boys again. Is that what you want?"

"Of course not. That is the last thing I want," Ilya said.

"But we are running out of options, and you are running out of money. I know you used that woman's credit card, but for the ferry from Mariehamn, you paid cash. And the food and the room tonight costs money. Tomorrow, what are you going to do tomorrow? Do we even have enough money to take a taxi? Is there enough to buy the boys lunch?"

"Yes, there's enough for that."

"It's raining again. You said this hotel is near the city square?"

"Yes." Anya waved at a taxi sitting at the curb. Moments later, they were winding their way through the narrow cobblestone streets of the medieval city.

"Can we afford this?" Ilya asked when the taxi stopped in front of a hotel.

"Yes, I didn't want to use it in Mariehamn, but I have my own credit card. No one knows who I am, even that American woman. So, I can use it. I'll figure out how to pay for it later."

The clerk was unsure about the boys.

"Will they be okay?" he asked in Russian as he slid their passports back across the marble counter. "They won't cause trouble, will they, Mister Popoff?"

"They are fine, only tired and hungry," Ilya said. "Are the rooms connected?"

"Yes, third floor."

"Is there a pizza place near here?" Ilya asked.

"Around the corner, sir. That way, called Pizza Magnifico. I believe they are open now for lunch."

"Boys, we are going to the room. I want you to wash and put on a clean shirt. Then we are going for pizza. That sound good?"

"Pizza, pizza," the two chimed.

"I need some exercise," Anya said. "You three have lunch. I am totally pizza'd out. I'll check on you when I get back. Gavril, can you take my bag to the room?"

Gavril reached out, and she put the strap in his hand.

"Thank you," Anya said.

"Me?" Pavel said.

"Pavel, you make sure your brother doesn't lose the bag. Take the other strap."

Pavel took the other strip of leather. Gavril gave a tug, Pavel tugged back.

"Stop it," Ilya said to the boys. To Anya, he said, "Don't be too late. We need to talk about the next few days."

"I won't be." She turned to the clerk. "Do you have an umbrella?"

"There are two in the room, and there are some at the door," the manager said, pointing to a tall cylinder basket stuffed with umbrellas.

"Thank you."

"I hope you enjoy your stay, Mister Popoff," the clerk said. He looked again at the boys.

"Thank you, and thanks for the recommendation," Ilya answered.

Anya grabbed an umbrella as she walked out the door. A block from the hotel she extracted a cheap phone she had bought on the sly in Mariehamn, turned it on, and waited. The signal strength was excellent. She continued to stroll up the cobblestone streets. Even in the summer mist, it was thick with visitors. She guessed they were from the cruise ships tied up near the ferry terminal; like in St. Petersburg, the tourists helped to keep the city's economy alive. She walked up the hill to the square that fronted the town hall; the clock high on its façade read 1:03 PM. She took a seat at one of the outdoor restaurants that faced the square. She tapped in a number on the phone.

"We're here," she said in Russian. "Yes, I know . . . It has been difficult . . . Right now, I want to see you . . . I don't care, now . . . I know we agreed to tonight . . . I also want half now as well; I need the money . . . If not, I'll take them to the train station, then to Berlin or somewhere else, someplace you will not find us . . . There's an outdoor restaurant on the square across from the town hall; it's called Saku. I'm in the corner table, black hair, pink striped top . . . Good, thirty minutes."

Anya had called this man the day she discovered that Ilya had emailed the Americans in Iowa. His laptop had been open, so she read the missive. She had an idea, and that idea turned into a plan. She desperately needed money—it would be her way out of Russia, and Ilya had given her a way to make it happen. She had demanded euros, a lot of euros; the amount was not to be questioned. After he asked a few questions, the man agreed to her demands. They worked out the logistics. She was sure the woman, Lois Stapleton or whatever her name was, had not suspected her. Ilya never knew—he was doing this for his boys. Anya had grown fond of them, the Sokolovs, even felt sorry when she heard what happened to the boys' mother. But, hell, life was hard, especially in Russia. She'd lost both her parents to drugs and alcohol. She raised herself from the age of twelve; did things, creepy things she would never talk about, and survived. This was one more turn down that road. By tonight, she would be free, free of all of it.

The rain had changed to a heavy mist; there was no wind, the temperature pleasant. The thick fabric of the restaurant's overhead awning kept her dry. She ordered a beer and a toasted cheese sandwich; she was so hungry that when it was set on the table, she immediately ordered another. The market square was full of stalls; many purveyors had spread clear plastic sheets over their goods to protect them. When the rain stopped, they would reopen. The cruise ship tourists persevered; a little rain would not stop their adventure. One day here in Tallinn, the next Copenhagen or St. Petersburg—only the fun seekers knew.

"*Ty Anya Bel'skaya,*" the man asked in Russian. He was tall, neat, bald, thick mustache, horn-rimmed glasses, and American. He wore a dark blue polo shirt under a sports jacket. His jacket was open, and she saw the leather strap of a shoulder holster.

"*Da, ya Anya Bel'skaya. Priyatno poznakomit'sya s vami, Spetsial'nyy Agent Robb Case. Sadites', pozhaluysta.*"

"It is good to meet you," FBI Special Agent Robb Case said. He did as she ordered, pulled out a chair, and sat directly across from Anya.

"You are alone?" she asked, looking around.

"Of course not, but he will not bother us."

"Do you have my money?"

"That is something . . ."

She leaned in. "My money—half now, and the rest when I hand over the Sokolovs."

* * *

Gavril and Pavel, bellies full of pizza, danced silently back and forth on their heels. They shared an umbrella between them. Ilya was behind them, also with an umbrella; the trio walked along a row of stalls filled with handcrafted towels and linens at one corner of the market square. He was always amazed at how in sync his boys were; their physical and emotional bonds went beyond what he understood.

Looking across the square, he spotted Anya sitting under an umbrella at an outdoor restaurant. Her back was to him, yet he knew the pink blouse she was wearing; she had changed into it on the ferry during the night. She was talking to a man. He looked military, well dressed, and wore dark-rimmed glasses. He'd never seen the man before, but Ilya's first impression was that he was a Cossack. Anya was obviously agitated, moving her hands about as she talked. The man nodded a few times, then pointed his right index finger at her and said something. He then reached into his jacket and removed a buff-colored envelope and slid it across the table. Ilya couldn't believe what he was seeing; Anya Belsky was selling them out.

"Come, boys, we need to get back to the room. We are going on another trip," he said.

"Home, home?" Gavril asked.

"Home?" Pavel said.

"Yes, we will be going home, soon," Ilya answered.

Theirs was a rush against time. He did not know how long they would have until Anya and the man or his people would arrive at the hotel. He threw their bags on the bed; they hadn't been opened since they arrived at the hotel. He rifled through Anya's backpack and found an envelope with more than eight hundred and fifty euros and twenty thousand rubles. There were ten American fifty-dollar bills. He was pissed at himself for believing the woman. No money?—such bullshit. This had to be the money she'd taken from the American woman while Ilya had been gathering up the boys for their rush to the train the day before, or was it two days before? Time had gotten all out of whack. He stuffed Anya's passport and the money into his jacket pocket. He remembered Anya taking her purse; in her hurry to go for a walk she'd forgotten the passport and credit cards stowed in her backpack. Her obvious rush was to meet this man, whoever he was.

"Hurry, boys, we need to catch a train," Ilya said, urging them to the door.

They took the elevator to the lobby and hurried out the main doors. Ilya glanced up and down the cobblestone street—no Anya. A cab waited at the curb; Ilya waved; the driver gave him a thumbs-up.

"Train station," Ilya said in Russian.

"Going home?" the driver asked.

"Yes, home. It's been a long trip."

"*Otlichno, ya iz Gatchiny.*"

The cab driver was from Gatchina. Ilya knew the small town south of St. Petersburg; a lot of Russians had left his country since the fall of the union. However, he did not want to talk to anyone more than absolutely necessary.

"The train station, *spasibo.*"

"Yes . . . sir." The driver saluted in the mirror.

He made a U-turn and then went right at the corner. Ilya glanced back up the street toward the square and saw a woman in a pink blouse turn onto the street. Anya was on foot and walking rapidly.

The taxi wound through the streets; in less than ten minutes they stopped in front of the Tallinn train station. Ilya passed the driver a twenty-euro note. The driver said too much; Ilya said to keep the change, hoping the gesture would give them luck for the rest of the day—they would need it.

The station was crowded even for midafternoon. People dragged suitcases en route to and from the platforms; some queued at the ticket dispensers, others sat in the coffee shop. Ilya knew this would be the first place Anya and the military man would look. They had to get on a train, any train, and get as far from Tallinn as they could. He scanned the electronic schedule; one destination caught his eye: Narva. Narva, Estonia, the city on the frontier with Russia—that would work.

"Boys, we are going home." Ilya pointed up at the sign. "That is a city on the border with Russia. We will head there; then in a few days, we will head home."

"Papa, where's Anya?" Pavel asked.

Ilya took a deep breath; he'd known this was coming. "Anya is a bad person. She wanted to hurt us, so we are going home without her."

"Home, home," Gavril said.

"Yes, boys, we are going home."

Ilya put a twenty-euro note in the ticket machine, punched in what he needed, and took the tickets. The overhead schedule read the train for Narva was leaving in ten minutes. It was also highlighted as one of the trains that would stop at Tallinn Airport on this same route. He looked at the other stops; a name stuck out, Rakvere. When Ilya was eight or nine years old, before the collapse of the Soviet Union and before his parents died, his family vacationed for a week in this region of Estonia. It was one of the last times his father had with the family before he went back to Afghanistan. Rakvere would be an excellent place to hide until he could figure everything out.

They walked to the platform where the train, red with great swishes of white lines on its flanks, mercifully waited. Ilya checked their tickets against the numbers on the cars, found the right one, and after jostling with dozens of tourists heading to the airport, found their seats.

At precisely the time shown on their tickets, the train slowly and silently left the station. The boys, after looking out the windows, turned to their father, and with expressions that nearly broke his heart, looked at him expectantly.

"In an hour and a half, we will be there, so please relax. Play your Nintendos." Ilya retrieved the two devices from his bag and handed them to the boys along with their earbuds.

"I want no yelling, understood?" he said as the boys plugged in the earbuds.

"Yes, Papa. No yelling," Pavel said. In minutes, they were engrossed in their games.

Ilya knew if they had been followed, this is where they would be caught—trapped on a train, no place to hide. He waited and watched his sons; they clicked away on their devices, looked at each other occasionally, then went back to their games. He listened to their small squeals of enjoyment, relieved they did not know what was happening. He carried the anxiety of this shit all on himself. His sons had no idea of the pain they initiated when they accessed the Russian server, pain that resulted from great government secrets, evil secrets, and immoral programs that, when opened, unleashed unimaginable horror and death. He hoped to God they never found out what they'd done through their naïve curiosity.

Ten minutes after leaving the station, his anxiety lessened. He was confident they were not followed. Whatever Anya was going through, he didn't care. The tall bald man, even though he looked like a Cossack, must have been an American. The envelope he slid across the table was a payment, a payment for their lives and souls. He would never forgive Anya. Two years earlier, he'd saved her from a terrible fate, and this was how she repaid them. He felt sorry for his boys; they liked her, and he had believed that she liked them. Maybe she did, but right now, after what she had done, and where she had brought them, she could rot in hell.

He glanced at his sons; they were asleep, their Nintendos on their laps. The boys had leaned into each other; he'd seen this a hundred times. Their bond was stronger than steel. Then again, his love for them was as strong.

After the stop at the airport, the car almost emptied; there were only three other passengers left in their car as the train continued on toward Rakvere and Narva. He needed to pee. The restroom was at the end of the car. He checked that the boys were still sleeping, walked down the aisle, pushed the restroom door release, and went in. Moments later, when he returned to the seat, the boys were wide awake. Gavril was still leaning in toward his brother. To Ilya's shock, Pavel held his phone, the one the American called Robert had given to Ilya the night they met in the park in St. Petersburg. Pavel looked up at his father and then reached out to hand the phone to him.

"It is the woman; we like her. Talk, Papa, talk."

CHAPTER 19

The TSD Gulfstream pivoted on its wheels as the aircraft tractor repositioned the jet. Alex, sitting in the lounge of the private jet center, noticed the registration number on the cowling of the engine: N013TS. The number thirteen as well as the "TS" for Teton Security stuck in her head. Chris, Linda, and Jack were headed to Helsinki. The plane taxied out to the runway. According to the pilot, Jack, they would be back in less than five hours. Thirty minutes earlier, Chris had received a text message from Jimmy Cortez in Dallas informing that Micah Lynch had called after being released from detention by the security police. He'd returned to his room at the Radisson, found it empty, and placed a call to TSD headquarters. Chris and Micah had spoken, Alex waiting nearby while Chris carried on an animated conversation with her partner. Micah was pleased that she got their human package out of Russia; he wasn't pleased to learn what happened after that. Micah decided, while still in the good graces of the Russian government and before they could change their minds, to take the next train to Helsinki. There Chris would pick him up.

It was also decided that Alex would go back to the Stockholm ferry terminal to wait for the next boat in from Mariehamn, due in two hours, in the slight chance Ilya and the boys were on it. After clearing the debarking passengers, she would return to Bromma Airport with or without the Sokolovs. In the lounge area, she saw a man sitting in one of the leather chairs; he wore a military-like officer's uniform. He was talking on his phone as he gathered a few items he'd set on the table next to him. She guessed he might be the pilot for the other private jet sitting on the tarmac. She knew cars, at least old classics; she did not know jets. But the other plane did look nice, a bit fatter than the Gulfstream, but nice. She half-smiled to herself, knowing that Jack, or Linda for that matter, would not be happy for her lack of interest.

She pushed her handbag into the backpack and hiked it up on her shoulder. She still had her own American Express card; why Anya hadn't taken it puzzled her. They took the cash, all of it. But her passport and wallet with the American Express card were in the bag when Chris found her. She needed money; Chris gave her two hundred euros.

She watched the TSD jet accelerate down the runway; in moments, it disappeared into the low clouds. She walked to the front of the terminal to hail a taxi. Standing against the wall of the building, under the wide eave and out of the rain, she watched a blue van similar to the one at the ferry terminal drive past the drop-off and turn into the adjacent parking lot. Golubev and her two henchmen exited the van and walked directly to the jet. The pilot—she'd guessed correctly; it was the man she'd just seen in the lobby—was jogging toward them. He activated the aircraft's door and a stairway folded outward. They all disappeared inside.

Alex took a chance and waited. Ten minutes later, the jet began to taxi toward the runway; it duplicated the air path of the Gulfstream and in seconds, it too disappeared into the clouds.

She shivered and felt a foreboding. Here she was in a country that was four thousand miles from her home, alone, a failure with the one job she was assigned to do: protect a family.

For all she knew, Chris might decide not to come back and pick her up. That was just crazy; of course, he would be back. Somehow, they would find these four people. Somehow all this would be made right. She would make it right.

The phone in her pocket began to buzz. Hoping it was Chris, she looked at the screen and read the name: *Fyodor*. The only Fyodor she knew was named Ilya, and the number belonged to the phone Micah had given the Russian the night they met him in St. Petersburg.

"Hello?"

There was a pause, then a voice she knew said, "Aaaa-lax, Aaaa-lax. *Pozhauluysta, pomogi nam.* Help."

"Gavril? Pavel?"

"*Da.* Pavel."

"*Papa, spacibo, Papa.*"

Ilya started to speak.

"How do the boys know my name?" Alex said, interrupting him.

"We found your passport. I told them your name. They said they liked it; it is the name of an empress of Russia. Some things stick with these boys."

"Thank you for leaving me my passport and credit card."

"Anya wanted to take them; I told her to leave you something."

"So, it *was* Anya who knocked me out. How nice of her."

"What? I don't understand."

"It's nothing. Where are you? What are you doing?"

"Okay, it was Anya who hit you. She tricked us into following her. She is working with someone, an American. She was going to turn us over to him."

"Slow down, Ilya. First, how are the boys?"

"They are tired; we are all tired."

"Where are you?"

"We are on a train in Estonia."

"Estonia?"

"We were in Tallinn; that's where the ferry landed from Mariehamn. We were going to stay there a few days, but then I saw Anya talking to this man. He handed her money, or I think it was money. I believe she was going to turn us over to him."

"Okay, where is Estonia? And who was this man? What did he look like?" She could hear the boys in the background; they were saying something about her. She heard her name repeated a few times.

"Where are you?" Ilya asked.

"I'm in Stockholm. I'm waiting for you to get off the ferry."

"Anya tricked all of us. We got off the ferry in Mariehamn, and then she made us take another ferry across the Baltic to Tallinn. That's where I saw her meet with this man; he looked like an American."

"How could you tell?"

"Americans look different from us. He was bald, had a thick black mustache, and wore round black-rimmed glasses. He was large, tall, looked like a soldier."

"Are you sure?"

"Yes. When I saw Anya talking to him, I knew I had to get the boys away from both of them. We immediately went to the train station and took the first train leaving. It was headed to Narva on the border with Russia."

"You can't go back there."

"I know, but there is a small village I know on the way—it's called Rakvere. We can hide there. Can you come and help us? The boys like you, and we need you."

"I hardly know you, Ilya. Right now, you have a chance to get away from all this. Why don't you?"

"I will never get away from this. You know that. I don't have any money, we have nothing. Our only chance is for you to come and provide some protection. You are our best hope."

Alex signaled to the single taxi waiting at the stand. The driver responded with a thumbs-up.

"Can I call you back at this number?" she said into the phone.

"Yes, it's the phone you gave me. Anya didn't know about it."

"The computer?"

"Anya made me leave it on the ferry to make the FSB think we were onboard. I kept everything important on a thumb drive." There was a pause. "It's in my pocket," he added as if having checked to make sure.

"It worked; the Russians were at the ferry terminal in Stockholm. The lead agent is a woman. Do you have any idea who she is?"

"No. Just a moment, Gavril wants to say something."

"Aaa-lex, *pozhauluysta, pomogi nam. Pomogite, Papa.*"

"What did he say?"

"My boys have their issues, but they are smart, sometimes too smart. He asked for you to please help us, and to help me."

"I will do what I can. When I land in Tallinn, I will call you. You can tell me where you are, and then I will find a way to help you and the boys."

The taxi driver tooted his horn, earning an annoyed glare from Alex. A glare was international. He responded with a hand gesture that asked, *What's happening?* Alex tossed her bag in the back seat and climbed in after them.

"International airport," she said.

"Arlanda International?" the driver asked.

"I need to get to Tallinn, a plane to Tallinn."

"Arlanda it is, boss," the driver said.

"You speak English?"

"Some. I lived for a time in London. So, you going to Tallinn, boss?"

"Yes."

"It will take thirty minutes to get to Arlanda. Sit back, relax."

Alex took the driver's suggestion and leaned back in the seat and finally took a breath; all the craziness was catching up with her. She tried to call Chris. She got his voicemail; she didn't leave a message. Bald man, thick mustache, black-rimmed glasses . . . she only knew one person who fit that description: Special Agent Robb Case. If it was him, why was he cutting some deal with Anya Belsky for the Sokolovs? Why was he even in Tallinn? How did he know? Anya had to have contacted him sometime earlier, probably before they left St. Petersburg. She'd made a deal and sold the Sokolovs to the American government.

Shit—what the hell? And the FBI didn't think it was worth telling Chris and me?

Interagency rivalry—that was supposed to have gone away after 9-11. People were the same; they never changed, thought Alex. Egos, turf, power, budgets: they all got thrown into the mix. And two children, two extraordinary children, and their father were the prize.

She tried Chris again—nothing. Their flight time to Helsinki was about an hour, but according to Jack, the pilot, they could be on the ground waiting for Micah as long as four or five hours because of the train connections. Micah would try to reach the station closest to the airport.

Alex walked into the Arlanda terminal, spotted the massive overhead display, and checked for departures to Tallinn. There were three flights during the next four hours. Her next stop was Scandinavian Airlines. Fifteen minutes later, she was waiting at the gate; still no answer from Chris's phone.

After takeoff, she had barely settled into her seat when the plane, a narrow-body A320, began its descent into Estonia.

She took a few minutes to study the map in the inflight magazine to get her bearings. Estonia was bordered by Russia to the east and Latvia to the south and shared maritime borders with Finland and Sweden. Tallinn, the capital, was in northern Estonia, perched on the shore of the Gulf of Finland. Alex traveled her eyes down the map and saw the port city of Gdansk on the Baltic coast of Poland. Somewhere in that faraway country was her family's home; her world was a strange Alex Polonia world these days.

She walked through the Tallinn terminal to the information desk, wanting to be certain she was heading the right way to the trains. Along the way, at a food kiosk, she filled a bag with sandwiches, a couple energy drinks, some chips, a chocolate chip cookie the size of her hand, and packages of moist and dry toilettes. At another kiosk, she bought a train ticket for Rakvere, strolled out to the platform with twenty minutes to spare. All in all, she was damn proud of herself: *Logistics is my middle name.*

She tried Chris again, this time on the sat-phone. No answer, but when she had boarded and took a seat, he called her back.

"Have you been trying to reach me?" Chris asked.

"Yes, I'm in Estonia. Ilya called; he's hiding. Lots of things happening, strange things.

"Estonia? Jesus Christ, how did you . . . What happened?"

She told him about seeing the Russians arrive at the airport and then watching them leave; the phone call from the boys; the conversation with Ilya; and her suspicions about Robb Case.

"Are you sure it was him?" Chris asked.

"Of course not, I wasn't there. This is based on what Ilya said. But it does make some sense; somebody had to be directing Anya. She may be bright, but this is spycraft way over her head. She's obviously in it for the money. And now that the Sokolovs have split, my guess, she's scared as hell—and that was five hours ago she met Case—she's probably gone. Took the money and literally ran. Have you caught up with Micah?"

"No, his train was delayed leaving St. Petersburg and then at the border."

"Was it something to do with all of this?"

"No, or I don't think so. A choir group on a charter was late, stuck in traffic during the bad weather in St. Petersburg. The train was an hour late leaving. The delay at the border? God only knows, but Micah's about two and a half hours out. We won't have wheels up for at least another three and a half hours at best. And we have weather closing in here, heavy stuff. So, figure at least five hours to reach Tallinn."

"I'm going to the Sokolovs. According to Ilya, the village they are in is just sixty miles from the Russian border. Looking at the map, Linda's buddy, Tanya Golubev, could have a special ops team there in an hour if she knew where they were."

"Be careful," Chris said.

"You're letting me go?"

"Of course. It's the right decision; you are the closest asset. I've got no one else in the country. In fact, the nearest TSD asset is Yuri in St. Petersburg, and I need him there. Besides, he's a Russian bear in a china shop when it comes to these things. You're up to bat. Keep me posted. I will quietly follow up on this Case adventure, try and find out what the hell he's doing. Maybe it's just the usual Potomac poker game, and he's upping the ante, but I will find out. And watch those two boys; I'm not sure what's happening there. But we cannot allow another power grid failure. The media is screaming; there's serious political finger-pointing going on back home, and even some rumblings of nationalizing the power grid. So, when you get to them, watch them."

Alex placed the sat-phone on the bench beside her and stared at it, expecting it to catch fire like in some *Mission Impossible* vignette. Ten minutes later a train slid silently into the airport station; hundreds of tourists and locals disembarked and headed toward the airport terminal. Alex checked to make sure it was the right train, boarded, then settled into one of the single seats. According to the schedule, Rakvere was one hour and ten minutes away.

She called Ilya; he answered on the first ring. He and the boys were in the Rakvere hotel, a few blocks from the town's small train station. The boys needed to be settled in, he said. Alex promised to call back in another hour.

She took out a sandwich and one of the bags of chips, then opened a can of caffeinated punch. She was more than hungry; she was ravenous. She ate half of the second sandwich. What she was really doing was setting up her stomach for the cookie. It was delicious.

In the early evening light, the landscape, flat and verdant, slipped by the train window. She still wasn't used to the sun being up until almost ten o'clock in the evening, and it never got completely dark. The more annoying part of this trip was that the train stopped at a small town or village every ten to fifteen minutes. Some on the train were asleep; they probably were the regulars. Others, she guessed, were heading on to Russia. They had bags full of stuff—she wondered what. What was cheaper in Estonia than in Russia? There was no chance for Alex to sleep; she could not afford to miss her stop.

CHAPTER 20

Tanya Golubev knocked loudly on the massive oak door to her boss's office; the sound echoed throughout the floor of the building.

"Come in, Tanya. It is impossible not to hear you marching up the hall. This whole thing has become a fucking disaster," Ivanovich said. He slowly stood behind his desk and scowled as she crossed the room and stood at attention in front of him. She had seriously screwed up, and the hacker was in the wind. There was a time, not so long ago, when this kind of blunder would have ended her career, or worse. "What happened?"

Golubev went through the Helsinki train fiasco, the Lahti disaster, the flight across Finland to Sweden—he knew she hated flying—and the waiting game for the ferry to arrive. All a bust. When she brought up the blonde who challenged her in Stockholm, Ivanovich's interest increased.

"Any idea who she is?"

"None. However, I'm not sure she was alone, either. We immediately left after I was identified. I initially assumed she was Swedish police, but when she spoke English, I knew she was American. How did the Americans know they were on the ferry?"

"They weren't on the ferry, Assistant Director Golubev."

"I know that now, Director. Obviously, neither of us knew

that then. Have there been any additional attempts to access the program?"

"Not since early morning yesterday, but we are closely monitoring it. If this hacker tries again, I want you ready to send in a team, and I want you to be there to lead that team. I want this over. The political ramifications are building in the United States. If word gets out about this being our program—I have been told directly by the president himself—no further fuckups will be tolerated."

"I understand."

"I hope you do. You are an essential part of this office, and I would hate to have to *reassign* you."

Tanya kept her expression neutral. "Any information about the American aircraft at Bromma Airport?"

Ivanovich rummaged around his desk and picked up a piece of paper. "Yes, and what we found was interesting and a bit disquieting. The Gulfstream G280 is registered to an American security company headquartered in Washington, D.C.—Teton Security and Defense, LTD. They are an international firm specializing in providing security and protection services in both the private sector and governments. They are very selective when it comes to their clients. Their website is impressive. We have had a few minor run-ins with them, once in Nairobi and a few times in Yemen and Somalia through our proxies there. They are professional, hire the elite, employ international personnel, and it's possible this woman may be working with them. Our best guess is that the woman who blew your cover is one of their top operatives. She matches the description you gave; we are looking at video of her with Sokolov on the train. Then again she could be CIA and is using this TSD organization as a cover."

He took out a cigarette without lighting it. "Only an experienced individual would have the hubris to call you out," he said. "Sandy Dumbrowski?"

"Yes, that is her name, or at least that is the name she gave. Is this Teton Security a CIA front?"

"We do not think so; we believe that would compromise some of their American government contracts. The owner of the firm, Christopher Campbell, was seen earlier this week at one of the press conferences after the incident in Iowa. Our analysts believe his personnel were involved with the removal of the hacker from St. Petersburg. The registration number you noted from their plane, I believe, confirms it."

"And Lynch?"

"Yes, Mr. Lynch, he has been released and is being followed. We assume he will meet up with the TSD Gulfstream at the Helsinki airport. We will see who he meets. We will track them from there."

* * *

Alex stood on the narrow asphalt road that doubled as the Rakvere platform and watched the red and white train continue eastward. The sun was low in the western sky; it just topped the line of trees across the street. A dozen other people left the train, most carrying bags and goods bought in Tallinn or other villages along its route. At least she knew she was in the right town; the word *Rakvere* was displayed on signage on the side of the adjacent one-story building, the train station. Alex walked with other passengers between the ties, rails, and gravel, and then through the small stucco-faced train station. It felt like she'd taken a step back in time.

She had spoken with Ilya just before disembarking; he and the boys were in a nearby hotel. The appearance of the village shouldn't have shocked her—there was a familiarity about it. Her first impression was that it resembled a typical town in northern Ohio; the land was flat with large trees, open spaces, and the occasional dilapidated building. It even smelled like Ohio: thick air, green, humid, mowed grass, and a hint of farm animals.

The Wesenbergh Hotel sat directly along the main road, a few hundred meters from the train station. Alex walked into the small lobby. Sitting on a sofa in the corner were Gavril and Pavel; Ilya sat in the adjacent chair.

She looked at the Sokolovs and sternly said to Ilya, "Don't ever do that again. See what it got you into."

The boys ran to Alex, and she was stunned that they grabbed her and hugged.

"They must really like you; they don't do that for anyone," Ilya said. "And I'm sorry it ended up like this. If I had known . . ."

"And how could you know Anya was a gold digger?"

"Gold digger?"

"American figure of speech—an opportunist, someone out for themselves. But you are all well; that's good. Now we have to figure out what's next."

"I got you a room next to ours. All they need is your signature and a look at your passport."

"And you are registered under . . ."

"Popoff, Fyodor." He smiled. "Maybe I'll keep it. As you saw coming here, the hotel is only two floors; our rooms are directly above us and face the street."

Alex talked briefly to the desk clerk, signed in, and asked about a rental car. The clerk spoke some English, but she was more comfortable with Russian. Ilya helped with the translation.

"A car rental is just a block away," Ilya said. "Why a car?"

"We will talk about this later. Right now, I need a shower and something to eat."

"I bought food at the grocer just down the street. The boys

are tired and need sleep. We can talk after I put them to bed."

"Thank you for staying with us," the clerk said as she handed Alex a key. With Ilya translating, the clerk explained she was Russian and that this was a summer job; the hotel closed in the winter. "We have Internet throughout the hotel, and there are two computers in the room down the hall for access to airlines and emails. You can use them any time you want."

"Thank you," Alex said. "Please contact the rental agency. We will be here a few days and want to see the countryside."

"I will send them an email; I know the manager," the clerk said.

Alex's room was remarkably comfortable and clean, connected to Ilya and the boys' room by a common door. She added what remained of her sandwiches, drinks, and bags of chips to the groceries Ilya had bought earlier. His contributions were cold meat-filled piroshkis, bags of chips, cheeses, and a dozen small salamis. The boys had cans of Pepsi, and Ilya poured a generous glass of a local vodka. When the boys saw the bottle, Gavril said, "Be careful, Papa."

"What did he say?" Alex asked.

"They remind me about my drinking; it's a little game we play. They are my conscience. My wife, she drank too much, they remember. They remember too many things. Yes, Gavril, just one," he said, smiling at his son.

"One, just one," Pavel said, holding up a finger.

After they ate, Ilya tucked the boys into bed. He joined Alex in her room and poured another glass of vodka for each of them.

"Just one," Alex said.

"Yes, my *prekrasnaya sovest'*," he answered. "When you say it, I will obey."

"It must be difficult raising the boys on your own. You are a good father."

He shrugged. "I try. They support each other and also feed off each other. They have come close to full Chernobyl, as I like to call it, a few times since we left St. Petersburg. But there was usually something to distract them; now they are bored. They want their games, their toys we left, the computer. Alex, to them, this is a game. How they found the back door to that government program, only they know. And I'm not sure they could tell you. The day it happened . . . I was asleep."

She gave him a knowing look.

"All right, I was drunk, passed out on the couch. When I awoke, I heard their chattering; they have some language they use between them. I looked at the computer and saw lines of code scrolling down the screen—every few lines, they hit a key. The lines jumped. It was only later that I learned it was their actions that began to turn on and off the electrical grid in America. But it was the program, the Russian government's software, that was actually doing it. Pavel, he's the real genius. He learned to build algorithms when he was just six. Like others who learn to play the piano, he learns or intuitively grasps mathematical concepts. His brother is the instigator and the technician. Between them, they've hacked into computers and servers all over the world. But they do it out of curiosity. They don't do it to steal money, which means nothing to them. I believe it is the challenge. Some children push the envelope when the parents say no, don't do that. In their case, it was a site that was telling them no, you can't come in. They take it as a challenge and eventually do get in. They did not understand what they did that affected Iowa. They still don't. It is the challenge—and to be honest, while Russia is known for its hackers and dark websites, this government site was too easy to get into. The government believed hiding it was the best way to keep it secret, yet Pavel somehow found it."

"You contacted us—why? You could have easily remained

hidden; we certainly didn't know where precisely to look. The Russian infrastructure is well defended. Their firewalls and other devices prevent this from happening. That is what I have been told."

"I could go into the detail, but I don't think you would understand, and please, I'm not trying to patronize you. Some of this—and I teach this at the university—I don't understand myself. Imagine a grove of trees, and each main trunk of each individual tree has thousands of branches going in every direction. And the leaves on that tree are individual servers, and connected to each of those servers are millions of computers—the pores in the leaves. And to complicate it all even more, all the trees in that grove share the same roots. So, everything is interconnected, root to leaf to pore. There are interconnections from leaf, to branch, to trunk, to the other trees—this is a simple explanation for the Internet. So somewhere, a leaf is the Russian government's server with a program that, when switched on, looks for and finds a particular leaf on another tree, and tells that server to find a particular computer with a particular operating system, and to turn it off. This is a simplistic explanation. In their curiosity, the boys found that particular government leaf and had it activate its primary program. When I eventually saw this, I shut it down."

"When did you begin to believe the Russian government was after you?"

"Almost immediately after I found out what the boys did. This would not be a surprise to them—they would want the person who broke into their program. And we know they are after me. This is a big deal; it is the stuff that can start a world war."

"I ran into one of their agents when we were in Stockholm waiting for you. A woman, blonde, Russian, was accompanied by some military-looking guys. We can agree they want you, but do you know exactly why?"

"Because they must keep their secrets secret, and I know a huge, embarrassing one. The government has a way of dealing with people who have the skills my boys have; they are asked to become volunteers. I'm afraid they would, effectively, weaponize my children, make them do things for reasons the boys wouldn't understand. They would use their innate curiosity to turn them into weapons of the Russian state."

"Do you believe we would act any differently?" Alex said, and as she said it, she wondered what made her say it.

"I hope and believe you Americans will. I must protect my boys."

She looked at Ilya and told a lie. "My superiors believe you are the one who committed this act of violence against America. No one will believe that two ten-year-olds have the skills to do what the CIA and the NSA have been trying to do for years: hack the Russian intelligence system."

"What your superiors believe, I have no control over. I must do what I can. What about this American that Anya met in Tallinn? Do you know him?"

"A little, if he is the man who you described. He is running the investigation for the United States government into who is responsible for the disaster in Iowa. They will sort out the why after you are taken into custody. Ilya, hundreds were killed and injured through the actions, no matter how naïve, of your boys. My government needs explanations and someone to hold responsible. This man is looking for the truth, and all I can figure is that Anya contacted him, she cut a deal, and it was for you and the children. Now that you've run, they are even more sure you are the hacker behind all this."

"You must help us. We have no one else to turn to. I don't know what I'd do if Gavril and Pavel are taken away. And if they are separated, I honestly believe they would wither and die."

CHAPTER 21

With a start, Alex bolted awake. The only sound was soft snoring coming from the other room. The usual morning halo of light around the window shade provided the only light. She pushed the door open and walked into the separate room; Ilya was asleep in a chair at the end of the bed, an empty bed.

"Shit—Ilya, wake up. The boys are gone, again."

The digital clock on the bed stand read 7:42 AM. Alex had been asleep for six hours. They hurried down the stairs to the lobby; the front desk was empty. From the back, beyond the signs that Alex assumed indicated conference rooms, they heard laughter. The two boys were sitting at one of the business center's computers. Ilya stood behind them for a moment, leaned in to see what they were doing, then reached between his boys and clicked a few keys. The screen went black.

"*Vernuvshis'v nashu komnatu, ya skazel vam ne igrat' na komp'yuterakh. YA ochen' razocharovan v tebe,*" he said sternly.

There was a long soft wail by both children, but they stood and dutifully walked out of the small room. Ilya followed closely.

"I told them we are going back to the room, and that they were not supposed to play on the computers. I also told them I was disappointed."

"You know what this means?" Alex said.

"Yes, the FSB probably knows where we are. The time stamp on the billing login says they were on the computer for more than two hours—more than enough time to pinpoint our location."

"And this close to the border with Russia, we need to get out of here," Alex said.

As they walked back through the lobby, the young Russian clerk had just returned to the desk. She watched the boys stop at the base of the stairs.

"They okay?" she asked. "I watched them on the computers; I didn't know what they were doing. They said they were okay."

Ilya translated as Alex said, "Car rental? Did you get a response on the rental?"

"Yes, madam. They will deliver it shortly; is that acceptable?"

"Yes, that would be great."

"I will call you when it is here."

"Do they take credit cards?"

"Madam, we can put it on your room. You are here for a week; we would be pleased to help."

"*Spasibo* . . ." she looked at the woman's nameplate . . . "Katrina."

"You're learning, *khorosho*," Ilya said, then pointed to the stairs. "You two, up to the room."

Ilya made the boys take a quick shower. Then he put clean shirts on both and told them to brush their teeth. The phone rang. Ilya answered. He listened, then said, "The car is here, a blue Kia in the side parking lot. She said she would be away from the desk for a few minutes; the keys are on the sun visor on the driver's side."

"God, I could use a cup of coffee," Alex said. "Give me two minutes; then we are leaving."

"I never realized how easy it is to rent a car," Ilya said.

"You've never rented a car?"

"Alex, I can't even drive."

She smiled; how simple life was for some. She went into the bathroom off her room. As she splashed water on her face, she heard voices, loud voices, voices that were not the children's. The loudest was a woman's.

Alex slowly opened the bathroom door; there was no one in her room, and the door to Ilya's room was open only a finger's width. She glanced around her room; the closet sliding door was open. A dozen hangers hung on a wooden rod. She quietly placed the hangers on the bed and removed the rod. It had the weight and heft of a long police baton. She moved to the door.

The woman's voice screamed something in Russian.

Then Ilya said, surprisingly in English, "Who are you? Why are the two of you here? Leave us alone; we are on vacation. We're Americans."

The woman yelled again; a large man passed by the gap in the door.

Alex recognized Tanya Golubev's voice, but she couldn't decipher any of the Russian words. One of the boys screamed; Golubev yelled something else. Then both boys screamed again, and Ilya was shouting. Alex jerked the door open; a man held Pavel by the back of his shirt. Gavril was pulling on the man's other arm; he was trying to bite it. The man's back was to Alex. She swung the stick hard and clipped him on the back of the head. He dropped like a stone. Golubev whirled on her. Alex saw a pistol in the Russian's hand as she sidestepped the fallen man. Golubev's aim was hasty; the shot she fired went high, and the bullet slammed into the plaster wall just beyond Alex's head. Alex spun the rod upward and dropped the end on Golubev's right forearm. There was a crack of wood on bone. The pistol spun out of the Russian's hand and onto the bed. Golubev shrieked and grabbed her arm.

"Ilya, put the boys over there." Alex pointed to the corner. "First, toss me the pistol."

Ilya did as told. Alex, the stick still in her left hand, pointed the pistol at Golubev. The FSB agent cradled her bruised arm with her good left hand. She glared at Alex.

"In the chair, there, now," Alex said, waving the pistol. Golubev sat.

"Ilya, see if he has a gun. Check his ankles too."

Ilya removed another Makarov PM from a shoulder holster, and a small revolver from the man's ankle holster. Golubev made a noise.

"Say nothing, or I'll hit you again, this time across your face."

"He had these in his pocket." Ilya held up a bundle of black Plasti-cuffs.

"Secure his feet and hands. Do it quickly before he comes to."

Ilya immediately went to work. The boys held each other, quietly watching.

"You know you can't get away; I will follow you; I will find you. I will personally enjoy killing you," Golubev said. "I know you are CIA."

"Lady, if you only knew the half of it," Alex said. "Ilya, tie her arms to the chair and her ankles to the chair's legs. And stuff a handful of Kleenex in her mouth; she is annoying me. Check her ankles, too, for a pistol. Tell the boys to come over here."

Golubev screamed again when Ilya pulled the black strap tight to her arm. Her rants grew muffled after a fistful of tissue was forced into her mouth; it had taken the threat of another whack on her arm to make the Russian open her mouth.

"Grab the bags; we need to go."

Alex pushed the boys out of the room; Ilya followed. "The stairs, in the back," Alex said and slipped the small revolver in her pocket and the other pistol in the back of her waist.

At the door to the back of the hotel, she turned to Ilya. "Wait a second."

She slowly opened the door. A large man stood next to a BMW sedan in the parking lot. Seeing Alex, he immediately reached into his jacket. Alex was quicker; she aimed the pistol at the man's head. "*Nyet!*" she yelled. "Drop the gun. On the ground."

From behind her, Ilya yelled, "*Bros'pistolet. Seychas na zemie.*"

The man slowly removed his weapon; it was a match to the one Alex held. He slowly lowered himself to the ground. "Secure his hands and feet." Alex saw the blue Kia and pointed. "Then put the boys in the back seat."

The man glared at Ilya as his hands were zip-tied. Ilya pulled the loose ends tight.

"Get in the car," Alex said to the boys.

Ilya hurried the boys to the car; they said nothing, though Alex was sure they would erupt any moment. "Check for the keys," she called to Ilya. He reached in and then held up the keys.

"Good." Alex turned back to the BMW, and the man on the ground. She quickly ran her hand down his legs and found the ankle holster and small pistol it held; it was a Beretta 950. She put the semiauto in her pocket, took out the small revolver, and quickly fired one shot into the sidewall of each of the four tires. She then opened the revolver's cylinder, dropped out the casings and one remaining bullet, and put them in her pocket. She tossed the weapon into the shrubbery next to the building. A minute later, they were halfway through the village of Rakvere. At the intersection in the center of town, three police cars raced past with sirens wailing, heading in the direction they'd just come from.

"Ilya," Alex said, "we need to get out of town, and I have no idea which way to go."

He peered over the back of the seat. "There, that sign is for Tapa. Turn that way."

She did as directed. After five more blocks, another police car, lights flashing, raced by.

"There, follow the roundabout, then veer to the right," Ilya instructed. "The sign says thirty kilometers."

Alex drove through the countryside, one eye on the road ahead and one in the mirror. She fully expected to see a police car come from behind, lights flashing. Singsong sounds came from the back seat. "They okay?" she asked.

"I gave them their Nintendos; they are playing."

Shocked, Alex asked, "They aren't shaken?"

"They don't understand fear. Pain, yes, loss, yes, but fear, not really. What's done is over in their heads; they don't think of the future like we do."

Alex continued, wondering when another black BMW would come speeding up behind them, roll down its windows, and shoot the living hell out of the blue Kia.

Chapter 22

"Where are you?" Chris asked as the Gulfstream taxied to the end of the runway at Helsinki airport. "Why didn't you call me last night?"

"We're all good, thanks for asking," Alex answered. "Having breakfast. Nice little place."

"What happened?"

He listened as she told him about the boys playing on the hotel computer, Tanya Golubev arriving with two other FSB operatives, and their escape. "We're in Tapa, a little village about fifty miles southwest of Rakvere," she said.

Chris inwardly admired her innovation and adaptability. He hoped it wouldn't get her, or the Sokolovs, killed. "The weather has kept us grounded—thunderstorms and heavy rain," he relayed. "We picked up Micah at the train station; he's good. And we all slept on the plane."

"That must have been fun."

"No, it wasn't. This little bit of snatch and transport has gotten out of hand. Our client is getting antsy; they want a resolution."

"An hour ago, the Russians in that hotel also wanted a resolution. Is that where we are headed, Chris? They weren't playing games; I think they would have disappeared with the Sokolovs if they had a chance. Me? Probably dumped in some forest around here. What exactly does our client want?"

His pause was punctuated by the whine of the Gulfstream's engines. "We don't work that way; you know that," he said to Alex.

"Then why the hell was Robb Case in Tallinn? Have you figured that one out? . . . No? Then I'm not sure who I can trust. I've got Russian special ops, run by a wacky blonde from Moscow spy central, flying all over hell and gone, chasing us—who, by the way, may have a broken arm thanks to yours truly. She is pissed at me."

There was another pause, this time on her end. He guessed she was moving away from Ilya and the boys.

"I have three exhausted people wondering who to trust and what to believe," Alex said, her voice angry but controlled. "Remember, Sokolov came to us, and the package he offered is worth a lot, but it's all screwed up now. And the client is getting impatient? Screw them."

"I get it; trust is a hard thing to keep in situations like this."

"Really? Philosophy this early in the morning? Where are you, and where are you going?"

"Leaving Helsinki, heading to you, Tallinn Airport. The flight is less than fifty minutes. Jack says we will roll out to the private jetway of Baltic Aviation; they are on the north side of the airport. We will meet you in the airport lobby; we can talk then. I want options."

"You want options? I want this to be over before I have to shoot someone."

"That seems to be the answer you have for everything."

"It's only my excellent restraint that keeps me free of doing just that. The Russians were lucky this morning. My pancakes are getting cold."

She hung up.

Chris turned to Linda and Micah. "That woman will be the

death of me yet."

"She is resourceful," Micah said. "The initiative she took getting them out of Russia was what I would have done. I like her."

"You stay out of this," Chris said, pointing his finger at Micah. Then to Linda, "Is there fresh coffee?"

The plane banked to the right toward the Gulf of Finland and leveled off. Linda went to the galley and returned with coffee.

"I like her too, boss," she said. "She's nicer than most of the macho-whack-'em-upside-the-head guys you hire. She brings a much-needed balance to this organization."

Chris rolled his eyes as he took the coffee. "You too, Linda? As if I don't have enough to deal with, I have feminists pushing their way into this whole mess."

"Then it wouldn't be such a mess now, would it?" She smiled and went back to the front of the plane.

As a seagull flies, it was almost exactly one hundred kilometers, sixty-two miles, over the Baltic Sea between Helsinki and Tallinn. The plane was barely pressurized before Jack began the descent. The sky had cleared, and a sharp, cool front had pushed in from Norway, blowing out the bad weather. The sky was the bluest blue Chris could remember ever seeing. They did a pass over the old city of Tallinn before making their approach. Their rollout placed them on one of the concrete pads outside the hangar for Baltic Aviation. The attendant signaled Jack to shut down the engines. In moments, it was all quiet.

"Now what?" Micah said.

"We wait," Chris answered.

"I'm famished. Alex is at least an hour out," Linda said. "There has to be a place to eat somewhere near here. Micah?"

"All I've had since, like forever, was that frozen pizza you microwaved—I need protein. Chris?"

"You guys go. I'll stay with the plane. Jack, if you and Linda want to go, I'll cover. Be ready to leave as soon as they arrive. I'll call you."

"Got it, boss," Micah said. "I have no money; Alex took it all when she left. So, Jack, you are buying."

Chris watched the trio cross the tarmac and walk into the airport lobby. A moment later they exited, a car pulled up, an Uber sticker in the window.

Chris poured himself another cup of coffee and found a couple PowerBars in the small galley cabinet. He went back to his seat, unwrapped a bar, took a bite.

What the hell is Alex up to? And for that matter, what is the FBI up to?

The operation was designed to be a simple in and out. Bring back the perpetrator of one of America's most horrific terrorist attacks—that's what the press was calling it now—and show the world that the United States would not allow these things to go unpunished, ever. The problem now was that if the Russian government was behind the attack, however inadvertent, it was still their technology, their computers, their programs that led to the deaths of one hundred and fifty-two Americans and the injury of hundreds more—what would be America's response? Was that why the FBI was here? Did they want the glory of the arrest? Or, he wondered cynically, was there a greater game being played out?

Chris looked at his watch; it had been ninety minutes since he'd talked with Alex. He pulled out his phone intending to call her when the whine of jet engines flooded through the open door of the G280. Out the starboard window, he saw the fuselage of a Gulfstream V. The ground attendant directed the jet to the pad next to the TSD plane. The arriving plane rolled to a stop; the attendant tossed yellow chocks around the front tires and then backed away.

As the massive private plane sat there, an ominous feeling grew in Chris's gut. He looked at the tail number: American registration. This was not a coincidence, not today. He punched in the phone number for TSD's Dallas operations office.

"Jimmy, Chris here. I need a name to go with a tail number for a G-V sitting next to me on the tarmac in Tallinn, Estonia. N-3-7-2-K-L. Thanks, Jimmy . . . I know, whatever you can get."

Chris sipped his coffee. He was sure he knew who was inside the waiting plane; he wanted confirmation. Five minutes later, his phone buzzed.

"Jimmy, what do you have? . . . Really? Fascinating . . . the Department of Justice? . . . Thanks."

Chris clicked off the phone and kept watching out the window. The door of the jet opened, and the stair lowered toward the concrete pad. A broad-chested muscular man in a sports coat paused at the door, then took the steps to the tarmac. Reaching the ground, he scanned the area. Then Special Agent Robb Case appeared. He looked at the G280 and smiled.

Chris picked up his phone and typed.

Double-time it back to the plane—trouble.

Chris exited the Gulfstream and walked toward the G-V. Case stood at the bottom of the steps, waiting.

"Why the hell are you here, Case?" Chris asked. "You should be back in the States. I heard there was another outage last night, not as long as the others, but still frightening."

"You know damn well where that came from," Case answered. "What we don't know is how they are doing it. Where are they?"

"Who?"

"The Sokolovs. I know all about them."

"You heard it all from the nanny? She's the one you were paying off to turn them over to you."

"What I do is none of your concern," Case said. "But, since you know all about this and her, can I assume that you have them?"

"No, as a matter of fact, I don't have them," Chris said. "But I might know where they are. It seems the Russians will do anything to find them as well. My people are protecting them; there was an attempt on their lives by the FSB."

"Protecting them? The FSB? Bullshit. Campbell, I could charge you with a dozen felony counts of obstruction, aiding a fugitive, breach of contract . . ."

Micah strode across the tarmac toward the two men. "What the hell are you doing here, Case? This is way the hell out of your jurisdiction."

"I go where the American people need me to go."

"That's a load of bull. We have this covered and under control, so get back on your fancy jet and go home. We will bring these people to the United States."

"Who's playing games now, Lynch? I never play games with the lives of Americans."

"Bullshit," and Micah threw a punch that clocked Case in the jaw; the big man staggered.

Case's man took two steps toward Micah.

"Stop. I'm good. He punches way below his weight class."

"Fuck you, Case," Micah said, as Chris grabbed his arm to prevent another punch.

"Stop this playground shit. I'm stunned," Chris said, letting go of Micah's arm and stepping between the two men.

"Campbell, this is no game," Case said. "Over one hundred and fifty people died, and many more are injured because of what that hacker did, and you two are hiding him. I want him today. If not, there will be hell to pay. I'm staying here until you turn him over, and you aren't going anywhere until you do."

CHAPTER 23

Alex glanced over her shoulder at the back seat of the Kia. Ilya sat between his sons; the boys were both asleep, while he silently looked out the window. How he managed these two was beyond her skills. She babysat for her brother's kids, organized birthday parties, even got them tours of the police department when they were working on school projects, but that was it. Beyond her involvement with children she'd encountered during her job as a cop, she knew little about being a parent. Her total miss on her ex-husband's activities was a good signal that she would be an easy mark for the machinations of a ten-year-old.

The freeway sign ahead read *Lennujaam Airport*, the ubiquitous silhouette of a jet next to it. She left the highway and turned onto the frontage road, looking for the signs for Baltic Aviation. Their building was one of the most prominent structures adjacent to the runway.

"We are almost there," she said to Ilya. "The boys, they okay?"

"They go a hundred kilometers an hour, then crash. I think we are at that point."

Alex stopped the car at the curb and looked out through the chain-link fencing to an open area between the buildings. Two small jets sat next to each other on the apron. She recognized the tail number for the TSD jet; she could not forget the *13TS*. The other plane she didn't know. A car pulled up to the front of Baltic Aviation, and three people climbed out. She recognized every one of them: all were TSD employees. She was glad Micah was free from Russia. They all quickly walked into the Baltic Aviation building. A moment later, they were on the pavement and heading to the jets. Two men stood on the tarmac: Chris and Special Agent Case. The conversation seemed intense.

"What's going on?" Ilya asked when Alex made no move to exit the car.

"I haven't a clue," she answered. "But I can tell you I do not like the look of this."

"What?"

She pointed toward the tarmac. "Do you recognize that man on the left, the bald man?"

Ilya leaned forward and craned his neck to look out the driver's-side window. "Yes, that's the man Anya was with in Tallinn. He's somebody I will never forget."

"His name is Robb Case. He is an FBI agent."

Ilya looked at the approaching group. "Isn't that your husband?"

"That was an alias. He's actually an associate of mine; we work for the man talking to Case."

They watched Micah walk up to Case. Something was said, and Micah took a swing at Case.

"You said he's an FBI agent?" Ilya said.

"Yeah," Alex said, drawing out the word.

They watched as more words were exchanged, then Case turned and climbed into his jet. His associate remained at the bottom of the stairs, watching.

Chris led his group onto the TSD jet. The airstairs on both planes remained down and open.

"What is going on, Alex?" Ilya paused, then said, "I get it.

First you get me out of St. Petersburg, and I trust you, then to Tallinn, where Anya sells us out to some bald guy, who you tell me is an American FBI agent . . . then this? This is wrong, so wrong. Get us out of here. I want my children away from all this."

"I'm not turning you over to anyone. I don't know why my boss is talking to that man, and I don't know why the FBI is involved here in Estonia."

"The FBI, good God. What have you done to us?"

With that outburst, the two boys woke. Their eyes were wide and confused.

"*Chto proiskhodit, Papa?*" Gavril asked.

"*Gde my, Papa,*" Pavel added.

"What do I tell them, Alex? They want to know what's happening, and where we are."

Alex had a hundred questions, questions she would ask Chris, but right now . . . she put the Kia into drive and slowly drove away from the facility. Her assignment was to protect the hacker, even if that hacker turned out to be two ten-year-old autistic kids.

"What do you think the capabilities of the Russian government are for surveillance and tracking people?" Alex asked.

"My guess, better than almost anyone's. When there are no laws against it, such as you have in the United States, and you have a paranoid government like Russia, I assume they can find anyone, anytime, anywhere. I have read about facial recognition that can scan millions of faces and pick just one out of the crowd. I have heard the Chinese are also doing this. Then there are license plate scanners, CCTV cameras everywhere, and the ability to locate computers anywhere—like last night in Rakvere. We can only stay a few hours ahead of them. The Russian security forces have no qualms about hacking into any system in the world, especially one that is directly on their border. And, Alex, I believe that the United States can do this too—anywhere in the world."

"*My golodny, Papa,*" Gavril said. "*Pizza.*"

"I get that one," Alex said as she followed the signs back into the center of Tallinn. She had an idea, one that would take advantage of this Russian paranoia. "Tell them we will get pizza in a little while, not too long."

"Where are we going?" Ilya asked.

"Back to Helsinki," Alex answered. "They might know the color of this car, though I'm not sure about that. We got out fast, and unless they asked the clerk about the rental agency, they won't know the car or license number. I'm sure the police pulling up to the hotel didn't help their case. Maybe we got lucky, and they were arrested or at least detained for a while. But that will end, then they will learn everything."

"Yes, it is only a matter of time," Ilya answered. "They will learn about this car; it has been more than six hours. They will find us."

"I'm counting on it, now."

A massive panel sign extended over the roadway. Arrows back to the airport pointed right, others went straight to downtown—TALLINN was in bold letters. Below that, the universal image of a ferryboat and the distance: *4 km.* An idea was growing.

On a city street, Alex stopped and pulled out her phone. There were two text messages from Chris. She'd get to those soon enough.

The schedule she retrieved on her phone read that the next Tallinn ferry for Finland and Helsinki was leaving in one hour. At the moment, this was the best bet in a very bad game. If she pulled it off, they would have gained at least two hours, maybe more. She draped her arm over the seatback and turned to look at Ilya.

"Ilya, I have to trust you, and you have to trust me. I don't have any idea what that was about at the airport. Right now, we have to get everyone, the Russians and my people, to believe we are leaving the country. I need time, we need time, to figure out what to do. I saw a pizza joint across from the parking lot to the ferry; I'm going to leave you and the boys there. They can get lunch, and you eat too. I will be back to pick you up in an hour. Can you do that?"

Ilya looked at Alex and briefly clasped the hand she'd draped over the seat back. "Yes, I trust you."

"Thank you." She gave him a handful of bills. She smiled at the boys. "You boys be good; how do you say that, Ilya?"

"*Vy, rebyata, bud'te khoroshimi.*"

She shook her head and tried.

The boys laughed.

"What did I say?"

"I have no idea, but they understand."

She dropped the three of them at the curb in front of a long façade of tourist shops, eateries, and bars. The last was a pizza restaurant; she guessed that because it said so on the door and a colorful wooden slice of pizza hung from the eave of the building.

After the boys entered the restaurant, Alex drove around the corner and pulled to the curb. She made a phone call.

* * *

"Where the hell are you?" Chris demanded.

"Keeping everyone safe," Alex said. "I saw the little play that went on at the airport. There's no way I was turning the Sokolovs over to Case after that. I don't know why Micah punched him, but I'm sure he had a good reason . . . nice right-hand shot. Chris, until I'm sure that Ilya isn't just going to be thrown into jail and the kids into one of those children's detention facilities, they are staying with me. I'm sure the Russians are very pissed at me now after my little face-to-face with Tanya. And with what I've learned about Case, I need time."

Chris looked at the faces of his team; Micah's expression showed both curiosity and concern.

"You do what you need to do, but there has to be a resolution soon," Chris told Alex. "I'm not sure what will happen if Case goes full government action on this. We've been under the radar—even the Estonians don't know why we're here. I haven't seen customs yet, but we could anytime. So, keep them safe. When you can, let me know what you are up to. We will talk soon." He clicked off his sat-phone.

"She okay?" Micah asked.

"Yes, she's good. Wants me to pass on her compliments about your boxing skills."

"She saw that? She must have been in the parking lot. Interesting, and she decided it wasn't the right time to end this?"

"I assume so. You heard my side of the conversation. What I'm doing could get me thrown in jail or, worse, I could lose millions in government contracts." He rubbed the back of his neck. "That woman is driving me crazy."

CHAPTER 24

Alex passed through the Tallinn ferry terminal gate, showed her passport, and paid the required fare for the crossing to Finland. She was surprised at how inexpensive it was for a two-way ticket. As she drove to her place in the line in the parking lot, she noticed at least four CCTV cameras mounted on the parking lot lights. The massive ferry, with the word TALLINK painted on its port side, blocked her view across the harbor. She was fifth in the short queue of cars. Thirty minutes later she drove the blue Kia onto the ferry, parked where directed, and then locked the car. She then walked through the maze of cars, campers, and trucks already loaded, found the stairway, then followed the signs up to the passenger decks. After stopping at the gift store for a sweatshirt and hat, she casually strolled through the press of walk-on passengers boarding the ferry from the terminal. At the ship's entry, she mentioned to an agent that her daughter had forgotten her backpack in the waiting room and that she would return shortly. She waved her ticket.

"Do not be late, ma'am. We will not wait," the man said with a smile. His English was quite good.

Alex weaved in and out between the boarding passengers and eventually made it to the waiting room on the pier. Leaving the terminal, she crossed the street to the pizza restaurant. She spotted the Sokolovs; Ilya was holding a large slice of pepperoni pizza, while the boys shared a cheese pizza. To her surprise, they were all smiling.

* * *

The two jets still sat on the runway. Jack and Linda remained onboard the Gulfstream. Jack started the engines to provide ventilation and power. An hour later, Chris and Micah took a walk inside Baltic Aviation.

"Stalemate?" Micah asked, looking out to the apron area.

"Yes. And a temporary one at best," Chris said. "There is more to all of this than anyone knows, and it revolves around the Russian's program that accesses our grid system. Alex doesn't believe we can protect the Sokolovs, and to be honest, I'm not sure we can either. She saw us with Case."

Micah nodded. "Now she is questioning our motives along with his."

"Micah, this whole thing has gone sideways."

"What has gone sideways, Campbell?" Case said as he walked into the lobby.

"God, you are like a bad penny. Can't you just leave?" Micah said.

"I have a job, and a contractor is not going to foul it up. Chris, you know where they are. Just tell me, and this will be over."

"Robb, believe me, I do not know where Alex and the Sokolovs are."

Case's phone rang at full volume. "Yes? . . . Tallinn . . . got it. Text me the specifics." He clicked off. "Gentlemen, I must leave you."

"You know where she is?" Chris asked.

As Case walked away, he raised his hand and showed them his middle finger.

Case signaled his man still on the tarmac, and they climbed into the G-V. Like Chris's plane, the G-V had been left running. In moments, an attendant jogged out to the plane and removed the wheel blocks. The whine of the jet's engines rose and then the plane began to slowly roll out toward the runway. In seconds it had cleared the Baltic Aviation portion of the apron.

"You thinking what I'm thinking?" Micah asked Chris.

"Yeah, my guess is that all our American spyware stuff, CCTV hacking, and eavesdropping just paid off. He knows where our girl is going, and he's going to meet her."

"Now if only *we* knew where she was."

* * *

As the ferry slowly moved away from the Tallinn pier, Alex finished her second slice of pizza. The Coke was the best she'd had in years—she usually stayed away from the sugary stuff. Remembering that she still had the car keys to the Kia in her pocket, she smiled. Someday there would be a reckoning, Chris would have to pony up a pile of money, and the rental car company would have to be mollified. But that was weeks away; right now, she needed to come up with a solution to the second part of her plan.

"Are you okay?" Ilya asked. "You wear a strange smile."

"A private joke, nothing more." She looked at the boys; it was hard to believe how well they had endured the chaos and confusion of the last few days. "And how are my two favorite young men?" she asked, knowing they would not understand.

They smiled back at her even before Ilya translated. Pavel said something to his father and then raised both his arms in fist pumps. Interesting, she thought.

"They have found the whole experience fun, which means stimulating," Ilya said, finishing a slice. "Alex, the most difficult aspect of their condition is boredom and lack of incentives. The world tries its best to ignore them, when all they want is to shine and be seen. There's confusion, but that's due to too much stimulation all at one time; they need time to sort it out. That's why people mistake their aloofness. I can assure you, with these two, it is often just the opposite."

Gavril leaned into his father and whispered. Ilya nodded.

"He says that you are now their good friend. And they want to know where we are going next. This is an exciting adventure."

"*Avtobus*," Gavril said, holding up a finger.

"Bus," translated Ilya.

"*Poyezd.*" Two fingers.

"Train."

"*Snova trenirovat'sya*," Pavel added.

"Train again."

"*Ogromnyy parom.*"

"Huge ferry," Ilya said with a smile and watched the boys count on their fingers.

"*Avtomobil'.*"

"Car," Alex said.

"*Poyezd.*"

Ilya nodded. "Train, again."

"*I neobychnaya sinyaya mashina.*"

"And a fancy blue car."

"You boys have good memories," Alex said. "Yes, lots of trains, and boats, and cars."

Pavel looked out at the departing ferry and pointed. "*Pochemu by ne poyti na parome?*"

"He wants to know why we didn't get on the ferry," Ilya said.

"For that, right now, I can't give them an answer. Ilya, I don't know who to trust, or who has the best interests of Gavril and

Pavel in mind. Until I do, I won't let anything happen to them."

"Don't make promises that you may not be able to keep."

"I will try."

"*Kogda my poyedem na samolete?*" Gavril said and pointed out the window to a private jet crossing low over the city.

"He wants to know when we will take an airplane."

"I have no answer for that, either."

Across the parking lot from the pizza parlor was a sign with red and white letters over a storefront; it was a car rental. Alex had her next idea.

"Ilya, we can't stay here. My little trick may give us a few hours. I'm going to rent another car. We need to go south, maybe to Latvia or Poland. Find a place we can hide, even if it's for a couple of days. The boys need sleep, a bath, maybe new clothes. I certainly could use a shower."

"You can't use your credit card; you know that."

"Maybe they will take cash if I show them my passport."

Ilya unzipped his bag. He rummaged around and pulled out a passport; the cover was dark red. He opened it, looked at the picture and then at Alex.

"This is Anya's. She left it in the hotel. I took it. You look a lot like her, though you could be her mother. They may ask about the hair. You could tell them you changed its color." He removed the credit card tucked in the pages of the passport. "She also left this."

An hour later they were fifty kilometers south of Tallinn on the A1, heading toward Riga, Latvia. When they reached the village of Pärnu, still north of the border, they eventually found a guesthouse that had one cabin left. Alex was told, or actually Ilya interpreted, that it was summer and that most hotels and inns would be full. The cabin had two bedrooms, a small parlor, and an attached kitchen. The boys saw the beach beyond the small complex of cabins and pointed excitedly.

CHAPTER 25

Tanya Golubev stood on the dock at the ferry terminal in Helsinki and watched a red and yellow tow truck as it slowly pulled a blue Kia sedan out of the guts of the ferry. She was beyond furious. Her people in Moscow said the blue Kia had entered the ferry in Tallinn thirty-two minutes before it sailed. The FSB team following Tanya's team into Rakvere had confirmed the rental of the blue Kia, and they were certain of the license plate, but Moscow could not confirm the targets were onboard the ferry. Nonetheless, Tanya knew they had to be there. After the fuck-up in Rakvere, the Sokolovs' escape, the three-hour detention by the police and their stupid questions, she had to endure the medical team in the Army hospital at Ivangorod and the cast they put on her fractured arm. Soon she would find this CIA bitch and put a bullet in her head.

The recent events had changed her respect for the American woman, whoever she was. The American was tough and not afraid of violence. Why the American was in Stockholm and not with the hacker, who presumably was with his children, Tanya would eventually find out. Her arm throbbed under the heavy bandaging and fiberglass wrap, but she'd accepted only Tylenol from the doctors; she wanted a clear head. There was much to consider. The Americans' motive for getting these people was revenge; Tanya's reasons were more subtle. She and the director wanted the man and his brain; the cover-up of their government's involvement in the Iowa disaster was a secondary bonus.

"Assistant Director Tanya Golubev, how is your arm?" a man's voice said from behind her. It was a voice she knew well. He was laughing. She wanted to shoot him.

"Director, you did not inform me that we were meeting here."

She turned to see Dmitry Ivanovich, dressed in a patterned summer shirt and slacks, followed by three men she knew well; they were from the same service branch as her team. Her day could not have gotten any worse.

"It is a day of surprises. Tanya, did you lose our targets again?"

"That is why you are here, is it not? You were informed that they were *not* on this ferry. I'm quite certain they did not jump off the boat somewhere in the Baltic Sea. It is now obvious they were never on the boat."

"I'm impressed by this American agent," Ivanovich said. "She is the one who met the Sokolovs in St. Petersburg, and she is resourceful. Please look at this."

Ivanovich held up a small tablet; an image was frozen on its screen. He tapped, and the video began to play. Golubev watched a woman come down an escalator, stop, then cross the ferry's entry concourse. She wore a sweatshirt that read TAL-LINN in bold letters across her chest and a wide-brimmed canvas hat. The video time stamp was the current date, just a little over four hours earlier.

"And this is supposed to mean what to me, Director?"

"Be patient, one moment," Ivanovich replied.

The video flashed to an outside camera. It was significantly brighter; the view was from above the doors of the terminal. The woman stopped, looked across the drop-off area in front of the ferry terminal, and removed her hat. Blonde hair tumbled out.

"Do you know this woman?" Ivanovich asked needlessly. "I believe you do. She is the one who broke your arm."

"That goddamn bitch, it's . . ." she paused for a moment. "She said her name was Sandy Dumbrowski. I told you that in my report two days ago. I am certain she works for the CIA or another American agency. She challenged me in Stockholm; I dismissed her out of hand. Then she appears in Rakvere. I will kill her."

The tow truck had stopped in the middle of the parking lot. A man in overalls and two official-looking people were talking; a clipboard was passed around.

"According to our investigation, Sandy Dumbrowski is the name of many Americans. Most are of Polish or Slavic descent. The spelling of Sandy varies; we are also looking into these."

"And your point, Director? It's a common name."

"Tanya, it is also the name of a character in the American show *Grease*. This woman is, how do the Americans put it—pulling your leg."

Golubev spun around on her boot heels. The tow truck was weaving through the parking area and heading toward the frontage road, the blue Kia in tow. This was the third time in less than a week that this American woman duped her; it was now more than personal. Tanya's professional reputation was at stake. She swung her arm around; the pain made her wince.

"Her name is not Sandy Dumbrowski," a man offered. Three more men were walking toward them. The taller man was bald with a thick black mustache and eyebrows to match, visible over his black-rimmed glasses. He reminded Tanya of someone she'd seen in newsreels from forty years earlier. His companion stood back about five paces. "I am not at liberty to give you her real name," the bald man said, "but needless to say she is good at her job."

"We know who she is, Special Agent Case," Ivanovich said. "Her name is Polonia, Alexandra Polonia."

Ivanovich's bodyguards turned and faced the FBI agent. Two of them had reached inside their jackets; the other took a position in front of the director.

"I am glad my reputation precedes me, Director Ivanovich. I have not had the pleasure of meeting your associate." Agent Case looked at Golubev. "I assume she works for you."

Ivanovich smiled—it was a look that only a spy who'd seen a lot could generate. It teetered between amusement and boredom. "Special Agent Case, yes, I have heard about you. It is a pleasure. I understand you are involved in the investigation of the Iowa disaster."

Case nodded.

"This is Assistant Director Tanya Golubev and, yes, she works for me, though we are on holiday, or what you Americans call vacation. For years, I've enjoyed the restaurants in Helsinki; they seem to catch better and fresher fish than we can in Russia."

"Yes, I've heard that," Case answered. "Excellent fresh fish here in Finland, especially the pickled kind."

"Why are you here, Agent Case?" Golubev demanded.

"Please, Tanya, he has come far for his . . ."

"Holiday," Case said.

"Yes, summer is a grand time to take a hiatus from the drudgeries of work. No cares, no responsibilities, leave all the problems of our jobs behind us," Ivanovich said. "Is that why you are here, Special Agent Case, to leave all the worries of the job behind you?"

Before Case could answer, an SUV pulled up next to the group. Three men exited and joined the little party. For Tanya

Golubev, the day had turned into a nightmare, again. Micah Lynch led the group. He and his companions were smoking cigars; how fucking aggravating these Americans had become.

Lynch was the first to speak. "I was hoping I would not have the pleasure of meeting you two again; strange how the world works. Director Ivanovich and Assistant Director Golubev, I would like to introduce you to Chris Campbell and Jack Monroe. Where are the Sokolovs?"

Golubev stared in growing wonder at the growing group of Americans. Thoughts bounced around in her head: Why were they here? Who else would be joining this impromptu meeting? And what did they want? She looked at the FBI agent; it was apparent he was not happy about the appearance of these other Americans.

"I'm sorry about the interview mix-up in St. Petersburg, Mr. Lynch. I was told there were passport and visa issues," Ivanovich said as he shook each of the newcomers' hands.

With her bandaged arm in a sling, Golubev declined any false show of cordiality.

"It is amazing what you Americans will do, especially when it comes to taking a holiday," Ivanovich continued. "We Russians go to the Black Sea. Personally, I love Sochi."

The director looked at Case.

Chris Campbell mirrored Ivanovich's look. The glare Tanya saw Campbell give Special Agent Case surprised her. *Interesting.*

"Director Ivanovich," Case began, "as a representative of the American government, I will ask you to turn over Ilya Sokolov and his family, and the employee of Mr. Campbell, Ms. Polonia, to me."

Golubev looked over Case's shoulder; two Helsinki police cars had stopped in the passenger drop-off zone a hundred feet from them.

"The Finnish government is monitoring us; they will be

handling the proper extradition papers," the agent continued.

"Special Agent Case," Golubev said, "the man you call Sokolov and his family are Russian citizens. We believe they have been abducted by this woman"—she held up her boss's iPad with the picture of Alex—"who works for Mr. Campbell. We do not take kindly to having our citizens kidnapped, especially on Russian soil. We are here to rescue them."

"Really?" Case said, interrupting. "You said you were here on holiday."

Ivanovich chuckled. He didn't say anything, but his expression was, as earlier, bemused.

"I am tired of this game," Golubev said. "It seems that we all have been fooled. If you are here, then you do not know where this employee of Mr. Campbell is. She identified herself to me as Sandy Dumbrowski. Our research assures me this is fake. We have a passport she left in St. Petersburg; the name on that document is Lois P. Stapleton of Dallas, Texas. Seems that she is married to this man here"—she looked at Micah—"that would be you, although I know your name isn't Stapleton. As you know, we have a copy of your passport. And this Alexandra Polonia is . . ."

". . . we are checking for additional information. Entering Russia with fake passports is a grave offense," Ivanovich injected. "But as you say—no harm, no foul—today. However, these people are no longer on Russian soil; as such, we no longer care about them. It has been a pleasure."

With that, Tanya, Ivanovich, and their bodyguards walked back to their rental cars. Golubev wondered what the Americans would do now.

"Do you have the appropriate surveillance in place?" she asked her boss.

"Yes, I have two," he answered. "Thankfully, they both are needed. One will follow each of them. It's good to confirm that the Americans also have excellent skills in hacking into the security systems of foreign interests, both government and private. We had not been sure about their abilities; now we are. I am shocked that you were surprised by this American, Alexandra Polonia. By the way, how is your arm?"

Her arm burned as if on fire. "And we are doing what?" she said, ignoring his question.

"Our people are scanning every digital data stream we can access, facial recognition, CCTV, especially in and around the Tallinn ferry terminal," Ivanovich continued. "We will find her. And, there is some confusion over the computer Sokolov was using. It *was* recovered on the ferry they were on from Turku. Unfortunately, it has been encrypted by this hacker; it is an encryption we have not seen before. We have not been able to break into it. This man is brilliant."

"He has a family. I saw them on the video feed we hacked. There was something odd about them."

"Yes, two boys," Ivanovich said. "Identical twins, we were told by neighbors. They are autistic, with special needs. According to the neighbors, they are good kids, but prone to explosive outbreaks and acting out; they are enrolled in one of the state's special programs during the school term. The neighbors say Sokolov had a babysitter that spends the day with them while he teaches. They only knew her name as Anya."

"Do we know where she is?"

"No, but we are looking."

CHAPTER 26

Looking directly at the FBI agent, Chris said, "Ah, the wonders of American intelligence and our own special version of hacking, am I correct, Case? You should be on your way back to the United States."

"Your fucking job, Campbell," Case answered. "All holy hell is going on back home, and fingers are pointing, heads are demanded. Everyone is looking for scapegoats: the power company, politicians who believe in global warming, those that don't; there are demands from the local governments, ethanol subsidies, mixed transportation systems, even AMTRAK. There must be a fall guy, someone to hang, as if any of that will make a difference to the dead. It was a huge deal, and now it's a huge political deal."

Chris took a long pull on his cigar, then looked past the FBI agent and at the Russians' car as it turned the corner and headed back toward downtown Helsinki. The car disappeared behind the wildly painted hull of a cruise ship docked in the slip a hundred yards away. Dozens of buses and taxis milled about in the drop-off area. It had the look of controlled chaos.

"And yet, you're here—why?" Chris asked, looking back at Case. "In Dallas we agreed everything would be neat and organized; my people would collect this hacker—and remember, he called you, then you called me to find and pick up this guy.

It was all going well—that is, until Micah got arrested."

"The Russians arrested you?" Case said, looking at Lynch.

"You didn't know that?" Chris said. "They let him go after a very long and inconvenient day of interviews."

"Still have all my fingernails," Micah said, holding up his hands and a cigar.

"This operation has been running a thousand miles an hour," Chris continued. "And it appears the Russians are good at hacking and surveillance; that's why they beat us here. And that's why you're here as well, I assume. We just followed the breadcrumbs all of you left."

"If that includes tracking my plane, I will see that you never get a contract again."

Ignoring the comment, Chris said, "A question, Special Agent. Before she disappeared, Alex said that Sokolov saw someone who fits your description sitting in a café in Tallinn's market square, talking with the boys' babysitter. This woman, Anya Belsky, came along for the ride and clocked Alex in a hotel room in Lahti. So, Case, if you are involved in this attack on my employee, I will let everyone know. What was that about?"

"Cool your fucking jets, Campbell," Case said, putting up his hands. "Here's the story. Anya Belsky contacted me directly. She saw me on TV, called the FBI office, said the right things to get our attention, and I talked to her. She said she could produce the hacker, said she was close to him, gave me a price."

"So, we are now paying for information?" Micah said.

"You and TSD are questioning the use of dollars to open doors? Please."

"How much?" Micah asked. "Just professional curiosity. I always wondered what a stool pigeon gets these days on the international market."

"Twenty grand, that's it. Hell, the G-V cost more to fly here than what she wanted. I gave her ten; then she took off. She didn't show for our meeting that evening. My guys followed her; she was staying at a local hotel. It seems the hacker and his kids took off, leaving her high and dry. Then she bolted. If I cared, we would go after her."

"Chris, this is how to fuck up an operation royally," Micah said.

"Whatever Alex is doing," Chris said, "she is protecting that man and his family. Why, I don't know, yet. There is more to this, and before we go handing them to you with black bags over their heads and you shipping him off to Guantanamo, I want to know why. You said this had become a big deal, a big political deal. It sure as hell is. The hacker says it was the Russian government's programs that initiated the collapse of the grid in Iowa. They are responsible for this disaster."

"Bullshit," Case said.

"According to Alex, that's what he said," Chris continued. "His kids broke into the Russian security system, accessed programs, which they opened—we don't know how—and it triggered some secret Russian government program."

"You will say anything to protect your ass," Case said.

"Robb, I don't care what you think," Chris said. "This is what we were told. Sure, it needs to be verified. But if this is true, it confirms what we've been thinking for years, and we need to find ways to protect ourselves from these electronic assaults. I will take care of this problem here in the Baltic. I would suggest that you get together with Homeland and begin to review procedures and what needs to be done to protect the American grid system. We will confirm all of this—you and your people need to be ready, get ahead of it. If the word gets out, it will drop like a bomb."

The conversation ended. Chris, Micah, and Jack walked back to the SUV, then watched Case and his two men walk up the pier to a waiting car, drive past the cruise ship, and like the

St. Petersburg White

Russians, disappear.

* * *

Alex sat in a canvas sling chair; she was barefoot, squishing the damp sand between her toes. The water of Pärnu Bay was like glass. After the morning clouds had cleared, the heat returned, and so had the humidity. The water of the bay was warm, probably due to the long days—earlier, when she waded in, it felt like bathwater. The boys sat in the thin sheet of water on the shore; it softly rose and fell, and they continued to dig in the sand. There were no waves. It was as if the bay were breathing. The boys' laughter was infectious; it had an edge to it, a little more demonstrative than another child that age might make. They were remarkable; that's the only thought that came to Alex's mind. Two geniuses, each locked in a brain that sometimes trapped them, confused them, and tricked them. Her experience with autistic kids was limited. Cops were trained for a lot of things, but a pair of autistic youngsters, acting out and seemingly bent on mayhem—they were not in the manual. The world was becoming more aware, fairer, more understanding, but many only saw dysfunction, retardation, and danger.

The boys walked toward her; they carried a metal bucket from the guesthouse between them.

"*Aleks, chto eto?*" one of the boys asked.

Alex looked at Ilya.

"What are these?" he translated.

She looked in the bucket and smiled. "Those are clams, Gavril. The animal lives inside the hard shell. Some people eat them."

Ilya translated; the boys squished up their faces.

"He's Gavril," Ilya said, pointing to the other.

"Yes, Gavril. Sorry, Pavel, I get confused."

"Papa gets confused all the time," Ilya translated with a nod and grin.

"As I said, you crack them open, and the animal lives inside. The shell protects them," Alex said.

Gavril turned and tapped his brother on the head with his knuckles. "Like your hard head, Pavel. All hard on the outside, can't see inside." Ilya emphasized *inside* and *outside* to Alex in the translation.

Pavel smiled at his brother's joke. "*Vnutri, snaruzhi, vnutri, snaruzhi.*" It rolled into a made-up song.

Alex looked out at the bay. "What do you see out there, boys?"

Ilya repeated, "*Chto ty tam vidish?*"

The twins put the bucket down and with childish eyes looked out at the sea. The horizon was an indistinct grey band. A seagull squawked, dipped low to the water, and grazed the glassy surface, leaving a V-shape arrow of ripples.

Ilya translated.

"Alex," Pavel said. "I see forever."

"Gavril, what do you see?"

"I see a bird and forever."

"And I see a boat, and a bird, and forever," Pavel said. He held his hand up to his eyes and looked through his fingers, then slowly waved them across his face. Gavril mimicked him. "And now I see me walking across the water, to forever."

"You know you can't walk on water," Alex said.

"Alex, I know that, but I can wish." Pavel took his brother's hand.

Ilya made the boys take a nap that afternoon. The heat pushed its way into all their heads. Alex joined Ilya under the shade of a tree in the lawn area in front of the cabins.

"Why are you doing this?" Ilya asked. "You owe us nothing; my children made a mistake. They are curious and made a mistake. My heart breaks for the damage they caused—actually, what I caused by not keeping them away from the computer.

To them, the damn thing is just a toy, something to occupy their minds. It's like a car. You can drive very carefully, slowly, and it will take you where you want, but if you drive fast, ignore the rules, and go where you are not supposed to, people will get hurt. Let me take the boys and go home. You can put us on the train, leave us. We can be in our beds tomorrow, and you can go back to America. We will be okay. I have been through so much in my life. The changes to Russia are the most confusing; there are good days and bad days. I believe things are getting better; however, *gorbatovo mogila ispravit.*"

"Meaning?"

"It means that only the grave will cure the hunchback. In English: A leopard cannot change his spots. Russia will be Russia. So, here we are. I don't want you hurt because of us. I will take the boys and go home."

"Ilya, you can't, and you know it. I knew a few Russians in Cleveland, that's my home. Are all of you so depressed, so fatalistic?"

"To be Russian is to be stoic and resigned to our fate; that is, unless you are a criminal. Then the world is your oyster or something like that. We Russians have been peasants for a long time."

"Good God, no wonder you drink. Nonetheless, Ilya, too many now know; too many want you; too many want to make sure you tell no one what you know. I want to find a way to help you hide. You owe it to your boys; they need to be safe."

"That's impossible. Our narrow escapes over the last few days have shown that this is true. Cameras are everywhere; scanners read license plates—even your credit cards will be checked. Soon they will make the connection to Anya's credit card, and this hiding place will no longer hide us. It won't be one car with that agent and her men; it will be a dozen."

"Then we have to find a better hiding place."

CHAPTER 27

Alex knew that Ilya was right about the eventual connection to Anya's credit card. Between the NSA, FBI, and the Russian secret police, one of them would stumble over the car rental. It occurred to her the car might have GPS or something similar. She talked it over with Ilya, and they decided to pull the leads off the battery; it might help. It would delay their escape if they had to run, but it would also delay their being noticed. They decided it was worth the effort.

She'd slept well the previous night, finally. There was nothing she could do if Ilya took the boys and ran; the train station was less than a mile away. He could be in St. Petersburg before the day was over. When she woke, she heard noises in the other room and was pleased he was still there.

She had to call Chris, tell him what was going on, try to explain why she was doing what she was doing. Would he understand? She barely understood herself. The boys were entertaining themselves with their Nintendos again; who knew how long that would last? The television broadcasts, such as they were, were in Estonian and Russian. It was strange to watch episodes of *Married . . . with Children*, called *Tuvikesed*, dubbed in Estonian. She needed to move the Sokolovs and soon.

It was now standard operation to pull the battery from her phone. Once a day she would insert the battery, check for messages, then pull it. She had done this with the sat-phone as well. She heard the rustling of plastic and the thud of cans against the countertop. She looked into the kitchen area. Ilya was pulling groceries from paper bags and placing them on the counter. The boys sat around the small dining table, both engrossed in comic books.

"Later, I'll make spaghetti for dinner. The boys love it," Ilya said when he saw Alex. "I asked the owner if there was a grocer nearby. There is a Selver grocery store just up the street. Since we've run out of everything, I borrowed a few euros from your bag and got eggs, milk, cereal, meat, sauce, and pasta. Even the liquor is cheaper here than in Russia."

Alex saw the vodka bottle on the counter; an inch was missing. It was a lot to process. She knew that Ilya could have just walked a few more blocks to the train and disappeared.

"You are probably wondering why we are still here," Ilya said as he pulled out pots and pans and began to organize the kitchen for later. "I would."

She looked at the boys and then Ilya. "Okay, why are you still here?"

"I have decided the best future for my boys is in America. They have nothing in Russia. They are very smart but are halves to a whole. If they stay in Russia, they will be separated. One of their teachers, with good intentions, tried to do that to the boys when they were younger, declared I couldn't take care of them. The authorities wanted to send them to a home. They called it something else—I knew it was an institution. That's what the government does in Russia with things or people they don't understand, commit them, and hide them away. I do not think they do this in America. I have read about schools and universities that can help on websites and have listened to your TED talks. I've learned much. My boys need to be in America."

Alex looked at the boys; both quickly put their heads down

and were back to their magazines.

Ilya slid a glass along the counter to Alex.

"My boys are everything to me. They are a challenge, but they are also an opportunity. I could never have their IQs tested; the government had already written them off. But based on tests I've given them, they are somewhere above 170 on the chart, genius level. I also learned that autism is shared by identical twins more than fraternal twins, and if one of the twins is autistic, it is a good chance both will be. I find nothing on this in Russian literature. Alex, I am a computer scientist. I see connections and interconnections that build programs. We humans are the same, an assembly of billions of genes. If one is missing or defective, we have the possibility of autism or a hundred other syndromes or diseases. With autism it is more complicated; nonetheless, my boys are brilliant. They are trapped in minds that don't function like ours. I've tried to teach them, but they are now beyond what I can do. They must be allowed to grow, to learn, to apply themselves—that can only happen in America or someplace as free."

Alex sipped her drink. The boys, with their cherubic faces, were once again looking at the two adults.

"*Aleks, my khotim poyekhat' v Ameriku,*" Gavril said, and he looked at his brother. They both smiled and began to rock slowly back and forth as if the energy in the phrase *poyekhat' v Ameriku* was powering their need to move.

"Even I can translate that," Alex said.

"Yes, they want to go to America," Ilya said.

They spent the rest of the day back along the shore and, after returning to the cabin, Ilya made sure the boys took a nap. When they awoke, he was browning the beef and preparing the sauce.

"I'll let it simmer awhile," he said to Alex, then poured an inch of vodka in his glass. He joined her in the spartan living room. "I wish to God they hadn't found that back door in that system. If there was only a way to turn back the clock."

Alex took another sip of her drink and watched the boys as they played their Nintendos.

"Clocks can be turned back, reality can't be," Alex answered.

The smells coming from the small kitchen were the most intoxicating aromas she'd smelled in weeks.

* * *

Tanya Golubev stood in the window of her office in Lubyanka and watched the traffic in the circle go around and around. She hardly acknowledged the woman standing behind her.

"They have dropped off the face of the earth," the young woman said. "We have looked at more than a dozen data sources in Tallinn and the surrounding region. Airport cameras, train stations, CCTVs at all the ferry terminals, and traffic cameras on highways. We have also looked for the same credit card that was used in Rakvere to pay for the room and rent the Kia you followed to Helsinki; the card has not been used since. Either they are in a hotel in Tallinn and are staying out of sight, or they found another way out of town. They could have used Uber."

"Do not ever talk to me about that blue car again, or Uber for that matter. I know they are still in Estonia. We would have seen them at the border if they tried to leave."

"Assistant Director Golubev, there are hundreds of places where they could cross into Latvia or even farther south into Belarus."

Golubev glared at the impertinent staffer. "Well then, check all of them."

"I don't know what I'm looking for."

"Your job is to find something suspicious and then tell me. I will determine if it is what we are looking for."

The staffer turned and left the office. Tanya turned to the man sitting in the chair in the corner. "Comrade Director, where do they find such idiots? My nephew could do a better job."

"Don't be too hard on them. They have been up two days straight. We have had difficulties tracking credit card purchases. The firewalls for American Express and Visa are very good. We are told by the Kremlin to walk softly and try not to leave footprints. In time, all this will become even harder; for some reason, people don't like others looking into their bedrooms. Consider these the halcyon days of spying. Who knows what we will be doing ten years from now."

"I don't give a shit," Golubev said. "Right now, we have the tools, and we should be using them."

"That crew you just berated built the AI program that can spot a particular ant on a mountain of ants."

"I'm not looking for an ant; I want this man, this Ilya Sokolov. I want him here to build programs like the one he used to crash into our servers. And, if I can't get him, I want no one else to have him either."

"You've said that. Be patient. Even a lizard has to come out from under his rock sooner than later."

"Yes," Tanya said, "but the Americans are doing the same thing, and they have better stuff than we do."

"Maybe, maybe not," Ivanovich said. "Our programs are like sledgehammers; theirs are like scalpels. We push our way in and take what we can. They pride themselves on being able to slip in and out unnoticed, or at least not immediately noticed. There is something to be said for that. That is why this program, and the two others like it, impress me. They too are elegant and surreptitious. That is why this man must be caught. He was not supposed to be able to do what he did. Look at this."

She took the folder Ivanovich held out and looked at the photos that had been placed inside. The woman in the newspaper photos was not identified in the copy. The location was conspicuous and obvious; the Grand Canal was behind the group that included a woman, a man, and four Carabinieri officers. Tanya studied the photo, then rummaged around her desk until she found the photo from a CCTV camera in Tallinn; it was the same woman. It was the woman who had left the blue car on the ferry. It was Sandy Dumbrowski, real name, possibly, Alexandra Polonia.

"Interesting," Golubev said to her boss.

"And why is that?"

She held up the photos. "The woman in Rakvere and Tallinn with the blue Kia; the woman who has taken our Russian citizen, Ilya Sokolov; the woman in Stockholm; the woman who is leading this wild goose chase—this Alexandra Polonia. She must be a CIA agent."

* * *

Chris, Micah, and Linda stood next to the stairs of the Gulfstream. They were still parked on the tarmac of the airport. Jack had gone inside to start the engines. An hour earlier, they had watched Robb Case's plane take off; he said he was heading back to Washington, D.C. The FBI agent had seemed both frustrated and livid over the exposure of his failed special operation to acquire Ilya Sokolov. Micah mentioned something about his tail between his legs. Chris didn't have the complete story of what went down, but whatever it was, it failed miserably. However, he'd been there himself a few times; you took your chances when you played these games, and sometimes you lost.

They had arrived at the business jet area of Helsinki-Vantaa International Airport prior to the Russians flying off in their respective French-made jets, and just minutes before Case left. Their departures left the impression that they could not leave fast enough.

The three colleagues discussed why Alex had disappeared.

"She said the two boys were autistic," Linda said. "They are maybe nine or ten years old, identical twins, and were with Sokolov when he met her at the St. Petersburg train station. It was a surprise."

"An understatement," Micah offered. "I get why Sokolov didn't say anything when we met him the night before. I'm not sure what I would have said or done if I'd known there were kids involved. She made the right call."

"And now she's disappeared," Chris said. "If the Russians had them, the FSB would not have been here in Helsinki waiting for the ferry. Alex and the Sokolovs would be sitting in a cell in Lubyanka prison—and that idea pisses me off. I'm glad we put tails on them in Tallinn."

"Our Dallas team did have some help," Linda said. "Though if the FBI learns about our friends at the NSA passing on flight data to us, there will be many doors slammed in our face."

"It was a chance we had to take." Once the Russians landed in Helsinki, it hadn't been too hard for Chris's team to follow them. "So, the Russians don't have Alex or the Sokolovs," he said.

"She's gone dark," Micah said. "We know she believes she can't trust anyone—and I can't blame her. She tricked the Russkies into thinking she was on the boat, and she was right—they do have the skills to scan surveillance digitals. They showed their hand and their access and talent of accessing civilian cameras and surveillance scanners. That idea gave her time. She knows that we can follow her by her credit cards, and maybe the Russians can too. Trains, boats, and planes are out; only a car is left—and the agencies require a credit card to rent."

"You think she has another card?" Linda said.

"Case met with Anya Belsky in Tallinn," Chris said, reminding everyone. "She was the nanny for the boys. This Belsky was the one who knocked Alex out and fled with the boys and Sokolov. Later, Alex somehow tracked them down. Maybe they used Belsky's credit card; maybe this Sokolov guy has a card."

"Alex will call when the time is right," Micah said. "Meanwhile, I suggest we look into the car rental agencies near the ferry terminal; that was where she was last seen. Check for someone with the name Anya or Anna, Anita, and even Anastasia."

Linda pulled out her phone.

"Chris, I know she's still in Estonia," Micah said. "It's the two boys; she's taking care of them. Maybe this Ilya Sokolov is a genius, maybe he's a crank, but if he's the one who created this problem, we want him as badly as the next guys. I get what Case tried to do; that's his problem."

"So, we chase down the car rentals," Linda said. "What else?"

"Don't know," Chris answered. "Maybe Case will keep this in his back pocket, for now. Someday, he will need it. It's the way Washington works—favors and forget-me-nots. When you need one or both, it's a good idea to have a shoebox full."

CHAPTER 28

For Alex, trust was something earned. She didn't give it away or assume it was a two-way street—now, anyway. If she'd ever considered trust and her marriage, things might have been different. For Ralph Cierzinski, trust was one-way; he didn't trust you. However, you were expected to trust him—until he put a .38-caliber slug in your ear. She was glad she was five thousand miles away from that asshole. She hoped someone would be there for her—even if it turned out to be only her family. The rest, even people she considered friends on the force, had turned away. The things you learn after the shit hits the fan.

She looked at the two boys asleep on the couch, exhausted from their day at the beach. Ilya was also asleep, with a little help from the vodka. The aroma of Italian spices still hung in the air. She took another sip of her vodka; the label on the bottle said *Poland*. Her favorite was also Polish, Belvedere. This was a brand she'd never heard of, but at least there was a warm kick to it. Had she become this desperate?

The right thing to do was call Chris, have him fly into Estonia, and pick them up. They would be in the United States in less than twenty-four hours. Her job done. Let the government deal with Ilya and the boys. She'd tell them everything she knew, support Ilya where she could, make sure they were treated appropriately. Maybe even find support and help for the boys. Then the cynical angel on her shoulder whispered, "Don't believe a word of what they tell you. They want a fall guy. Someone has to pay; someone will be going down for this. And this Russian hacker fits the bill perfectly." Her own government would believe nothing she had to say about Ilya Sokolov and his sons.

She tried to brush away the pessimistic attitude, but she knew after what she'd been through in Cleveland, the cynical angel was closer to the truth she didn't want to accept. After what she'd seen on the Tallinn tarmac, and Lynch and Case's little dance, she was sure that Ilya would disappear, lost in some ten-by-ten cell in Guantanamo, Fort Leavenworth, or some other dark site. America wasn't that different from Russia in some ways: if left at the mercy of U.S. officials, the boys would be sent to an institution. Sure, they would live out their lives, but they would never see their father again. They would, like their father, disappear. That was the way the real world worked, unlike the fairy tale of righteousness and justice. Politicians needed a head, and Ilya's would do nicely. Everyone was looking for a stick to put it on. *Shit!*

* * *

Golubev had her people chase down every possible connection that would identify Alexandra Polonia. There had to be some trail she'd left somewhere, though she was experienced and crafty and a woman who was not afraid to use force. Tanya respected her, and it would be a pleasure to stop her. The FBI agent Case, through a backchannel, made an offer. She knew he had offered a small prize: the woman. He left the door open, even stuck his shoe in the door, for her people to chase down who Polonia was. A trade? Was that what this was? Let her and the FSB track this man down and then maybe turn him over to the FBI, a detente between agencies, something left on the table for later? Special Agent Case obviously didn't know the truth about the hack, or he would never have given up the woman and the people she was hiding. If she, Tanya Golubev, were to apprehend this Ilya Sokolov, he would never be allowed out of Russia.

Dmitry Ivanovich stood in the doorway of her office; he was smoking one of those infernal foul cigarettes, Belomorkanals; their stench would remain for hours.

"Must you stink up my office with that vulgar thing?" she said.

"I don't think you will mind when I tell you the news," Ivanovich said.

"And what can you possibly have that will allow me to permit you to keep smoking that shit in here?"

"We have confirmed your Stockholm and Rakvere lady friend is *not* a CIA officer." He held up a thick folder, then placed it on her desk. "She was a cop. We have also confirmed that she is a contractor working for that American, Christopher Campbell, who owns Teton Security and Defense. Last February, there was a Venice terrorist operation and explosion. I'm sure you remember. Our people believe she was involved with a man we believe was a CIA officer. She may have been working for this TSD company even then—we are checking on that. But just before the events in Venice, she was a detective on the Cleveland, Ohio, police force. We found numerous articles in the newspapers. It seems she was implicated during a nasty trial in which her husband was convicted of operating a drug lab and selling drugs; there are other indictments as well. He was sent to prison, and within a few months, escaped. Soon after, she quit the police department, though she was not indicted in any of his activities."

Tanya slowly rose from her desk. "Alexandra Polonia is not a CIA officer. Interesting. That means she may not have the resources they have. She may be out there on her own."

"She does have Campbell and TSD," Ivanovich said.

"After our conversation at the ferry, maybe she has gone rogue. Campbell may not know where she is. Why is she protecting this Russian? I haven't a clue. Maybe it's his boys; women will do that—become protectors."

"I do not have to worry about that with you, do I, Tanya?"

"Fuck you, Director Ivanovich. Everything I do is for Mother Russia, no matter who is the director."

"At the moment I *am* your director, so be civil." He crossed the room and pointed to the file. "We have confirmed her name; it is Alexandra Polonia."

"We knew that."

"It has been fully confirmed through AI and facial recognition."

"Polish?"

"We believe so, or at least at some time in the past. Downstairs, they are working up a profile and background. I will see that it gets to you. It might prove helpful."

Ivanovich left a thick cloud of foul smoke drifting in the still air as he departed. She admired the man, like the way the young beta wolf respects the older alpha wolf. Sometime there would come a day . . .

For the next hour, she poured through the file and began constructing a scenario that supported the facts and variables of the situation she now faced. She stared at Polonia's face in a news photo from the *Cleveland Plain Dealer*. Alexandra Polonia was clever and resourceful and managing to stay a step ahead of Tanya and her teams. The operation in Rakvere should have worked, yet they escaped. Her arm throbbed.

Behind Golubev's desk hung a map of western Russia and Europe. She had overlaid another map, in a larger scale, that focused on the Baltic Sea and the surrounding countries. Pins had been stuck where her quarry had been. A thin string was strung between the pins, creating a spiderweb of their escapes and known locations. It was worthless. She wanted to know where this Polonia was now. Something had to happen, a mistake had to be made, an image caught in a camera lens. There was a knock on the door.

"Madam," the young women said. "This just came in. The director said you should have it."

Golubev waved her hand, and the woman crossed the room. "We have found a possible connection to the Sokolov case."

Golubev's eyebrows arched up. "Sokolov case?"

"Yes, that is what we are calling it in research. It's easier if you have a name; it reduces the confusion with the others we are working on. Once the target was identified, the research director gave it that name."

"Okay, go on."

"Two things. The rental of the blue Kia in Rakvere was by the same person we have identified as Alexandra Polonia. It was her credit card that the rooms were registered to. Until research explored the Cleveland angle and this woman, we could not connect the two; we have now. We believe, with some certainty, that this same Polonia woman rented a car from another car rental agency directly across the street from the Tallinn ferry terminal. The time of this rental was within an hour of the departure of the ferry carrying the blue Kia. One of our agents in Tallinn went to the rental agency and retrieved the information. He believes Polonia used a credit card with the name Anya Belsky; we believe Belsky is a Russian national and is connected to Sokolov. We are checking in St. Petersburg."

Golubev looked at the assistant. "And?"

"The Tallinn rental interview was done quietly, and the remuneration was reasonable. We matched Belsky's passport with the credit card, though the employee at the agency wasn't sure if the woman was Anya Belsky. They rent dozens of cars every day."

"Your assessment?"

"It is the same woman, Alexandra Polonia. The rental car is a grey 2019 Toyota Corolla. There is a photo of one in the file, along with the license plate number. We are checking readers and scanners we have access to around Tallinn and in Estonia; nothing so far."

"This Belsky woman, what do we know?"

"She may be the woman who traveled with Sokolov when he left St. Petersburg. There is a record of her passport being scanned on the train. We are also looking at Finnish CCTV digitals to see if she shows up."

"If she does, it's irrelevant. That was days ago; however, she may be with the family now. Add her to the list of faces we have and make sure the Polonia woman is also in the database."

"Already done." The assistant left Golubev's office.

CHAPTER 29

After the debacle at the Helsinki ferry terminal, Chris Campbell decided to return to Tallinn. This all had to end. Alex needed to come in and bring the Sokolovs with her. Everything about the Russians read frustration, even desperation—and he never liked it when things became desperate. That led to decisions that were dangerous at best.

"Chris, Jack says there's a call for you. It is being routed through Dallas," Linda said. She handed him a cup of coffee. Lately, caffeine had become a meal replacement.

"Do you know who?" Chris asked as he reached for the phone secured to the panel near his seat.

"The secretary for Homeland Security."

Chris gave Micah a sour look.

"Secretary Tallmadge, what can I do for you?" Chris said.

"What the hell is going on there, wherever the hell you are?" Tallmadge said. "The FBI says you have this hacker, this killer, and that you won't turn him over to them."

Horus Tallmadge had been the governor of Wyoming until a problem developed within his committee for reelection that required that he step away from his political campaign. The problem, no matter how hard the press tried to expose it, never entirely surfaced. A year after his retirement from politics, he was tapped by the president for the position with Homeland;

he was approved by a partisan vote.

"Mr. Secretary, it seems that the Russians also want this man, as I'm sure Special Agent Case has told you. It is imperative that we keep him safe until we find a way to get him out. He is under the care of one of my best associates."

"Campbell, I'm in Berlin for the G7 security council meeting. How long before you can meet me?"

Chris looked at his watch and made a few calculations. "More than two hours. Where are you?"

"Ritz-Carlton." There was pause, then to someone else Tallmadge said, "Where the hell are we?"

"Secretary, I know where it is, Potsdamer Platz. Three hours. Anything else, sir?"

"No. Just get here. And if you have that son of a bitch with you, even better." The line went dead.

Chris tapped the keys on the phone. "Jack, change in plans. We are going back to Berlin. I have a meeting."

"Yes, boss."

"He seemed a little pissed," Micah said. "I could hear it."

"Politicians," Chris said. His sat-phone buzzed. "Alex, where are you?" he said.

"Safe. For how long, I'm not sure, but for now safe."

"The Russians are very pissed at you right now. My guess is they know who you really are and are doing everything they can to find you. Can you stay hidden?"

"A few days, maybe more. Just don't know."

"I need to have you come in," Chris said. "I'm on my way to Berlin. Secretary Tallmadge demands a meeting."

"I get it, and Ilya knew this was coming. We've talked. How and when?"

"There's an old Russian airport near the city of Pärnu," Micah said. "It's on the city's north side. We can pick them up there."

"Is that Micah?"

"Yes. We were in Helsinki meeting your ferry. Nice job, by the way. You managed to fool both the Russian secret police and the FBI at the same time."

"I was just looking for time, and I guess it's run out."

"Micah says there's an airport just north of Pärnu. Is it near you? Can you meet him there tomorrow morning? He will bring you back here to Berlin. I'm sorry this has to end this way."

"I get it, I really do, Chris. Just make sure that it's you and not the Russians. I've promised the family I will do everything not to have that woman find them. Six o'clock tomorrow morning?"

"Copy. See you tomorrow. Get some sleep." Chris clicked off.

* * *

"You okay?" Ilya asked Alex. "The boys say that you look unhappy. I told them you are just concerned. But their intuitive skills are way beyond mine. Gavril wants to know what is bothering you."

"Tell them that I am fine. All I want is to protect them," Alex said as she pushed the sat-phone back into her bag.

"And how are you going to do that? Besides, that's my job, not yours. Yours is to find us a safe place, and I will take care of them."

She told him about the plan to meet up with Micah. It was the only way to end this and to keep him and the boys away from the Russians. "Tomorrow morning at first light," she said.

"And you trust this man?"

"I do trust Chris Campbell," she said. "I'm not sure I trust the government we work for."

"I understand. That is good; my government has been saying for years to trust them. I trust them never to tell us the truth. Rather, never completely believe what they say. Governments are made of people, people have their own interests, and often these are more important than the citizens they are supposed to serve. So, trust only goes so far."

"Right now, Chris may be the only chance we have of getting out of this. Every minute, the FSB is closer. They *will* find out about the rental car, and Anya. For all I know, they may even have her in one of their prisons."

"You act like your American friends can't be trusted, either."

"Chris will do what is right. My concern is for those two boys. What may be waiting for them in America may not be the best for them."

"I understand," Ilya said as he poured a little more vodka in his glass. "I do not wish to spend the rest of my life in one of your prisons. There must be an alternative."

She smiled, then asked, "Is there someplace you want to go?"

"We Russians have our disadvantages when it comes to material goods and all the excessive trappings of the West. Expensive cars, the latest phones, Michael Jordan shoes, fancy homes, and what's the word . . . bling? That is the right word, is it not?"

"Yes, bling works."

"You have all that stuff," Ilya said with a shrug. "Me, in St. Petersburg, all I hope for every day is clean clothes for the boys and to live in a warm apartment. I dream of them in the best schools, universities that will expand their minds and allow them to grow. In Russia, they will become dishwashers. America has these kinds of schools, and Canada too, and some of the Scandinavian countries. But these are dreams, unreachable dreams."

"Canada? Why there?"

"I saw a video about an autistic boy who found his opportunity in a private Canadian college that allowed him to expand his interests, something that most Russian schools fall short of for these children. It seemed interesting. And there is a private school in Norway, near Oslo, that may also help. Money is the issue; money I don't have. You asked where I would like to go; I would like to take my boys to Canada. Do you think this boss of yours can do this?"

"I can't answer that. Nonetheless, I'm willing to try."

"I am willing to try too; you have done much for us." Ilya paused, then said, "We will try this together, yes?"

Alex nodded gravely. She sent a text to Chris, confirming the pickup. He responded in minutes.

> *Jack and Micah will meet you at Pärnu Airport, 6:00 AM Estonia time. Jack checked the maps; he will hold just south of the small terminal building there. Please move quickly to the plane; we will need to leave immediately.*
>
> *CC*

"Then where will we go?" Ilya asked.

"First Berlin, then maybe where the dream for your children will be become real."

Ilya just shook his head. "You Americans dream, and then your dream becomes real. For Russians, we just dream of a warm coat."

They spent the rest of the day at the beach. Alex bought a picnic lunch at the Selver grocery store: cold pizza for the boys, sandwiches and beer for the adults. That evening they drove past the airport; Alex wanted to know where everything was. She gave Ilya the money to pay the owner of the guesthouse, a stout middle-aged woman named Helena. They would be leaving early in the morning and didn't want to disturb her. They sat around the cabin until late in the evening, then managed a few hours of sleep. They didn't tell the boys anything. An hour before they were to leave, they loaded the few things they'd bought in town—shirts and underwear for the boys—into a single canvas bag.

As they drove through Pärnu to the airport, a murky grey overcast drifted in from the bay. Raindrops appeared on the windshield. Alex still couldn't adjust to the early morning light. The terminal, a bland two-story building with dozens of square windows covering its façade, faced the two-lane road that fronted the airport. A control tower rose off to one side. There were no cars in the small parking lot. It was as desolate a place as Alex had ever seen; it was fitting.

"*Kuda my idem seychas, Papa?*" Pavel asked as he stared out the window.

Alex looked at Ilya. He said, "Pavel wants to know where we are going."

A lone airplane sat on the tarmac just beyond the terminal.

"*My budem letat', kak ptitsa?*" Gavril asked.

Ilya said something to the boy; then to Alex, "He wants to know if we are going to fly like a bird."

"*Da*," Alex said.

Both boys grinned.

The plane was early. She studied the jet as they carried their things through the open gate at one end of the building. The registration number on the fuselage matched the one in her memory; the jet was Chris's. As they walked the last hundred feet, the whine of another jet came from within the clouds overhead; it seemed to materialize out of the grey. It banked, aligned itself with the runway, and within a minute was taxiing toward them.

"Who is that?" Ilya asked.

"I don't know," Alex answered.

This jet wasn't as sleek at Chris's Gulfstream, but there was something about it that was familiar. The four of them stopped at the edge of the tarmac, and Ilya suddenly dropped the bags to the pavement. The door to the Gulfstream was open and the stairway was down. Micah and Jack stood at the bottom of the stairs; Micah had a gun pointed at the pilot.

"Did you think it was going to be easy?" Micah said to Alex. "Alex, I want you and the boys over there; leave the bags. Ilya, I want you here." He pointed with his free hand to a spot about twenty feet away.

The whine of the approaching jet drowned out all conversation and the boys' protests as their father moved away from them. Micah leaned in and spoke directly into Jack's ear. Jack nodded, then slowly walked over to Alex and the boys.

The jet pulled to an abrupt stop fifty feet behind the Gulfstream. When Alex saw the Russian numbers posted on the engine, her heart sank: now she knew the jet and who would be inside. The stairs unfolded out from the fuselage and down to the pavement. Within a second, two men exited. The first, holding an AK-47, held the top step, while the other continued down the steps to the tarmac. Tanya Golubev followed; she took the stairs carefully, using her left arm to steady herself. She walked directly to Micah. He had moved over to stand next to Ilya. Golubev's man fell into step behind her, keeping his weapon pointed at Alex and Jack.

Golubev kissed Micah on the cheek.

"Damn, this sure as hell surprises me," Alex said. "Really, Micah? You, a fucking traitor? Chris wasn't paying you enough?"

"Oh, he was paying me enough," Micah answered. "It's just Russia would pay me more." He looked at Golubev. "How is your arm?"

"It hurts to high heaven; I should shoot her right now and get it over with."

Golubev turned on Ilya. "My God, for such a little man, you certainly have caused a lot of trouble. Get on my plane. We have a lot of questions. And your answers had better be right." She looked at her subordinate. "*Poluchit' yeg v samolete!*"

The man looked at Ilya and pointed at the Dassault with his rifle. "*Seychas.*" Then in English, he added, "Now, or I shoot one of these brats."

Ilya turned toward the Russian plane. Golubev's man poked him in the ribs and yelled again. Ilya looked back at his boys, then Alex. "Take care of them. I will see them soon." In Russian, he said to Gavril and Pavel, "*Bud' khoroshim, skoro uvidimsya.*"

"I really doubt that, Ilya Sokolov," Golubev said. "I'd take them with us, but I don't want to deal with a pair of retards."

Ilya lunged toward Golubev, his hatred evident. Her man smashed him in the back of the head with the butt of the rifle, knocking him to the tarmac. Both boys screamed and tried to run to their father. Jack and Alex held them tightly as they twisted and tried to break free.

"Micah, get the hero on the plane. The police will be here soon, and I do not want to be here." She looked up at her pilot and waved her good hand in circles. The jet's engines began to wind up. She then crossed over to Alex. The boys were screaming at her.

"Tell them to shut the fuck up. I'm trying to do business here. They need to be quiet."

"Fuck you," Alex yelled back. To the boys, she said, "Scream all you want. Shake the ground. Let the whole world know that this is not right."

"I should shoot you, or just break your arm—tit for tat,

as you Americans say. But that will just bring down more shit from your CIA. I know all about you, Alexandra Polonia, a fine adversary. Someday, we will meet again." She glanced at Pavel and Gavril in turn. "Shut up, you brats."

"Damn, Tanya, are you always this talkative? Blah, blah, blah. Either shoot me or get on your plane," Alex said. "And you, traitor, we are not through."

Micah looked at Alex. He and the second guard supported Ilya's unconscious body between them.

"Tell Chris it was strictly business," Micah said.

"Micah, you hurt me. Business?" Golubev said.

"I'll make it up later," Micah said, then stopped. "Just a minute." Leaving the guard to drag Ilya toward the plane, Micah pulled his pistol from his shoulder holster, walked up to the front of the Gulfstream, and put one bullet each into the sidewall of the front tires.

"*Do svidaniya*, Alexandra Polonia," Golubev said.

Two minutes later, Alex, Jack, Gavril, and Pavel stood at the edge of the runway as the Dassault disappeared into the thick overcast. The sound of its jet engines lingered until that, too, was gone. Only the damp wind off the Baltic Sea rustled the dry grass that held close to the edge of the asphalt.

"Well, we're stuck, Alex," Jack said. "I can't go anywhere with two flat tires, and I'm sure as hell not leaving this jet. You need to get out of here with the boys, go back into hiding. Micah still believes Ilya is the hacker, but Chris told me it was the boys." He looked down at them; they were tightly holding each other. "Hard to believe these fellows could be such masterminds. When that Russian agent finds out, there will be hell to pay. You need to be gone before she turns that jet around and returns."

"What are you going to do?"

"Baltic Aviation in Tallinn can get me tires, maybe even today. They are just eighty or so miles away. But you cannot stay here. Find a place to stay. I'll call Chris. When he finds out about Micah, there is going to be serious blowback. You keep these kids safe. And if any word of this gets out, shit, the international situation can only get worse. Go, get—I'll take care of this."

Alex knew he was right. She looked at her two young charges. How the hell was this going to work? Especially with the language problem.

"Gavril and Pavel, pick up your bags. We are going back to the car." She pointed to the bags and then the grey Toyota. "Car."

"We heard you, Alex," Gavril said. "When will we see Papa?"

"English, you speak English?"

"Yes, not so good, but we were learning," Pavel said. "Papa told us never to speak English, but to listen. Now, he's gone. We need to find him, to get him back. Now, Alex, we need to find him now."

"Now, Alex, now," Gavril added.

"We will go back to the beach and the cabin, for just a little while. Then we will find your papa. This man must stay with the plane."

"We know; we heard."

A car pulled into the parking lot next to the rental office; the driver came walking toward them. When he reached them, he pointed at the car and said something. Alex shook her head; she didn't understand. She assumed he was asking if the car belonged to her. She thought of the only word in Russian she knew: "*Da!*"

The man continued to follow them and began yelling as they walked to the open gate in the fence at the end of the building.

Gavril stopped and looked at the man and said something in

Russian. The man replied, clearly startled, and Pavel answered. The man threw his hands in the air and walked away.

Alex looked at the two boys. "That was Russian. He understood?"

Both boys nodded. "*Da*," they said in unison.

"What did you say to him?"

"Gavril told the man we were on a secret mission to save the world and that I was his sidekick. If he didn't let us go, there was an excellent chance the world would end tomorrow."

"You didn't say that," Alex said.

"Yes, Alex, that is exactly what we said."

Ten minutes later, Alex pulled into the driveway of the guesthouse they had left earlier that morning. The manager, even this early in the morning, was hanging laundry on a clothesline. Alex smiled at the matronly woman. She was maybe forty-five, with blonde hair and blue eyes. At one time, not too long ago, Helena had been a beauty, thought Alex. Helena said hello back, her expression one of concern. The boys, haltingly, did the talking and the translating. It was apparent to Alex that they had not had many conversations without their father being present.

"We would like our cabin back," Alex said.

"It is still available," Helena said. "Where is your husband?"

That question caught Alex off-guard, but the boys smiled and nudged each other.

"He is away on business; he will be back in a few days. There was an emergency—he is an important man in the government. We took him to the airport in Tallinn."

"Which government?" Helena said.

"The Russian government."

Helena frowned, then spat on the ground. "If I had known he was a Russian official, I would never have rented you the cabin. But you, you are American—I know, I can tell—so your connection to that man confuses me. Then again, I am easily confused. That's what my ex-husband would say: 'Helena, you are the prettiest empty head I know.' Now he's dead." She quickly crossed herself. "And I run this place and make more money than that drunk ever did. I do not like Russians. I remember, as a young girl, when they believed they owned everything in Estonia; however, they never owned our hearts. It was the greatest day in the wretched last century of my country when they packed up and left."

The boys had difficulty translating the Russian and Estonian mix that Helena used. But eventually, Alex got the gist of the long answer.

"I understand. The cabin?"

"I'll get the key. Price is the same, and I prefer cash, just as before. I haven't even had time to clean it. There's still some of the food you left in the refrigerator. I'll come by later with clean sheets. What is your name?"

"Alexandra Polonia."

"Pretty name, for an American. The boys?"

"This is Gavril and Pavel."

"I am Gavril, he's Pavel," Gavril clarified.

"Sorry. I am their temporary guardian."

"Temporary?" Helena asked as she pinned up another sheet. "You are not their mother?"

"Yes, temporary until their father returns. And I am not their mother."

CHAPTER 30

After they settled back into the cabin, Alex made the boys breakfast. They'd eaten earlier that morning, but she wanted to make sure they were well fed. She wasn't sure what the next few hours would bring. Then she called Chris. It was 9:33 AM; she left a message. While she waited for the return call, she made herself an egg sandwich. When Chris returned the call at 9:45 AM, she was still eating her sandwich. The boys were watching television; there was a soccer match on. She had no idea who was playing.

"I talked with Jack. I'm so sorry, Alex," Chris said. "I had no idea, none, and when I find the son of a bitch, he's dead. When we get back together, we need to talk. I can't believe I've been so blind when it comes to my people. I'm such a fool."

"In a cabin on the southern side of Pärnu," Alex said, when he asked where she'd taken the boys. "We've been holed up here the last few days, nice place, reminds me of a cabin along Lake Erie. But that was a lifetime ago. The boys are good, though I'm not sure when they might explode. The same can be said for me."

She walked outside, out of the boys' earshot, then told him about what happened, every sordid and sad detail. Chris said nothing.

"Say something, damn it," she said.

"I can't; this whole thing has gone so upside down. I'm like you, about to explode. Jack says they have to get the tires from Sweden. That will take at least a day. He says you need to get away from all this. I agree. He will, hopefully, get to us in Berlin tomorrow."

"How did your meeting with Secretary Tallmadge go?"

"I believe I have a new one, as the phrase goes. He's such a political putz, but he is right about one thing: we need a resolution and fast. The president and the Iowa governor are pressing everyone, and I'm sure that Robb Case is chomping at the bit to add his two cents. However, you and the Sokolovs have not made the news, but it is only a matter of time. We were this close to being done; do you understand that? Goddamn it—so, how are we going to get Ilya back?"

"Right now, I'm concerned about the twins. I need to get them out of Estonia and to someplace safe. They need to rest at least for a day; they are exhausted. Me? I'm not far behind."

Another pause. "Are you safe where you are?"

"As safe as anywhere."

After she pulled the battery from her phone, she went back inside the cabin. The boys were intently talking between themselves while writing on sheets of paper.

"Where did you find the paper?" she asked.

Gavril pointed to the desk. A drawer was open, and other blank pieces of paper lay loosely in its bottom. They continued to draw, and strange patterns filled most of the page, lines interconnecting other lines. What looked like formulas were written along the edges.

"What is this?" Alex asked.

"An algorithm that can search and then access particular files in the *Federal'naya sluzhba bezopasnosti Rossiyskoy Federatsii*," Gavril said. "It will help us find Papa."

"The what?"

"Papa calls them the FSB, the secret police. They are the people that took him, isn't that correct, Alex?"

"Yes, that is correct. How are you going to search for him? You don't have a computer."

"Helena has one," Pavel said.

"How do you know she has a computer?"

"We asked her," Gavril said.

"How do you know all this? First the English, now this? You never said anything to me about speaking English; your papa didn't either. Why?"

"Papa told us to speak only Russian," Pavel said. "There was not a reason for you to know we can speak English. When they took him, we decided to talk to you."

"When we were six years old," Gavril started, "Papa gave us books and magazines that were about math and computers. We learned all the math, algebra, calculus, trigonometry we could—that took a month—we like number theory and game theory the most. We learned English from both Anya and Papa, and from the Internet. That's when we began to find new games on the Internet; some were a challenge to get into . . ."

"That was fun," Pavel said. "They would try and stop us. We would find ways to work around their firewalls—that's what Papa called them. We got into trouble."

"We are also very good at not getting caught."

"Not anymore," Alex said. "I am here because you left a trail that led us right to you."

"That is impossible. No one could have found us," Gavril said.

"We did, and so did the FSB."

The boys looked at each other, then whispered something that Alex didn't understand.

"*Da, da, dolzhno byt',*" Pavel said.

"What? What are you talking about?"

"The only person who could have allowed us to be discovered was Papa. He has to be the one that left a trail for you to follow."

"Do you understand what you did? Do you even know what happened after you accessed the FSB programs?"

"Yes, we turned it on and off; in fact, we have a program that would do it automatically. We weren't hurting anyone. We wanted to show them that even kids could mess with their programs. They think they are so smart."

"Your father never told you what happened?"

"No, he just took away the computer. Locked it too, but it was easy to unlock."

Alex debated whether to tell the boys what happened after they accessed the Russian program. How responsible were they for what came after the power in Iowa was turned off? The issues of responsibility and even morality seemed beyond them at the moment. How could two ten-year-olds—playing a game they constructed—be held accountable for systems that adults created to attack and hurt others? It was like a child finding a loaded gun. Who was responsible for the aftermath of the weapon accidentally being fired?

She decided this kind of a lesson would have to wait until they were older and more mature—and that would be Ilya's responsibility. She looked at the boys' drawings, grasping why Ilya had left the electronic trail of crumbs. He wanted them to be discovered; even though he initiated contact with the Americans, he needed to show them the proof to be believed. And now here she was, sitting in a cabin in a town she'd never heard of three days ago, talking to two brilliant autistic children about things she couldn't understand, plotting to find a way to persuade the Russian government to return their father. It couldn't get any stranger. But it did.

There was a tap on the door. Through the front-door screen, Alex saw Helena. She had a bag in her arms.

"Come in," Alex said.

Helena set the bag on the counter and talked to the boys as she took cans and jars from the bag.

"She has cans of spaghetti and soup," Gavril said. "They are for us."

"Tell her thank you."

The three carried on a short conversation; both boys' faces showed surprise.

"What's the matter?"

"She says that last night four men came to the office and wanted to know if a family with two boys were staying here. She told them no; they left."

Alex looked at Helena; the proprietress was shaking her head.

"Does she know who they were?"

"They spoke Russian and looked like the police."

Alex set aside her annoyance that Helena hadn't said anything until just now. She smiled at Helena. "Thank you."

Helena shrugged but returned the smile. She said something to the boys.

"She doesn't think they will be back, but maybe," Pavel said. "We think they were like the men at the hotel. Maybe bad guys?"

"Yes, probably bad guys," Alex said.

Should they stay or go? Would Golubev think they would come back here? Would she try to tie up any loose ends? Somehow, they had been spotted—maybe a scan of the car license plate, maybe when Ilya went to the store. There were a dozen ways the Russian team could have found them.

"Helena, we may be leaving tomorrow. Do you know if there is a car rental in town?"

"Which one?"

Alex told her.

She thought for a moment, then said, "Yes, on the road to the airport. It is just outside of town in a strip of stores."

"May I use your computer? I want to drop the car tomorrow."

"Of course, please come by later. Since I bought that computer, my cabin rentals have tripled. I couldn't get that no-good husband of mine to buy one. He said they were worthless, just toys. All he did was complain. Two weeks after he was buried, I bought my first. Best investment ever, and we Estonians are proud of our Internet access, some of the best in Europe. So, any time after three, that's when I'm back from my yoga class."

The boys giggled over the words *yoga class.*

Alex studied the woman; the first word that came to mind would not have been yoga. Then again, the first word concerning Alex would certainly not be teetotaler.

"Three o'clock, excellent. May I bring the boys?"

"Sure, if they have Facebook friends or Instagram posts, they can make them there. I assume they know about computers?"

"Some. Their father knows a little about them. They are fast learners."

The boys could barely keep a straight face as they translated this conversation. However, they admitted to Alex that they did not have a Facebook account; their Papa would not let them have one.

"He said our lives were our own. It was not wise to tell the world everything we did, especially in Russia."

"I can just imagine," Alex replied.

CHAPTER 31

Assistant Director Tanya Golubev sat at her desk; the fingers of her left hand massaged her temples; for twenty-four hours she'd tried every trick she knew to make this little man tell her what he knew about the secret programs he had accessed. The tension made her right arm throb.

"He'll break," Micah said from a chair in the corner.

"They all break," Ivanovich added.

"I'm not so sure," she answered.

Earlier, Ilya looked at her; in fact, it was a glare filled with hatred when he said he had no idea how to access the program. Sure, he knew something had happened. It was all over the news—the disaster in Iowa, the deaths, the shutdown of the power grid—but why did she think he had something to do with it? In the old days, which weren't that long ago, he'd already be shot and buried. She realized her tactical mistake when, early on, she asked about his boys. It was then that he completely shut down. Tanya also knew that she had completely underestimated the American, Alexandra Polonia. She looked over at Micah; he was now just one more complication.

According to Micah, the Polonia woman knew little about the operation, only that she was there to take care of the kids. She did a good job stepping in. More to the point, her actions blew up the intended apprehension of Sokolov at the train station in St. Petersburg.

"And, my dear, she turns out to be something else," Tanya said, looking at Micah. "Something that you did not know about. Who was managing who on this operation?"

"Yes, I'm impressed, and possibly Campbell could have had an idea about all this," Micah answered.

Then Tanya told him she believed Polonia might be a CIA officer. He said possibly, but he doubted it.

"We were sent in to be the pickup and delivery service. The American government wanted a show trial, the grand inquisition, the conviction, and—as had been the case with those who bombed the federal building in Oklahoma—a speedy verdict and just resolution. That isn't going to happen now."

This simple snatch and transport had turned into a manhunt and chase around the Baltic Sea, here and there, and back again. All orchestrated by that blonde, that so-called ex-Cleveland cop, Polonia. Ivanovich said she wasn't a foreign intelligence agent; Golubev still believed differently. In fact, she was positive that Alexandra Polonia was CIA. Right now, she wanted to wash her hands of all this shit, including Ilya Sokolov, who currently occupied one of the nicer cells in the lower levels of the Lubyanka detention facility. He'd asked for pizza with sausage for dinner.

"So, the little shit won't talk?" her boss said from the door. "We have his computer and him. There have been no attacks on our system in the last few days—you have accomplished your operation."

"I'm not sure," Micah said. "According to your people on the third floor, Sokolov has no record of dissent or political activity; he has been an instructor at the ITMO Institute in St. Petersburg for the last eleven years. He is a widower. We know his wife was murdered; he is raising two, who we believe, are autistic twin boys—which would put a strain on anyone, and he is broke. He was an easy target for the CIA. He did what he did; then we came in to extract him. Whether the man is who you believe him to be, that's your problem. You needed to know."

"Thank you for thinking of us, Mr. Lynch. And, as you well know, half of Russia is broke or worse," Ivanovich said. "This whole country is like a debtor's prison. If Sokolov is as smart as you think he is, smart enough to break into our computers and hack our systems, why the hell hasn't he stolen millions and run off to Monte Carlo?"

"Not everyone is as larcenous as you, Director," Golubev said. "Right now, I want to know what he is hiding. Maybe he *is* working for the CIA, and that is why that Polonia woman is here, to make sure Sokolov does his job."

"Possibly, but I doubt it," Micah said.

"He could access the program from the moon if he could get there," Ivanovich said. "I do not believe the man is a spy or a CIA operative. If he is, they have lowered their standards."

"We believe the hacks came from the computer we recovered from the ferry," Golubev added. "The computer is Sokolov's; it was issued to him by the institute. We believe he left it on the ferry as a diversion, a trick to make us think he was still on the ferry."

"It worked. How did you enjoy Stockholm?" Ivanovich said.

Golubev glared at him. "Yes, we did recover the computer. The encryption is so robust we haven't broken into the system to understand how he did it."

"Interesting; it is *our* encryption program."

"They say most of it is, but it has been altered; it is better."

"Sokolov did this?" Micah asked.

"We assume so. I am going to charge the man with espionage, intent to sell state secrets to a foreign power, and stupidity," Golubev replied.

"Be careful with that last one; it may be too close to home for some in this building," Micah said.

"Very funny," Golubev said. "Maybe he'll loosen his tongue after we file the charges."

"And his twin boys, where are they?" Ivanovich asked. "And, why did you leave them with that American cop?"

Golubev paused and looked first at Lynch then the director. She abruptly stood, walked to the window, then stopped and dramatically turned. She was grinning mirthlessly. "Director, it is the boys, the twins. It is them. They are autistic, sure, but maybe they have Asperger Syndrome. Maybe *they* are the geniuses who accessed our systems. Maybe we have the wrong Sokolov downstairs. That's why he says nothing, says he doesn't know anything—that's the truth. It was his boys that broke into our system; they reconfigured the encryption on the computer. I'm sure of it. I want them. They would be incredible assets for Russia."

"It's possible," Micah said.

Ivanovich produced one of his foul-smelling cigarettes. "Yes, that is possible—in fact probable. But I remind you, *you* do not have the children." The smoke began to fill her office.

"We obviously know now that Sokolov was in the Pärnu area two days ago," Golubev said. "We have since identified him from surveillance footage we accessed from a Selver grocery store there. He was in the area; our people made inquiries, stopped at guesthouses in the area, and we found nothing."

"People have been known to lie."

Ignoring the obvious, Golubev continued, "I believe the woman took the boys back there, to one of the guesthouses. We have the identification of the car she rented in Tallinn, a grey Toyota. It has a GPS locator; we are trying to access it. Maybe, just maybe, we can find them there. I'm sending a team in to recheck the area. Then, when we have the boys, serious pressure can be used on Ilya Sokolov to find out how to access his children's brains."

* * *

"What are we going to do?" Linda Monroe said to Chris. "The Russians have Sokolov—after they squeeze him, he'll disappear into some Gulag somewhere. Alex has the boys, a small consolation. We can't go public with any of this, at least not yet. The media has bought, at least temporarily and it will be temporary, into our government's latest notion that it was an unfortunate series of accidents and coincidences—no matter what pound of flesh the Homeland secretary wants. That won't last. Too many people know that the power hack came from outside the United States. We need the man; we need Sokolov."

Campbell didn't answer. He stared out the window of his Berlin office.

"Damn it, Chris, get over Micah," Linda said. "We will deal with that later. Jack will be back this morning. The wheels are replaced, peace has been made with the Estonia police; they believed Jack's story about an emergency landing. And the boys are safe. When this is over, I know you will forgive Alex. Among the dozens of good choices she's made during the last week, I believe she will find a way to get Sokolov back."

"And why should the Russians give him up?" Chris said. "He's a nobody, some guy who was at the wrong place at the wrong time. We still don't fully know what happened. Damn it, we still don't know if he is actually involved in any of this. We only have his word, some electronic mumbo-jumbo, and the plea for help—maybe he is simply looking for a way out of Russia with his boys. He's smart; maybe it's all staged. Maybe it's a setup by the FSB. Shit, I don't know."

"Alex knows; that's why she's been hiding the family," Linda said. "She knows how they did it and how to stop it."

"Yes, maybe. So, tomorrow we pick her up, find out what we can from the twins, and see if there is a way to get their father back. Then we are back to square one—all good, with leverage."

"Somehow I don't think it will be that easy," Linda said. "The Russians are hiding something big, and Sokolov somehow knows about it. I feel it in my gut."

Chris looked at her. "Really?"

"Years of working against these guys while I was at the CIA tells me they don't go to this amount of effort over a hack that doesn't even affect them—unless of course, it does."

* * *

Late that evening, Alex pulled a blanket tightly over the boys; a cool breeze now blew in from the bay and knocked twenty degrees off the heat and humidity. She walked back into the kitchen, found the nearly empty bottle, and poured herself the last of the vodka. Before she lowered herself into the single overstuffed chair, she removed the pistol she'd kept hidden in her waistband; the two Makarovs she acquired in Rakvere were wrapped in a towel in her backpack. It was a nice compact piece, a Beretta 950. From the visible wear, she guessed it was at least twenty years old. She smiled. The Russian she took it from would miss this pistol. She dropped the magazine; it was fully loaded with eight rounds. She cleared the weapon; it didn't have a round in the chamber. She reloaded, racked the slide and chambered a round, and then placed it on the small table next to the lamp. After aimlessly paging through an Estonia travel magazine, she placed it over the gun to hide it from the boys, sipped the last of her drink, and spent the next ten minutes trying to figure out what to do next. Sokolov didn't deserve to be the victim of her screwup. He was a nice guy, doing the best he could in an impossible situation. Now he was sitting in a Russian jail. And it was her fault—or at least the last few days were her fault. She had to find a way to get Ilya out. She slowly closed her eyes.

The next moment, she was staring into the black hole at the end of a pistol; the barrel was less than six inches from her face, and someone was kicking her in the leg. When she refocused and looked upward, a broad-chested Neanderthal stood directly above her. He was the one holding the pistol. Another man, obviously from this same species, stood off to the side. The flash of chrome in the second man's right hand blatantly showed that he was also armed.

"Where are they?" the Neanderthal asked hoarsely. He obviously smoked too much. "Where are the fucking boys? Give them to me, and you will live." He said "leeeve"; Alex almost laughed. His English was mangled enough, but his base Russian accent garbled everything.

"Boys?" she said, thinking quickly. "I don't have any boys; it's just me here on holiday." She looked past the other man to a window; early morning sun streamed through.

"Bullshit. The woman said you came with two boys. I want them. Where are they?"

"Look," Alex said as she slowly raised her arms in an open gesture, "I haven't any idea what you are talking about. You didn't hurt Helena, did you?"

"No. Maybe a bruise or two—fuck this shit, where are the boys? They were here, in that bedroom. It's empty."

"That's not the only thing that's empty," Alex answered, looking up at him. "I don't know anything about two boys. Can't you get it through your thick brick of a head? I was asleep earlier, in there." She pointed. "I came out here, sat down, fell asleep. That's it—so, go back to your boss and tell her I don't have the boys."

"So, you *do* know about them."

"Who?"

"The boys."

"What boys are you talking about?"

"Look, you goddamn—" the man raised the pistol to strike her; that was her opening. Before he could bring down his weapon, she pulled the Beretta from under the magazine, fired a round into his thick upper leg, swung the gun across the room, and fired once into the other man's shoulder. The first man dropped to the floor; the second man spun from the impact and fell. Catlike, Alex was on her feet and slammed her heel onto the first Neanderthal's hand, breaking fingers; his pistol slid across the wooden floor. For a big man, he screamed a lot. One bloody hand was now covering the wound on his leg; the other, fingers awkwardly bent, clutched to his chest. Alex quickly collected both assailants' weapons—more Makarovs. She frisked both men, removing their cell phones. Covering the man on the floor with the Beretta, she checked the bedroom. The man was right about one thing; the boys were gone. She jerked the cords out of two of the lamps, and using a kitchen knife from the counter, cut the wires and then tied the legs of both men. The one with the shoulder wound was still wide-eyed but worthless. If he didn't get to a doctor in the next hour, it was a good chance that he'd be dead.

Alex tied the Neanderthal's arms together, retrieved a towel from the bathroom, and tied it tightly over the bloody finger-sized hole in his jeans. She was amazed at how much the man whimpered.

"Now be a good boy and don't go anywhere. If I can, I will find someone to get you to a hospital. I don't care whether you live or bleed to death, but your buddy over there is in worse shape." She heard the faint sounds of sirens in the distance. "Got to go, and please tell Tanya to go fuck herself. This is not over."

She slipped the still warm pistol into her waistband and put the other two handguns and cell phones in a grocery bag, added her phones and some of the boys' things, took another look at the two men, and went out the door. The rental car sat in the parking lot. Hers was the only sedan; a BMW SUV sat ten feet away from it. Helena had said they were the only ones in a cabin tonight.

"*Ty v poryadke?*" a voice asked, startling her. Alex spun and pulled the pistol—it was Helena; the boys were standing next to her. Helena screamed.

"She wants to know if you are okay?" Gavril said, staring at the pistol.

"Are you? They didn't hurt you?" Alex asked.

"She is okay. She has a bruise; she didn't tell them anything. Somehow, they knew we were here," Pavel said, then Helena added something. "She heard pistol shots and called the police. They will be here soon; we need to leave."

"There are two wounded Russian bad guys in the cabin. Sorry about the mess. Were you boys with Helena?"

Gavril translated. Helena then said, "Yes, the boys have been with me the last two hours. They told me you were asleep. Then those two Russians showed up; they were two of the ones from last night. The boys hid in the back."

"What were you doing at Helena's?"

"We were on her computer; it is a very good one," Pavel said. "Almost as powerful as Papa's."

"You were on a computer? Oh, shit."

"You need to go *now*. I will make up some story," Helena conveyed through Gavril, who likewise emphasized the word *now*. The woman smiled at Alex. The sirens were louder. "This is the most fun I've had since my husband died. Someday, you must come back; I think we could become friends."

CHAPTER 32

Alex drove into the early morning sunlight. A thin band of orange spread along the northeastern horizon, the sun just breaking the tops of trees.

"Tell me the truth, boys. Are you two okay?" she asked. In the rearview mirror she saw that the boys were sitting close to each and slowly rocking back and forth.

"Yes, Alex, we are okay. We like Helena. She's nice."

"Why weren't you sleeping?"

"We couldn't; we were just rolling around, missing Papa. Then Gavril said, 'Let's see if Helena is up.' And she was. She wanted to come and tell you, but we told her it was okay, you were sleeping."

"What were you doing on the computer?" Alex asked, not sure if she wanted to know the answer.

"We were looking for Papa; you said the police took him. We told you we could search the FSB, their files and programs; it is easy. All we need is a computer. Helena left us alone and we found him."

"Your father?"

"Yes, Papa is in a jail cell in Lubyanka. That's the FSB head-quarters in Moscow."

"Were you discovered? Did they find out you were in their system?"

"No, our programs are excellent; theirs are not. It is way too easy. Papa is okay, we think. Maybe we can find a way to make them send him back to us."

"I have been trying to find a way."

"Alex, you said your friends are coming to pick us up in Tallinn Airport," Gavril said.

"Yes."

"We can't go there; they know we will be there," Pavel said. "The woman who took Papa is flying to meet those men who were at Helena's."

"She won't be meeting them; I can assure you."

"She doesn't know that. She will arrive later this morning; we can't be there."

"How do you know this?"

"She posted her schedule on her computer. That is how we got into the FSB system the first time—through the scheduling program they use. Do you know Dmitry Ivanovich?"

"No."

"He is maybe Tanya Golubev's boss," Gavril said. "We looked at his schedule; he is staying in Moscow. Only she is coming."

"You two are very sneaky."

"What does that mean, sneaky?"

"It means you are very good at looking for things you should not be looking for."

"If we don't, how will we find Papa?" Their rocking continued—the logic from the minds of geniuses.

Two miles outside of the Pärnu city center, she pulled into the parking lot of a small strip mall. She reloaded her phone battery and called Chris; his phone rang four times, then went to voicemail.

> *New plan; don't go to Tallinn. The Russians will be there. Had a little trouble with some of her gang; you*

*might check the local Pärnu hospital for particulars.
The boys and I are great. I will call you later. BTW,
the Russians do have Ilya; he's in Lubyanka. I'm pulling my battery, so leave a message.*

"So, gentlemen, where do you want to go?" she asked her
geniuses in the back seat.

* * *

Chris listened to the message from Alex. He shook his head.
Jack and Linda were sitting with him in the conference room
of the TSD office in Berlin. Chris let them listen to the message. Then they were shaking their heads.

"Fine kettle of fish this is," Jack said.

"Yeah, pickled and all," Linda added. "We wait?"

"No choice," Chris said. "She will let us know."

This whole adventure had more twists than a Chubby Check-
er dance contest, Chris thought. Pärnu was on the west coast
of Estonia, about one hundred and twenty kilometers south
of Tallinn. If Alex were to go anywhere in Estonia where they
could land, it would be east, maybe Tartu. She wouldn't do
that. The best airport in the region was in Riga, Latvia. Chris
left a text message.

*Go to Riga. Radisson Blu Hotel on Elizabeth Street.
Suite reserved for you. We will be there tonight.*

"How long will it take us to get to Riga?" Chris asked.

"A couple of hours at most, plus taxi time into town," Jack
said. "Latvia is about as quiet a country as you can have in
today's world."

"Like Estonia," Linda said.

"Yes, just like Estonia," Chris said.

The TSD Team White took an entire floor of an office building on Charlottenstrasse, across from the Hilton on Mohrenstrasse in the heart of Old Berlin. The historic Gendarmenmarkt, German Cathedral, and concert hall were across the street from the hotel. Chris always wanted to be in the middle of things, and this was the center of old East Germany before the reunification. Today, the middle of things was deluged by a thunderstorm that had pushed the pedestrians and tourists off the grand square and into the shops and restaurants that catered to the new Berlin.

"This will blow through by noon," Jack said. "We will head out at 2:00 PM and beat the freeway traffic."

Chris's phone dinged. He looked at the message, then held it up so the others could see.

See you in Latvia.

"That was easy," Linda said.

"There is nothing easy with that woman," Chris answered.

* * *

Golubev, for the second time in three days, stood next to the Dassault at Tallinn Airport, waiting. God, she hated to fly, and the last few days proved it. She kept up a good front for her men, but every time the jet left the ground her, she inwardly said a quick prayer. The weather front had begun to move in, bringing some relief from the heat. It would be raining in a few hours. She had not heard from the two operatives she'd sent to Pärnu until ten minutes ago, and the report relayed through Moscow was not good. Early that day, she had ordered the leader, Arsov, back into Estonia with his partner, Gubin, to recheck the guesthouses in the Pärnu area. They came through

Tallinn Airport and drove down to Pärnu. The pair were part of the team that blew the Rakvere operation. Golubev had given them a second chance. Now she wasn't sure what she would do with them after learning that both were in a Pärnu hospital with serious gunshot wounds: Arsov with a leg wound and broken fingers, and Gubin with a severe right-shoulder wound. As far as she was concerned, they could rot there. It had been a simple assignment: collect the woman and the two boys, and bring them to her in Tallinn where they would be reunited with their father, who was now sitting handcuffed onboard the Dassault. That was it. What could go wrong this time? Between the two operatives, they had twenty years in the military and four years in the service of the FSB. An American—a woman, no less—took them both out. And then disappeared—again. Tanya paced in a tight circle alongside the plane; her first thought was to reboard and go directly back to Moscow. And maybe, somewhere along the way, throw Ilya Sokolov out the door.

She positively knew now that it was not Ilya Sokolov who had caused the cascade failure within their systems. The only answer was that the cause had been his twin boys, the mutants who were declared autistic.

Autistic, my ass.

Golubev wanted them: Russia had a use for children with these talents. They would be critical to the security and future of the country. And, when she had the twins, their son of a bitch father would tell her everything; the twins would be her lever to pry the real story out of him. Except now, it was all a disaster—all caused by that Polonia woman.

She climbed into the cabin of the jet and glared at her prisoner. He stared back at her, a puzzled look on his face.

"You seem confused, Miss Golubev," he said.

Golubev looked at her associate; a pistol sat in his lap. His black eyes never left Sokolov.

"Where are my children?" Ilya asked.

"They are coming," she lied. "My men are looking for them. They will be here soon."

"Why do I not believe you?"

"Believe what you will, traitor. I do not like your kind. You think that by invading government systems, you can change the world. But you see what happens; the collateral damage is disastrous—people died. The Americans will take your children; they will be put in institutions, and it is your fault."

"I did not create the program; it was not my computer that activated the virus; those were your computers. It was not my fault—it was an accident."

"I do not believe you. It was you and your sons who caused all this. No, Ilya Sokolov, it is you who are responsible. And I believe the CIA paid you to do it."

Ilya looked long and hard at the woman. "Is it the gun that kills, or is it the man who pulls the trigger? Or is it the manufacturer of the gun, or the one who made the bullets, or the one who sold it? Who is responsible? My children were playing, they found a puzzle, they opened the puzzle, and people died. Was it my children, or was it the maker of the puzzle? That is what *you* have to live with. I have to live with two boys who see a different world than we do, a world that is strange to them; their world is one we do not understand. Where are my children?"

Golubev disregarded his philosophical questions. Of course, it was the man who pulled the trigger; it was as simple as that.

"I will watch him," she said to her associate. "There is a restaurant just outside the gate. Get us and the pilot breakfast—we will eat on the plane. We may have to leave in a hurry."

"Yes, Assistant Director." He slipped the pistol into his

shoulder holster, pulled his jacket on, and left.

"I am through talking with you," Golubev said to Sokolov. "You and your boys have been such a bother. I am consoled that this will be over soon."

Ilya smirked and looked out the window where a few raindrops spattered. "Maybe."

"What did you say?"

Ilya shrugged.

CHAPTER 33

The backroad into Riga, Latvia, from Pärnu, Estonia, reminded Alex of the country roads from Cleveland to Toledo. Flat farmland, broken with groves of evergreens and birch trees. Often, maybe every twenty kilometers or so, they crossed a river and had a view of the bay; it looked like a lake, but the map said *Riga Bay*. They stayed off the A1; she didn't want to take any chances with a license plate scanner. Still, she couldn't shake the sense of being in Ohio. They stopped three times, once because she needed to use the bathroom, the second because the boys did, and the third was to rid herself of the cache of weapons she'd accumulated. Stopping on the bridge that crossed the Salaca River in the town of Salacgriva, she unceremoniously dropped the five weapons out of the paper bag into the river. She kept the Beretta.

A couple of hours after leaving Pärnu, they pulled into the village of Saulkrasti. In a strip mall fronting the two-lane highway, Alex found a clothing store. Alex had grabbed her backpack and bags of guns and phones, but in the hurried departure they'd left most of the boys' personal possessions at the guesthouse. She now had enough weapons to outfit a four-man fireteam in her bag and no Nintendos to keep the boys occupied. Everything she'd bought for them, a few days earlier, was back at the guesthouse. With the boys in tow, she bought more shirts, shorts, and underwear. She found a T-shirt for herself and shorts as well. One look at the available Latvian underwear confirmed her decision to wash out what she had. Two doors down at a convenience store, she bought food that ten-year-olds would like (most with the nutritional value of potato chips). She let them pick what they wanted. She set up their picnic in a small park with a sandy beach, and was certain, standing in the parking lot, that Lake Erie spread out in front of them. For this Midwestern girl, the fact that it was saltwater was hard to believe.

"This is like my home, where I live," she said to the boys. They took their shoes off and walked in the shallows, kicking water on each other. They looked closely at the ground where water met sand.

"What are you looking for, Gavril?"

"Clams, like when we were with Papa," the boy answered.

"Where do you live?" his brother asked as he dredged his fingers through the sand. "It is like this?"

"Yes, some, but it is far away. In the summer it gets hot, too."

"Does it get cold in the winter?"

"Yes, it can be as cold St. Petersburg. Bitterly cold. I like the summers."

Later, as they sat at a picnic table, Gavril said, "So do we. We like summer." He took a bite from his sandwich, then a sip from his Pepsi. "Why did they take Papa?"

"They think he was responsible for what you boys did. They want to know how he hacked into their systems."

"He doesn't know. We know what hackers do," Gavril said. "We are excellent hackers."

"And we will make them give him back," Pavel said.

"And how are you going to do that?"

"A trade."

"What kind of trade?"

"One they understand, and the other to scare them," Gavril said.

"Where are we going?" Pavel asked.

"We are going to Riga; it is about forty kilometers from here. It is close, maybe an hour. We are meeting some people—"

"Who are we meeting?" Pavel asked, interrupting Alex. He began to rock nervously. "Not like those men this morning."

They had to have seen the men; Helena had to have said something. But they didn't need to know about the violence that had ensued in the guesthouse; Alex would never tell the boys that story, ever. The local police hadn't stopped them, so Helena must have given a good account of what happened or at least a story that gave them the time they needed to get to Riga. The sooner they were in the hotel, and she was done with the rental car, the better. She gathered up the rest of their lunch, made sure the boys used the restroom, and headed back on the road. The sun had disappeared; a thick overcast sky moved in. She could taste the rain.

Once they arrived in Riga, even with its winding streets, the Radisson Blu was not hard to find. It was one of the tallest buildings in the city. An hour later, after they settled in, she got the boys to take showers and wash their hair. She called the front desk to ask them to contact the car rental company, tell them their car was here, and to come and get it. Then she made the boys swear to stay in the room while she showered. She slipped the Beretta into one of the plastic bags from the clothing store and suspended it in the tank of the toilet. Hopefully, the boys would not think to look there. Thankfully they obeyed her order to stay inside; they were watching television while she dressed in the bathroom. The T-shirt she slipped on read LATVIA FOREVER.

"Are you hungry?"

Both turned and said, "*Da, pizza.*"

"Of course," she answered. She called room service. "Just cheese and sauce?"

"*Da*, lots of sauce," Gavril said. His eyes never left the TV screen.

Feeling somewhat settled, Alex looked out the window of their twentieth-floor room. Lush green parks surrounded the hotel. The river beyond, according to the city map in the *Where* magazine on the table, was the Daugava River. For a brief moment, she forgot they were wanted by the three most feared police organizations in the world. For a brief moment, she felt like she was on vacation. And for another brief moment, she forgot the last eighteen months. Each moment of forgetting the past felt distinct. She took a deep breath; the moments evaporated, replaced by overwhelming exhaustion. The one thing she'd desperately wanted was sleep.

A tap on the door roused her from her deliberations. Gavril stood up.

"Sit, Gavril. I'll get it." She looked through the peephole and saw the young face of a blonde woman. She opened the door, took the pizza and the cans of Pepsi.

Turning to the boys, she said, "Go wash your hands. No pizza until you are clean."

They dashed to the bathroom. In seconds they were back and sitting on the floor around the coffee table. When she opened the box, Alex had to admit the pizza looked good. She took a slice and sat in the chair near the window. It tasted as good as it looked.

She sent the boys to bed and remained in her chair, sitting upright until sleep overtook her. She woke with the sun shining directly into her eyes. Her mind, confused by a dream she couldn't remember, stumbled, then it recovered. The digital clock on the nightstand said 3:55 AM. She'd been asleep for almost two hours. The boys were gone, again. She hurriedly checked every corner of the room. The boys, where were the boys?

She ran to the bathroom and removed the small Beretta and snugged it in the back of her jeans. The LATVIA FOREVER T-shirt covered everything. Catching sight of herself in the mirror she mentally shrugged—*It is what it is.*

She took the elevator to the lobby. She forced herself to slow her pace as she approached the desk; a young woman stood at the counter.

Trying not to alarm anyone, Alex said, "My two boys, they came down here a while ago. They are age ten and twins. I told them to meet me here in the lobby and, like the little trouble-makers they are, they failed." This was accomplished with a smile. "Have you seen them?"

"No, madam, I have not. Do you wish to have me make an announcement?"

Alex considered the request.

"Excuse me? American?" The man was dressed in a nice suit; he was bald with a thick mustache. For a brief instant, she imagined he was Special Agent Robb Case; then, of course, she knew he wasn't.

"Yes, American. Vacation, and the boys have been on a roll since we landed, jet lag and all."

"John Deets, AmLat Communications. In fact, I'm on my way to the airport. I was getting my boarding pass in the business office and I saw two boys that fit your description."

"Where?" Alex asked.

"Around the corner there, third door. You can't miss it," Deets said.

"Thank you."

She quickly walked through the lobby to the far hallway.

At the third door, all-glass, she looked in and saw what was becoming an all-too-familiar scene: Gavril and Pavel energetically clicking away on two of the four computers on the long counter. They were so involved they did not notice her enter the room.

"I told you to stay in the room," she said.

"No, you didn't. You said to stay only when you were taking a shower," Gavril said, still looking at the monitor.

"We have found a way to make them give us Papa," Pavel said, pointing to the screen.

CHAPTER 34

Dmitry Ivanovich lit another cigarette; the ashtray was full. The reports from the third floor had been distressing. He had informed Golubev, hours earlier, about her men in Pärnu—such incredible incompetence. But in the new Russia they would return home, be given time to recuperate, and then, who knew. Probably receive disability checks and pensions. He longed for the old days when rewards and punishments were more equal to the tasks accomplished—or failed.

He also passed on the information to his protégé about a possible sighting of the American woman in Riga. Her face had been recognized during mass scans of hacked hotel security footage—always a good source of raw data. She had been seen at the Radisson hotel. She might have arrived by car. Checking license plate numbers revealed a car that had been rented in Tallinn and returned there from Riga. At this news, Golubev mumbled something and then hung up. He would make sure that Human Resources talked to Golubev about her attitude when she returned to Moscow.

Neatly arranged on his desk were mementos of his professional career serving Russia. A live 50-caliber bullet from his time in Afghanistan more than thirty years earlier; a polished stone from a riverbed outside of Grozny from the first war with the Chechens; in a clear plastic box a piece of shrapnel that had been dug out of his leg during the Crimea campaign; and a small teacup he'd scrounged from a collapsed building in Aleppo. He'd spent his life serving Mother Russia, and now it was all threatened by a worthless computer teacher from St. Petersburg and his two idiot children. He crushed out the cigarette and lit another. It was midafternoon; he desperately wanted a drink. He turned up the volume on the app on his phone; music from the Bluetooth speakers filled the office. It was a Shostakovich piano piece—one he'd learned to play as a child. Today was a day for reminiscing.

A knock at his door startled him. He looked up into the face of the president; the man was smiling.

Ivanovich slowly stood, turned down the volume to almost nothing, and nodded to his boss. "Please, Mr. President, sit. I was not told you were coming."

"That is okay, Dmitry, my old friend. I was in the area and wanted to talk with my favorite director."

The president eyed the cigarette and squinted. Ivanovich crushed it in the ashtray and removed the debris from his desk. He put the offending contents in a drawer. Usually, when he knew the president would be stopping by, he would have his office sanitized.

"Make sure it is out; I would not want a fire here in this fine building that serves the people."

"Yes, sir." He rechecked the drawer.

"Dmitry, I have been informed that we have a problem, actually that *you* have a problem. These unfortunate events surrounding the power outages in the United States have grown into an embarrassing situation. I have kept it behind the scenes, so to speak. Only a select number of people know about your failure. But it has evolved and now has become overly complicated. You will make it all go away. All evidence of Nightshade must disappear, and more importantly, all those who know about it need to be reassigned. I do not expect to see any of this—"

The president was mid-sentence when the lights in Ivanovich's office flickered, then went out. Ivanovich had earlier closed the curtains; now the room was almost black. The battery-powered emergency exit light clicked on: the word **ВЫХОД** glowed in the small sign above the door.

"What the hell?" the president said and quickly rose from his chair. In the dim light, Ivanovich also stood. Two men came through the door, shadows really; each held a flashlight and a pistol.

"Are you all right, Mr. President?" one of the guards asked.

"Yes, I'm fine. What happened?"

"We are trying to find out." The man put his hand to his ear. "*Da!* They tell me the power is out throughout all of Moscow."

As the man said that, the lights went back on.

"A momentary failure," the guard said. "That is the report."

"There is no such thing," the president said. "Director Ivanovich, please call the director of MOESK, and find out why the power—"

The lights went out again. For the next several minutes, the power went on, then off, in fifteen-second intervals. After three minutes of this, the president left Ivanovich's office and quick-marched down the long hallway. His guards followed him. The group started for the elevator, reconsidered, then took the stairs.

The seconds-long outages lasted for ten minutes. Ivanovich opened the shades and watched the chaos growing in the streets below. The traffic at the corner of Lubyanskiy and Bolshaya Lubyanka streets was jammed. Two cars had crashed into each other; the drivers were engaged in a shoving match in the street. People were shouting at the two men to move their cars. Others, with cell phones held high, were shooting videos.

The power returned for thirty minutes; then the outages began again, this time in twenty-second intervals. In less than an hour, the city of Moscow was in chaos.

* * *

Golubev's phone buzzed. The screen read *Director*.

"Yes, Director," she said.

"Where are you?"

"Just landed in Riga; we are taxiing to our—"

Interrupting, Ivanovich asked, "Are Sokolov and Lynch with you?"

"Of course. Sokolov is sitting directly across from me. Micah is forward with the pilot."

"Ask Sokolov about the power outages."

"What power outages, Director? We already believe he is not directly—"

"In fucking Moscow, Golubev. Here, in Moscow, right now! The lights are going on and off. What does he know?"

Stunned by the question, she looked at Ilya. "What do you know about the power outages in Moscow?"

A mystified look appeared on Ilya's face. "I don't know anything about power outages in Moscow," he said. "I've been with you the last twelve hours; in fact, I've never even been to Moscow. Why do you ask?"

"Director, why?"

"Are you that dense, Golubev? Right now! While the president of Russia was sitting in my office, the power was systematically turned on and off by someone. This has been going on for more than an hour. That someone must be Ilya Sokolov."

"It is the boys who hacked into our systems . . . and they are probably the ones controlling the power in Moscow."

"Two children? Two idiots? You are fucking crazy."

"Sokolov has had no contact with anyone. I talked with the

third floor; they confirmed that Polonia and the boys are at the Radisson here in Riga. When I find them, I will take them into custody."

"The president informed me of his displeasure about all that has been going on since the incident in Iowa. He has ordered that everything about Nightshade be destroyed—everything. He wants nothing to remain. I'm ordered to reassign staff and—"

"You can't do that; I am this close to capturing the children and forcing Sokolov to tell us everything. You must tell him no."

"You do not say no to the president. Do you understand? It is over. Dump Sokolov on the tarmac and immediately return to Moscow. We will talk about this later. And you might think about dumping Lynch with him too."

"Director, we can't stop now. We must learn how they accessed the servers. They are turning Moscow's power on and off; it's them, the twins. I know it. Don't you understand that this leaves us vulnerable to future attacks, especially if the Americans get them? They must be stopped."

"Do what I tell you," Ivanovich said and hung up.

"Ivanovich?" Micah said, walking back to her. "Problems?"

She passed along the news of the power outages in Moscow, adding her opinion that the twins were the cause. Micah couldn't believe two children had that much power. When she told him Nightshade was to be destroyed by executive order, he grew quiet.

"Sometimes a father can be so proud of his children. I think I'm having one of those moments," Ilya said.

Micah swung the back of his hand across Ilya's face, almost knocking him over.

"Stop that, I still need him," Tanya said. "And besides, you are not here to beat up my prisoner. I expect more from you.

We paid you a lot of money; I'll see that we get every kopek back if this recovery fails." She said nothing to Micah about the director's inclination to dump him in Latvia.

"You will not use my children for your games," Sokolov interjected. "Is this what Russia has come down to, arresting college teachers and ten-year-old children? I forbid you to use them."

"You are in no position to make any demands," Golubev said.

"I must be there to talk my boys out of their game. They can be so single-minded about something that they cannot see what the impacts might be. They aren't going to trust you or anyone else."

"You can make them stop and also tell us how they did it?"

"I don't know, but if my boys are harmed in any way, I'll see to it that you never find out how they did it, or how to stop it."

An hour later, the jet lurched to a stop in Riga. Golubev glanced out the window at the two attendants jogging through the rain toward the plane, and then turned her gaze on Sokolov. He responded with a blank-faced stare. She was sure Sokolov knew more about what was happening than he was letting on.

"And my boys? Are they here?" Ilya asked while he looked out the window.

She saw the sign for Latvian Air Center – Riga.

"You shut up. I'm very tired of you and your family."

The pilot, the man who had flown Golubev on every flight during the past week, stood in the door to the flight deck. "Your orders, Ms. Golubev?"

As the pilot asked the question, Micah looked back at Golubev, as did her associate, a big bear of a Russian seated directly behind Micah.

"Stay with the jet. Be prepared to take off as soon as we return. We will immediately head back to Moscow."

The pilot pulled the latch, and the stairway opened into the light drizzle. He handed Golubev an umbrella. She looked at it and then at her arm; her look said, *What the hell am I going to do with that?* He took the umbrella back.

Ten minutes later, Ilya, Micah, and the bear followed Golubev to a rental car parked in front of the facility. Two minutes later, they were driving through the rain into the ancient city of Riga.

* * *

Alex stood in the small glassed-in space that said *Darijumu Centrs* in large letters. Below, in English, it read *Business Center*.

"Please, boys, you're too smart to be so obtuse," she said.

"Obtuse?" Gavril said.

"It means stupid. You two know exactly what you are doing. You were supposed to stay in the room."

"We are getting Papa back."

"And how are you doing that?"

"We know where the controls are," Pavel said.

"What controls?"

"Who is being obtuse, now?" Gavril said and smiled.

"Russia? You are switching off the power in Russia?"

"Just a small part."

"What part?"

"The part that took Papa, Moscow. Let me show you," Pavel said.

He stepped aside and pointed to the screen; Alex didn't understand what she saw. Streaming lines of text and numbers; a box with a digital clock flashed in the corner; it was counting down second by second. A clock, maybe?

"It goes on and off. We have the program on a timer," Pavel explained. "Like the way their program turned on and off the power in Iowa."

"You understand what happened two weeks ago?"

"We didn't. We didn't know." Gavril looked at Alex. "Then we saw the TV news from America. We understand now, we think."

Alex took out her phone and typed: *Hurry. What's happening in Moscow?*

CHAPTER 35

The rain pelted the windshield of the TSD Gulfstream as it touched down at Riga's International Airport. Jack taxied the plane toward a complex of buildings on the north end of the airport.

Chris Campbell read the short, cryptic message from Alex. "Shit." He called Dallas; it was ten o'clock in the morning there.

"What's happening in Moscow?" he asked Jimmy Cortez. At Chris's specific request, Cortez was staffing the international control desk at TSD's main American office.

"How did you find out? You are in transit between Berlin and Riga," Jimmy answered.

"We just landed. What's going on?"

"There is an alert through international news outlets; BBC was the first to break the story. Electrical power has been going on and off throughout the whole region of Moscow since midafternoon, their time. The local time in Moscow and there in Riga is the same. One second . . ."

Chris told Jack and Linda what he'd just learned.

"Power has been back on for about twenty minutes," Jimmy said. "The news reports are sketchy. We are trying to get local Moscow television news on our monitors—no luck so far. I will let you know what I find out as soon as I know."

Chris clicked off. "We need to get to Alex. If I think what's happening is happening, she has her hands full."

The plane eased to a stop. Chris walked to the cockpit. Only Jack was manning the cockpit; Linda remained in the back. Looking left out the window, Chris saw the forward nose cowling of a Dassault Falcon 2000.

"I saw it when we rolled in. Look familiar?" Jack said.

"It's the Russian jet, Tanya Golubev's. Right?"

"Bingo."

"I can't believe she beat us here. Can you find out how long it's been here?"

Chris went back to Linda.

"Problem?" she asked.

"That jet there—" he pointed out the window—"is the Russian FSB."

"Ten minutes ago," Jack said over the intercom. "They just landed. A woman and four others left in one of their corporate SUVs. The woman said they would be back in a couple of hours."

"Does their business center have another car?"

"Yes," Jack said.

"Tell them we want to hire it."

"Got it."

Minutes later, they were crossing Vanšu Bridge and headed into the old section of Riga. The Radisson Blu dominated the eastern skyline. They pulled to the front and parked behind another car that said *Latvian Air Center* on the door and across the trunk. The figures of two men could be seen through the rear window. A young man came running to the car.

He said something they didn't understand.

"English?" Chris asked.

"Cannot park this place. Guests only," the valet said.

"Checking in."

"You want park?"

"No, it is good where it is. We're going out soon."

"You just came in."

"And we will be just going out." Chris handed the boy twenty euros. The valet immediately seemed more satisfied with the arrangements.

The trio went through the automatic doors and into the lobby; for late afternoon, it was busy. The clouds were breaking up after the rainstorm, and sunlight shone through the expansive windows, illuminating the lobby. Dozens of people were sitting and talking; others stood in groups along the edges. Noise and loud conversations spilled from the bar on the far side and added to the buzz of conversation in the lobby. Chris was turning toward Linda when the loud snap and report of a gunshot stunned the crowd. Another shot immediately followed. People began to run toward the doors; others froze until they saw people scattering and diving for the floor. A woman began screaming.

* * *

For several minutes, the boys tried to explain to Alex what they had done and how they had done it. She still did not understand when they said, "That's all there is to it." *Sure*, she thought.

"I want you to turn everything off and come with me. What you did is wrong, and I will tell you why when we get back to the room. But I want you to understand that people may be hurt by what you did."

"We want Papa. They must give us Papa. If they don't, we *will* make it bigger," Gavril said.

From the first day she met the boys, Alex believed that Gavril was the more serious mischief-maker of the two.

"As I said, we will talk about it. Grab your Pepsis, we are—"

"You are going nowhere," a voice said behind her.

Alex recognized the voice. "Of course we are, *Tanya*," she said without turning around. "We are going back to our room. You have no authority here, or anywhere in the civilized world. So just get out of my way."

"And if I don't?" Golubev answered.

Alex turned toward Golubev, letting her disdain show. "Someone will get hurt, again."

With her left hand, Golubev pulled a pistol from the waist holster under her jacket. She waved the gun at Alex and the boys.

Alex glanced at the black sling that held Golubev's right arm. "I see you've changed the bandage since our little escapade yesterday morning. Black, it suits you."

"Fuck you. They are going with me."

"I'm sure they don't want to go with you. Do you want to go back to Russia—with this woman?"

"No, Russia has Papa," Gavril said. "They must bring him to us. If not, we will shut the power off to the whole country."

"Not going to happen," Golubev said. "You can come willingly, or with help."

The big Russian stood in the door behind her, Micah next to him. Micah held a pistol as well. The big man pushed his way past Alex and headed directly to the boys. He grabbed each by the back of their new T-shirts and bodily lifted them off the carpet.

"*Vy poydete so mnoy, mal'chiki*," he said.

"We will not go!" Pavel screamed. "Get your hands off us."

"*Seychas. Priyti!*"

"*Net. Ni za chto, battkhed*," Gavril yelled.

Even Alex understood what that meant.

The Russian ignored their screams and began to drag the boys out of the small office. Alex swung an arm out to try and stop him. Using his massive shoulder like a fist, he knocked her into the wall; he did not let go of the boys.

"Stop!" Alex yelled. Recovering in a flash, she drew her pistol and aimed it at Golubev's face. "Stop now! Tell him to let go of the boys."

Standing less than ten feet apart, the two women stared at each other, weapons high.

"It's two against one, Alex," Micah said. "Just lower the weapon so no one gets hurt."

"We are leaving," Golubev said. "There is nothing you can do to stop us; you do not want the blood of innocent people on your hands."

"You have the audacity to say that to me? Your program killed hundreds of Americans."

"It was those brats' fault, not my government's."

"That's bullshit, and you know it. Besides, the brats, as you call them, left a little payback. Call Moscow. Your Nightshade clock is going to keep turning the power on and off until all the generating stations in Russia are affected."

"That's impossible," Micah said.

"I'm sure that's the same thing your tech people said when the grid collapsed for the first time, and each time after that," Alex said. "Scary, isn't it? It will take hours to reboot, right? Revolutions have started with less. Let them go, let them all go."

"Not a chance," Golubev hissed. "Take them to their father," she ordered. "I need to get this done."

"Ilya is here?" Alex said.

Golubev shrugged.

"Papa? Is Papa here? Alex, where is Papa?" Gavril said.

"She knows where he is, ask her," Alex said.

In one amazingly quick move, Pavel jerked away from the man's grasp and spun around to Golubev. "Where is Papa?"

"Grab the boy, damn you," Golubev yelled.

Pavel grabbed Golubev's injured arm and pulled, causing

her left to swing the pistol wildly, her finger on the trigger. He hit her broken arm again; her right fingers reactively clenched, and the pistol fired. The shot ricocheted off the floor; everyone ducked reflexively, except Pavel, who slammed both his fists against Golubev's right arm and sling. Golubev screamed. The pistol in her other hand fired once more before she dropped it.

Alex registered that the second shot had lodged in the wall behind her at the same time she heard shrieking and shouting from the lobby. As the shots were fired, Gavril had quit fighting and went slack in the big Russian's grip. The man quickly scooped up Pavel, and with a boy under each arm, ran out into the lobby.

"You stay right there, Alex," Micah said.

"How about you lower your pistol to the floor," Chris said, his own weapon not an inch from his recent associate's head. "Now, you fucking bastard."

Alex kicked Golubev's pistol away. She would have to fight her way past Alex to retrieve it in the narrow room. The Russian agent glared at the American cop, and then pushed her way past Chris and took off after her henchman and the screaming boys. Alex bolted after her, giving Chris a quick thank-you as she ran by him. She followed Golubev into the lobby. People were screaming and falling over each other.

The big Russian ignored them and, using the two boys as battering rams, attempted to slam into Jack, who was standing in the open automatic doors. Jack, with little effort, sidestepped the man, kicked him in the knee, and watched as the three tumbled through the entry. The big Russian collided with Linda, who slid as she fell, her eyes on the fleeing Golubev. The boys rolled away unharmed. The rear door of the SUV parked under the awning flew open and Ilya jumped out, his right arm handcuffed to the door handle. The driver swung open his door, stood behind the car, pulled a pistol, and aimed it at the entry. The boys, seeing their father, screamed with delight as they tumbled away from the Russian. They ran to his open arms.

A few steps behind and running to catch Golubev, Alex watched as Linda, still prone on the floor, grabbed Golubev's ankle as she ran by. The agent tumbled head over heels through the open doors. If less agile and well-trained, Golubev might have ended up with a concussion and dislocated shoulder. She nonetheless screamed in agony as she fell hard on her broken arm. The big Russian fumbled in his jacket, trying to pull his weapon. Jack yelled something in Russian and pointed a pistol at the man's head. The Russian stopped, slowly removed his gun with two fingers, and placed it on the concrete walkway.

Alex slid to a stop when she reached Golubev. Linda was on top of the FSB agent, her own weapon out.

"*Vse ostanavlivutsya,*" the SUV driver yelled from the drive-way. He pointed his weapon at Ilya and the boys. "*Ostanavli-vat'?*"

"*Vstan', ne strelyay,*" Golubev yelled; then, in English, "Stand down, do not shoot."

"Anyone hurt?" Alex asked and turned to Chris. He was marching Micah out through the lobby. He smiled at Alex.

"No one is hurt," Chris said as he looked around. "Thank God."

"Just my torn slacks and her pride," Linda said, standing up while still pointing her weapon at Golubev. The Russian agent remained on the floor, breathing hard but making no more effort to fight. She glared at Alex and Chris.

Across the drop-off, the boys, wrapped in Ilya's free arm, tightly hugged him. They would not let go.

Meanwhile, in Moscow, the power continued to go on and off every twenty seconds. This would continue for the next two hours.

CHAPTER 36

The questions asked by the Latvian police extended into the early morning hours. Two detectives, who had obviously watched too many episodes of the American police drama *Blue Bloods*, continued to interview everyone—at least three times. It was big news for the sleepy Latvian capital: Russians and Americans coming to Riga in private jets to battle over the fate and custody of two children with autism spectrum disorder. There were endless on-screen interviews with international autism experts about the current state of treatments and the difference in international organizations (and their quarrels). The story made the international wires; BBC did a short story from London. However, as with every news cycle, within a few days, the two boys were all but forgotten.

Chris and his PR people (by phone) were able to deflect the battle in the hotel from the real story. No connections to the power outages in Moscow and the disaster in Iowa were made. The story was kept local and focused on the children. Ilya Sokolov, understanding everything that was expected, and at the request of both Alex and Chris, addressed the cameras and microphones and refabricated the truth.

"I need to have special treatments for my twin boys, who are both autistic," he began. "Hopefully, I can find a private school where they will be able to lead, for them, normal lives. There is such an institution in Canada. I cannot name this school;

they rely on privacy for both their donors and their students. My friends here, Christopher Campbell and Alex Polonia, have donated their time and the use of Mr. Campbell's plane to take us there. Unfortunately, some in my home country did not appreciate my children's needs. I believe they were embarrassed that I, a private citizen, had to resort to this secretive process. That is why there was an unfortunate incident in the lobby of the Radisson hotel. It was a misunderstanding about custody and my right as a human being and father to choose what is best for my children. All the other issues are best left to attorneys and politicians, I believe, now that it has been resolved to the satisfaction of all those involved. Thank you."

The entire TSD group and the Sokolovs spent the night at the hotel. The next morning, Alex met with Chris, Jack, and Linda over breakfast. Ilya remained upstairs with the boys.

"I assume our pigeon has flown the coop?" Alex asked.

"Late last night, after the police completed their questions, Golubev, Micah, and her guys flew out. Flight plan was for Moscow," Jack said.

"I wonder if she will make it, or will she change her mind somewhere before reaching the border and make a left turn and head north and away from Russia?" Alex said. She looked at Chris. "I'm sorry about Micah."

"I should have shot the son of a bitch," Chris said.

"She's a loyal soldier," Linda said. "She will go to Moscow. What happened to the computers in the business office?"

"Just after the craziness in the lobby," Alex said, "I slipped back into the business office and cleared the URLs and anything else I could find that even remotely might connect us and the situation in Russia. One of the detectives asked if I knew the Russian woman. I stuck with the story, told him I believed she was from the Russian government agency who had a problem with the boys and their father leaving Russia. I knew they would get nothing from Golubev."

272

"I like your T-shirt," Chris said. "LATVIA FOREVER."

"A trophy and a memento. I also have one from the ferry that says TALLINN. I go to the Baltic Sea, and all I get is a T-shirt."

"You saved the twins," Jack said.

"Is there a T-shirt for that?"

"No, that's a victory we keep to ourselves," Chris said.

The next morning, they flew back to Berlin. Ilya entered the country as Fyodor Popoff; the boys were identified as Vadim and Boris. Alex didn't know who which was. Ilya agreed to meet with Chris and Alex at the TSD offices after he'd settled the boys in a hotel; in reality, he had no option. Linda stayed with the boys.

They met in Chris's office.

"Thank you for saving my children, Alex. And me as well," Ilya said.

"You are welcome," Alex said. "This is not over, and you know that."

"Yes, I understand," Ilya said.

"I have discussed this at length with those in the American government who understand what has happened," Chris said. "They don't like it but agree this might be a reasonable solution. It will require you to tell us what you know about the actions and programs within the Russian government, how your boys accessed those programs, how they can be identified, and how they can be deactivated."

"I understand but, unfortunately, I can't," Ilya said. "My boys told me they created self-destruct programs that would burn the bridges they built into the Russian systems. That was happening just before Alex caught them in the business center. Two hours after the boys' programs were initiated, they automatically shut down and backed out, leaving no trace or track to follow back in. The power returned to Moscow at the same time. I assume by now the FSB has either destroyed any evidence of their Nightshade programs or buried them so deep offline that no one will find them again. Without access to these programs, it is impossible to prove that they existed. My laptop is gone; there is no evidence that any of this even happened. I am profoundly sorry for what occurred, and for what my children did. And I will wish, to the day I die, that what happened could be undone."

Alex looked at Ilya and watched a tear slide down his cheek.

"My children found a loaded gun and it went off. It was not their gun; it was my government's, and my government had this gun because of their fear of your government and its guns. You, Mr. Campbell, know this. I wish to God in heaven that I could change all this, but I can't. I talked to my boys last night. They understand what they did was wrong, and in many ways, I am glad that their condition shields them, even if a bit, from fully understanding what happened. Someday, they may understand."

Chris nodded and turned to Alex. "Tell him what you have been able to do."

"Ilya, it's really with Chris's help as well," she said. "The school in Canada does have curricula to help autistic and special-needs children, like Gavril and Pavel. They will accept them into the school. They do not know anything about what happened or any of their connection to the events in Iowa. You must ask your boys not to tell anyone what they know or even where they came from. I know this is difficult, maybe impossible, but this is where we will start. There is also an open teaching position at this school, and they have offered it to you. While some might consider this to be a Witness Protection program, it does not include any formal American government involvement."

"What you don't know can't hurt you?" Ilya said.

"Something like that. You will be taken directly to this school the day after tomorrow; there is paperwork to clear up.

The Canadian consulate, here in Berlin, is sending over an associate to help with the papers and the immigration process."

"Will we keep our real names?"

"New life may require a new name," Alex said. She looked at Chris. "Next time, tell Yuri to be a bit more creative with the names. Boris and Vadim are boring."

"I'll tell him."

"Ilya," Jack said, "I'll walk you back to the hotel."

Ilya stood and walked over to Alex. She stood and they hugged; he kissed her on both cheeks. A tear rolled down Alex's cheek. She felt him grab her hand and squeeze—he pushed something into her hand.

After the door closed, Alex walked to the bar at the back of Chris's office, surprisingly found a bottle of Belvedere, dropped ice in a glass, and poured two fingers of vodka. She took a brief glance at the object; it was a thumb drive.

"Chris?" she said, holding up a bottle of bourbon.

"I am not happy with you, Alexandra Polonia," Chris said.

"A bourbon it is."

* * *

Anya Belsky sat on the worn wooden bench of the train station on the southern edge of the Lithuanian city of Vilnius. She had spent the previous night in a hostel three blocks away. The luscious red Michael Kors bag she'd bought in the downtown department store sat next to her. Her roller bag, an expensive small silver Rimowa suitcase, was filled with clothes she never imagined buying in St. Petersburg.

She couldn't make up her mind which way to go. South and east was Belarus; to the south and west was Poland. And beyond Poland was Germany and Europe. She'd already spent a quarter of the money the American had given her. She'd not been asked for a passport yet.

She wondered how long her windfall would last. An older man, distinguished-looking and in a black leather jacket, approached her. He looked her over approvingly.

"May I help you?" he asked. "You appear to be lost."

She considered the man and then her options. "Yes, I am a little lost. Maybe *you* can help me."

* * *

Mayor Elizabeth Nelson stood on the box that had been placed behind the podium. Ten microphones nearly hid her from the crowd of citizens, emergency personnel, and reporters. Behind her, a collection of federal officials, state law enforcement officers, Iowa government representatives, and local firefighters and police officers stood shoulder to shoulder. They were there to honor the fallen and praise the heroes who had saved the town of Maise.

Only three people—the secretary of Homeland Security, the governor of Iowa, and Special Agent Robb Case—knew what had happened (or to be more precise, believed what they had been told about what happened). They were there to support the mayor. They could live with the story she would tell, a story that she believed to be accurate.

"Ladies and gentlemen, the press, and most especially those who were here that awful day, two weeks ago, when our town and state suffered so grievously from one of the most horrific accidents that could befall our community, thank you for coming today. Behind me are many of those heroes: our police chief Clyde Dubban; our fire chief, who just this morning was released from the hospital; the members of the emergency crews that rescued hundreds of our citizens; Secretary Tallmadge of Homeland Security; Special Agent Case who represents those brave men and women who tirelessly investigated what happened that horrific day; and of course Governor

Smith for ensuring that every state resource was made available to us during this time of need.

"While there still is much to do, you can hear throughout our village the sounds of hammers and saws that tell you we are coming back. Maise, Iowa, will be better and stronger. Mistakes that were made are being addressed, changes are being made to the regulations for ethanol plants, and, I have been informed, we are on the way to better secure our interstate power grid.

"We offer prayers for those we lost, and for those still in pain. We want them home as soon as possible. We will move forward, knowing this is a warning and a lesson that will better protect our citizens in the future. Thank you."

A woman in the front row impolitely cut short the soft applause with a question.

"Madam Mayor, what do you know about the rumor that the Russians may have been involved in this incident? That it may have been their meddling in our power grid that directly caused this disaster?"

Befuddled by the surprise question, Mayor Nelson frowned before quickly regaining a degree of composure. She turned to Special Agent Case.

"Special Agent Case, can you answer this reporter's . . . uh . . . comment and question?"

Case, looking like he wanted to be anywhere but here, walked to the podium. He looked directly at the reporter, then the others to her left and right. "Currently, our investigation has turned up no direct connection to the government of Russia or any other foreign entity. If anything further develops, we will inform the public through the proper channels."

The End

A Note from the Author
The Alex Polonia Thrillers

There are two other Alex Polonia thrillers, Venice Black and Saigon Red.

Gregory C. Randall was born on a hot and muggy day in Traverse City, Michigan. He grew up in Chicago. Greg has never forgotten his Midwestern roots. Mr. Randall makes his home in California.

Mr. Randall is the author of fiction and nonfiction works available through the usual outlets.

For more information about the other books that Mr. Randall has written and planned sequels, please visit and connect with Greg online:
    www.gregorycrandall.info

See his blogs:
    http://www.writing4death.blogspot.com

Other books by Mr. Randall:
Fiction
The Cherry Pickers

The Sharon O'Mara Chronicles
Land Swap For Death
Containers For Death
Toulouse For Death

12th Man For Death
Diamonds For Death
Limerick For Death

The Alex Polonia Thrillers
Venice Black
Saigon Red

The Tony Alfano Thrillers
Chicago Swing
Chicago Jazz
Chicago Fix

Nonfiction
America's Original GI Town, Park Forest, Illinois

Additional copies can be purchased through Amazon.